TED TAYLER

ONE TRUE FRIEND

BOOKS

By Ted Tayler

The Freeman Files

Red Herring Season
Gathering Clouds
Still Standing

Vinci Books

vinci-books.com

Published by Vinci Books Ltd in 2025

1

Copyright © Ted Tayler 2022

A CIP catalogue record for this book is available from the British Library.
Paperback ISBN: 9781036705046

Chapter One

Tuesday, 25 September 2018

"WILL everything be ready for me to leave at eleven-thirty?" asked Gus.

"No problem, guv," said Alex. "We've added the finishing touches this morning."

Gus Freeman had been at London Road yesterday when news came through to the Old Police Station office that Oliver Rogers had been arrested at his sister's house in Mold, near Chester. The retired rare coin collector from Stratton-on-the-Fosse had moved to the village in North Wales in February 2017.

Peter Wright had insisted Rogers continue the two-mile commute from home to the lock-up on the industrial estate at Chilcompton until the right buyer could be identified for the one hundred and eleven Roman coins.

Oliver Rogers told police he had feared for his life. He hadn't agreed to broker a deal until Wright threatened him with a knife. His first instinct was to inform the authorities.

All finds of that nature should be reported. Rogers was well aware treasure recovered from underneath the earth belonged to the Crown, where the rightful owner couldn't be determined.

Gus took Rogers's claim with a pinch of salt. DI Gareth Francis contacted the office yesterday afternoon to tell Alex the pair's financials showed they split the money fifty-fifty.

"Rogers had one-hundred and eighty thousand reasons not to complain," Neil Davis had said when Alex told the others the news.

"If Wright could have cut out the middleman, he would have taken the full amount without a second thought," said Lydia. "They both deserve everything they get."

"Oliver Rogers should get five years," said Gus.

"What about Peter Wright, guv?" asked Blessing.

"I would hope for a mandatory life sentence."

"Do we deserve a celebratory drink this Friday, guv?" asked Neil.

"What have we got to celebrate, Neil?" asked Gus.

"We put the lid on our contribution to the Stan Jones case," said Neil. "Then we found evidence to nail Ralph Gibbons for murder. After that, Blessing helped make it a hat trick by unmasking Peter Wright as Clive Palmer's killer. I thought that was a decent return for ten days' work."

"It's what the public expects from us, Neil," said Gus.

"Come on, Neil," said Alex. "Surely you can see why Gus isn't enthusiastic. Its odds on Luke has left us for good, and for the next three months, we've got DI Packenham in the office."

"We don't need to invite her," said Neil. "Let's call it a farewell drink for Luke instead. We can't let him go without marking the occasion."

"I can live with that," said Gus. "Grace doesn't start

until next Monday. DS Mercer told me she had to finish her report on the administration set up at London Road first."

"The Waggon & Horses at nine o'clock," said Neil. "Melody will appreciate a night out. She's looking forward to comparing notes with Suzie Ferris."

"I'll give Luke a call," said Lydia. "He might want to invite a new friend."

"The more, the merrier," said Alex.

Gus hoped there would be other topics of conversation on offer than pregnancies and failed relationships. These social occasions were designed to allow the team to discuss something other than work, but there were limits. For example, sometimes he wished he were interested in sports like Neil.

Forty minutes before his midday meeting with the Chief Constable, Gus collected the relevant file folders and headed for the lift. As he drove towards Devizes, he spotted two council workers. One stood on the fourth step of a six-foot ladder, and the other watched his colleague from the safety of the pavement. Both wore ubiquitous yellow hi-viz jackets and hard hats. Gus couldn't imagine what they did that needed such elaborate precautions.

The usual delays frustrated Gus on his daily trips between home and work and journeys in between. Temporary traffic lights for non-existent road workers, mothers on the school run who couldn't walk their children half a mile to school, and the constant threat of a waste collection vehicle slowing progress to a crawl.

Somehow, he parked the Focus in the visitor's car park at London Road, negotiated Reception, and scaled the stairs to the administration area before the appointed time.

"Good morning, Gus," said Vera Butler. "How's the patient?"

"Suzie, or Bert Penman?" asked Gus.

"Suzie's fine, isn't she?" asked Vera.

"No problems, so far," said Gus. "As for Bert, Irene North is looking after him at home. I've not heard any complaints from Bert about his new walking stick either, so that's good."

"We heard the news about Luke Sherman's temporary replacement," said Vera. "Do you think you'll survive until the New Year?"

"There will be a period of change," said Gus. "but I'm sure Ms Packenham will cope. Geoff keeps insisting she's an excellent officer."

Vera smiled. If Grace thought she would get Gus to change his ways, she had another think coming.

"Kenneth's door's opening," she said. "He's wondering where you are."

"We're getting together at the Waggon & Horses on Friday night," said Gus. "You're welcome to drop in if you're free. It's a farewell drink for Luke."

"We might just do that," said Vera.

"Are you still seeing Rick Chalmers?"

"Heaven's, no. That was a one-off. Divya Yadav's husband, Arjun, has to work nights from time to time, and she hates being alone in the house. So we've started meeting two or three nights a week when Arjun's turn comes around."

"Friday, then," said Gus, crossing the mezzanine to the Chief Constable's office.

Gus tapped on the door and entered. Kenneth Truelove and Geoff Mercer were waiting.

"Time's short, Freeman," said Kenneth. "Is that the Palmer file?"

"Done and dusted, sir," said Gus, handing Kenneth the folder.

"Peter Wright played on Clive Palmer's past," said Geoff, "ably supported by that builder, Tom Angell. But, in the end, the case centred on pure greed. Wright suspected Palmer was searching for something valuable after his workmate borrowed his metal detector. So he followed Palmer, watched him retrieve something from John Oatley's land on Sunday afternoon, and killed Palmer the following night."

"Ben Moore couldn't see beyond the murder being related to the reason Palmer went to prison," said Gus. "He spent too much time on that facet of the case and ran out of time. Blessing cut to the chase and realised Palmer's killer lived in Purton during the ten months he was there and knew him well."

"That reduced the field of runners to less than ten," said Geoff.

"I don't suppose those rare coins will ever surface again?" asked Kenneth.

"Not a chance, sir," said Gus. "One unscrupulous collector may have them hidden away, but my guess is whoever bought them from Wright and Rogers sold them on, at a profit, to several unsuspecting buyers. Then, when the case gets to court, the odd collector might wonder whether what he purchased was part of the Purton dowry hoard."

"Do you think they would come forward?" asked Geoff.

"Don't hold your breath," said Kenneth.

"Thanks to Blessing's intuitive approach, we wrapped this one up far quicker than I imagined," said Gus.

"Do you know what the PCC complained about the other morning?" said the Chief Constable. "He said if your team was to continue solving these cases in double-quick time, it could reflect badly on other detective teams around the county."

"You must remind the PCC that we have a distinct advantage, sir," said Gus. "First, the original investigating team has covered the groundwork. We don't have to attend a murder scene, identify a victim, and determine the cause of death. We're not waiting days for forensics, identifying potential witnesses, suspects, and so forth because that's laid out in the murder book. Second, apart from last week, when we were tying up loose ends on other cases, we have one unsolved murder to concentrate on at a time and nothing else."

"Exactly, sir," said Geoff Mercer, "The only time I can remember having one case to handle was on my first day as a DC. Then I went for a coffee, and my DS sneaked a couple more into my in-tray while my back was turned. The detective squad at Gablecross runs between ten and fifteen separate investigations per officer at any time. Sometimes they get a good run and reduce the load. Sometimes nothing works, they can't make headway, and the numbers build up. But, unfortunately, the entire squad still has to drop everything for a major incident."

"I haven't forgotten what it was like at the sharp end, Mercer," said Kenneth.

"Sorry, sir," said Geoff.

"Apology accepted," said Kenneth. "Things have changed. We didn't have the PCC whispering in our ears about budgets, targets, diversity, and the role of the police in society."

"The good old days," said Geoff.

"When dinosaurs ruled," said Gus. "Are you suggesting we change our approach, sir?"

"Don't you dare," said Kenneth. "I want these files in

my drawer sorted before I retire. The next case I have for you has been with us for far too long. The murder of Katherine Alford? Does that ring a bell with either of you?"

"Did Trefor Davies run that investigation, sir?" asked Geoff.

"Wayne Barnett was a DI at Marlborough Police Station at the time," said Kenneth. "Trefor had a watching brief because Barnett's first murder was the Alford case. DS Anna Cromwell was Barnett's sidekick."

"She's an ACC in Dorset now, isn't she?" asked Gus.

"Have you crossed swords with her, Freeman?" asked the Chief Constable.

"The Katherine Alford murder was ten years ago, sir. It's one of those that sticks in your memory. A nasty business with no resolution. I found it best to keep out of the way of officers like Anna Cromwell on their fast track to the top. She soon left Wayne Barnett and her superiors at Marlborough in her wake. Rumours started early doors. Anna Cromwell trampled on anyone who disrupted her race to the summit. Therefore, I made a mental note and steered clear."

"It might be an idea to let DI Packenham drive to Dorchester to speak to her, sir," said Geoff. "They'll talk the same language."

"And Freeman can't say something leading to me getting earache from her Chief Constable," said Kenneth. "I like your way of thinking, Mercer."

"I've dealt with DCI Trefor Davies in the past, sir," said Gus. "He's a good sort. I don't foresee any problem with the crew at Marlborough. Can you run me through the details of the case again; to refresh my memory?"

"Katherine was a devoted mother of two, divorced and living in a semi-detached house on the Purlyn Acre estate with her ten-year-old son, Paul. Her twenty-four-year-old daughter, Emily, lived on the other side of town in West Manton. Emily was a single mother with a six-year-old daughter, Sophia. On Saturday, the twenty-eighth of June in 2008, Katherine was at home watching television. Paul was in bed, asleep. Katherine received a phone call at around half-past nine. The identity of the caller was never determined. Whoever it was, and whatever they said to Katherine, it was enough to get her to run next door to her neighbour, Lily Faulkner. Lily, fifty-six, agreed to return to the house and babysit. Katherine told Lily she'd be gone for ten minutes."

"That was the last time anyone saw Katherine Alford alive," said Geoff.

"Apart from whoever she met that night," said Gus. "Where did she go, anyway? How did she get there? Someone must have seen her."

"It was the last confirmed sighting of Katherine," said Kenneth. "She drove off in her red, ten-year-old Peugeot 306 at nine forty-five."

"I remember now," said Geoff. "The Peugeot was spotted the following morning at seven o'clock. A husband and wife from Clench Common, cycling along the A346, turned off past the caravan site and intended to follow the road to join the A4 Bath Road. Instead, they stopped at the West Woods car park. It's an ancient woodland site littered with walking trails to the south of town. There's a carpet of bluebells in springtime that attracts thousands of visitors, but late on Saturday evenings, it was popular with courting couples seeking privacy. As a deterrent, it was a regular occurrence for Marlborough police to send a car to the site. When DI Barnett checked with uniformed officers, he learned a patrol car had cruised the parking lot at twenty minutes to eleven that night. The place was empty."

"Who spotted the car?" asked Gus.

"Dominic and Amy Gray," said Kenneth. "Kitted out in fluorescent lycra and helmets. Unfortunately, their early Sunday morning ride to Bath and back was scuppered by a dead body."

"Why did they stop?" asked Gus.

"The husband was annoyed," said Kenneth. "He thought someone had abandoned the car."

"It was only ten years old," said Gus. "I would argue it was only just a run-in."

"Katherine Alford was inside the car slumped over the steering wheel," said Kenneth. "Dominic Gray told police she showed signs of strangulation."

"He watches cop shows on TV, I suppose?" said Gus.

"Dominic Gray's a doctor at Savernake Hospital, Freeman," said Kenneth. "Katherine was fully clothed, and although there were signs of a struggle, there were no apparent signs of robbery or a sexual attack. The post-mortem confirmed that Doctor Gray's observations had been correct."

"Was anything found at the scene?" asked Gus.

"Such as?" asked Geoff.

"A ligature, a cord, something of that nature. Or was it manual strangulation?"

"Police found nothing unexpected inside the car," said Kenneth. "Katherine left home in a hurry. She took her car keys and nothing else. There was no weapon, no evidence left behind by her assailant. Nevertheless, news of the murder shocked and scared the local community. Neighbours from the Purlyn Acre estate were eager to help in the police investigation. Nobody enjoys having a savage murderer on the loose. The residents of Clench Common also expressed concerns."

"Are you having second thoughts over your idyllic country cottage, Geoff?" asked Gus.

"I didn't mention the murder to Christine when she told me she had her heart set on Clench Common. We had looked at over a dozen places that didn't meet her approval. It was ten years ago, and West Woods is two miles from our cottage."

"What progress have you made, Mercer?" asked Kenneth.

"I put our place on the market in early August, sir. We've had several viewings, and the estate agent reckons we'll have no problem getting the price we're asking."

"They always do, Mercer," said Kenneth. "Is the cottage vacant?"

"No, but they are further along with the selling process, and I might go cap in hand to the bank manager for a bridging loan in a few weeks."

"You've got this to come, sir," said Gus.

"Don't remind me, Freeman," said Kenneth. "There's a lot to be said for finding a good place to live and staying put until they carry you out in a box. Moving house has to be one of the most stressful things anyone has to endure."

"Apart from having your mother murdered," said Gus. "How did Emily and Paul Alford handle the following months and years? Did the ex-husband step into the breach?"

"Not a bit," said Kenneth. "Katherine had reverted to her maiden name after the divorce. The ex-husband, Daniel Matravers, was forty-six and lived in Salisbury. He'd moved on. Paul went to live with his sister, Emily, in West Manton."

"Is everyone you've mentioned still alive and at the same address?" asked Gus.

Kenneth checked the murder file.

"There's nothing here to suggest either of the older witnesses has passed. Lily Faulkner hasn't moved from her semi-detached house in Purlyn Acre. She's had the same neighbours since Katherine Alford's murder. Bert Harris was walking home when he saw Katherine's red Peugeot. Harris was sixty-four back then and lived on the same estate."

"What time did Bert Harris say he saw the car?" asked Gus.

"Harris said he left home at half-past ten with the dog. He was halfway home from Coldharbour Lane when the car passed him. He told police it was his usual twenty-minute circuit with the dog."

"So, Katherine left home at nine forty-five in her car and was still driving at around a quarter to eleven," said Gus. "Where had she been? Was she alone in the car? Which direction was she heading?"

"Patience is a virtue, Freeman," said Kenneth. "DI Barnett's enquiries produced one possible sighting of interest. Witnesses came forward to say a woman matching Katherine's description was seen with a man outside The Roebuck public house at around half-past ten that Saturday night."

"That's a five-minute drive from her home," said Geoff, checking the details on his phone. "If that was Katherine, then the man could have been responsible for the phone call that caused her to drop everything to meet him."

"True," said Gus, "but Katherine told Lily Faulkner she'd be gone for ten minutes. Was Katherine with the same man for forty minutes before arriving at the pub? Or was it someone else? Did she meet another person there who persuaded her to extend her stay?"

"DS Cromwell interviewed Belinda Franklin, a barmaid at The Roebuck," said Kenneth. "The twenty-one-year-old told Cromwell she was busy serving drinks all night. Cromwell showed Belinda a victim's photograph, but she wasn't sure she'd seen the woman before. The other witnesses were Charlotte Ovens and Jasmine Park. Both ladies were in their early thirties and engaged to be married."

"Did they describe the man they saw outside the pub?" asked Gus.

"A vague description," said Kenneth. "The man wore casual clothes. He was of a similar height and build to Katherine Alford. Neither girl noticed any distinguishing features, such as rings, tattoos, or glasses. He had his back to them throughout."

"They were on a night out," said Geoff. "No doubt they'd had a few drinks. The last thing they thought of doing was taking note of a random couple in case the police needed to identify a potential killer."

"Yet they remembered that couple talking outside the pub and came forward without being sought out," said Gus. "Why did they remember them? Were they arguing and drawing attention to themselves? Was the man stopping the woman from leaving? Did Barnett and Cromwell get answers to these questions?"

"You know the drill, Freeman," said Kenneth. "Many answers will be in this murder file if you dig deep enough. I'm just giving you the headlines. Then, your team can ask questions not answered to your satisfaction when you speak to the detectives involved."

"From what I've heard so far, I'm struggling to find a

clear motive for Katherine's murder, sir," said Gus. "To add to our woes, police found no forensic evidence from the killer in the Peugeot. The murder took place in June. What do casual clothes suggest at that time of year?"

"Shorts and a t-shirt?" said Geoff. "Although, if her companion was older than Katherine, he might choose a short-sleeved shirt and slacks."

"If he strangled her with his bare hands," said Gus, "surely, he would have left prints somewhere inside the car, showing signs of a struggle."

"Nothing collected by forensics matched anything on record," said Kenneth. "The post-mortem report showed the killer wore light cotton gloves."

"Did those ladies at The Roebuck notice if he was wearing gloves at half-past ten?" asked Gus. "Or perhaps they were tucked into his back pocket, ready for later."

"We don't know whether the killer and this man are connected," said Geoff. "It might not have been Katherine, anyway."

"If I can add another question to the list," said Kenneth. "How did the killer get home from West Woods?"

"We don't know if anyone was in the car with Katherine when Bert Harris saw her drive past," said Geoff.

"We can visit the housing estate and the surrounding roads," said Gus. "I can't visualise the layout. Marlborough isn't a town I know well. But look, if Charlotte and Jasmine got the time right, and the victim was at The Roebuck, then Bert Harris would have seen a passenger in the Peugeot."

"Katherine and her companion must have left within minutes and driven towards her home," said Geoff, consulting the map on his phone.

"They were a fair distance from West Woods at twenty to eleven when the patrol car did its regular check," said

Gus. "I wonder which way the officers approached the car park and which road they took when they left?"

"The patrol wasn't looking for the Peugeot in particular," said Geoff.

"They would have had dashcams fitted a decade ago," said Gus. "I hope DI Barnett checked the footage to see whether the Peugeot appeared. It might give a more accurate time for the car arriving at the West Woods car park."

"Bert Harris's sighting puts them on the road leading back to Purlyn Acre," said Geoff. "Why change direction and head into the country, especially since Katherine had told her neighbour she wouldn't be ten minutes. She was driving, not her companion."

"Which suggests she went with the man willingly," said Gus. "Look, if you had a phone call late at night from a stranger or even a casual acquaintance, would you drop everything and go to meet them?"

"Not likely, so Katherine knew the man well," said Geoff. "But the police questioned her friends and family members, and they had alibis. None of them had a motive."

"Barnett and Cromwell were hunting for a mystery man," said Kenneth. "Someone Katherine trusted but who was unknown to her family and friends."

"No wonder they had trouble finding him," said Geoff.

"So, at around a quarter to eleven, Katherine was driving between Coldharbour Lane and home," said Gus. "How long would it have taken her to drive to West Woods?"

"Fifteen minutes," said Geoff. "Quicker on a Saturday night."

"There couldn't have been an argument at that stage," said Kenneth. "Katherine wouldn't have agreed to drive into the countryside if there had, surely?"

"So, they arrived at West Woods car park at eleven o'clock," said Gus. "Forensics found no signs of sexual activity. Katherine wore whatever clothing she had on when she left the house."

"A short-sleeved, off-white shift dress and a pair of strappy sandals," said Kenneth. "That was Lily Faulkner's description."

"What did the post-mortem report record as the probable time of death?" asked Gus.

"Between midnight and one o'clock," said Kenneth. "West Woods is an isolated spot. The killer could have chosen it because he hoped for something other than a chat."

"They had a lot to chat about if Katherine didn't die until midnight," said Gus. "Something sparked a violent argument which resulted in murder."

"What about the cotton gloves?" asked Geoff. "Are we saying her companion planned to kill her all along?"

"They're not a common item for a chap to carry on a Saturday night out," said Gus, "unless he's a snooker referee."

"Hang on," said Kenneth, "we don't know where this man was before he called Katherine. Perhaps he was at work, and she picked him up and drove him to The Roebuck for a drink and a brief chat. But, on the other hand, maybe they didn't bother with a drink, just stood outside the pub and talked."

"Belinda Franklin couldn't swear either person was ever inside The Roebuck," said Geoff.

"Nobody heard a heated argument lasting for up to sixty minutes in West Woods either," said Gus.

"No witnesses came forward to say they heard screams or sounds of a struggle at the murder scene," said Kenneth.

"The killer chose West Woods because they knew they were unlikely to be disturbed."

"Which adds further evidence that the killer was local," said Gus. "How long had Katherine lived in Marlborough?"

"She was born there," said Kenneth. "Matravers moved to Marlborough from Salisbury to work. They met in 1982, married the following year, and divorced when Paul was two years old in 2000."

"Katherine would have known the area was frequented by courting couples," said Geoff. "Why go there otherwise at that time of night?"

"Forget that for a minute, Geoff," said Gus. "Why did they divorce, sir?"

"Irreconcilable differences," said Kenneth.

"That sounds a cop-out," said Gus. "More likely to be how Katherine explained things to her teenage daughter, Emily. We'll ask Daniel Matravers for the truth."

"As much as I enjoy these get-togethers," said Kenneth, "the PCC demands my presence in his well-appointed office in an hour. So I can rely on you to do your best with the material at your disposal, Freeman; whoever is working with you will help sort out this mystery in short order."

"Has Rick Chalmer's future been determined, sir?" asked Gus.

"I suppose you would have preferred to see Chalmers in your office for the next three months?"

"He's a detective sergeant with bags of experience," said Gus. "Although Geoff keeps telling me what an outstanding officer Ms Packenham is, I haven't seen her track record on murder investigations."

"Grace was involved in the latter stages of the Stan Jones case," said Kenneth.

"I think DS Davis would say her contribution was

minimal at best," said Gus. "Much like a football team introducing a substitute in added time to run down the clock."

"Unlike you to use a sporting analogy, Gus," said Geoff. "You're right about Grace, though; she hasn't worked on a murder investigation."

"We don't get that many in the county, thank goodness," said Kenneth.

Gus looked at the folder on the Chief Constable's desk and thought that if they were all as puzzling as this one, it was just as well.

Chapter Two

KENNETH PICKED up the phone and called the administration area.

"Vera tells me our lunch is on its way," he said. "At least I'll get my ear bent on a full stomach by the PCC."

"If you're spending the afternoon with our Lord and Master, you had better stick to coffee today. Sir," said Gus. "No matter how inspiring the cakes are this week from the naked baker."

Kenneth glanced towards the bottom drawer of his filing cabinet and sighed.

"We won't have long to wait, by the sound of things," he said.

Gus could hear Kassie Trotter's strident voice outside the office. Then there was a sharp tap on the door, and she was marching into the room, pushing her trolley.

"A vision in pink," said Geoff Mercer.

"A homage to the naked baker, perhaps?" said Gus.

Kassie had spent part of the weekend at the hairdresser. Instead of her usual black tresses with a flash of red, green, or electric blue, she'd switched to one colour. Some might call it shocking pink, but nothing that Kassie did ever shocked Gus.

His young friend was searching for Mr Right. It was open to debate whether this was the best way to go about it. Gus wasn't one to pass comments on hairstyles. He didn't stick his finger in a light socket to get his hair to stand on end. It just happened.

"Good morning, gentlemen," said Kassie as she placed the tray of coffees on the desk beside the Chief Constable. "Everything you ordered was in stock this week."

"Great," said Geoff. "I can't do without my bacon bap."

"We've told the suppliers to stop pestering us with the vegan alternatives," said Kassie, handing Kenneth his plate of food first. "They're convinced they'll catch on, but a balanced diet trumps everything, doesn't it, Mr Freeman?"

"It's never done me any harm, Kassie," said Gus, tucking into his grilled chicken wrap.

"Do you have any other news, Kassie?" asked Geoff.

"Rumour has it Gareth Francis and Rebecca Gregory are an item," said Kassie.

"I think DS Mercer was more interested in his stomach than idle gossip, Ms Trotter," said Kenneth.

"Sorry, sir," said Kassie. "I don't know what I'm doing wrong. Everyone's at it, even Rhys Evans."

Gus had almost forgotten the Welsh, rugby-playing Police Surgeon who had arrived at London Road at the end of June. The last time he'd spotted Rhys was with Amazing Grace. They used to spend their thirty-minute lunch break together.

"Who's the lucky girl?" he asked.

"I should have guessed," said Kassie, "when Vera and I visited Rhys to welcome him to the town. He was more interested in where he could get his yoga sessions than popping into The Bear for a few drinks with us. Vera said she saw him with Jagvir, a chef from the Indian restaurant. I heard the others call him Jags when I went in for a takeaway a few weeks ago on a Saturday night."

Kenneth Truelove sat, sipping his coffee, listening to his young protégé and her troubled love life. Kenneth thought it was time to have a word with his wife. They had already saved Kassie from a painful life on the streets. Perhaps his wife could offer a solution to finding Kassie a boyfriend. Someone not necessarily Mr Right, just Mr Right Now.

"If you were forced to spend Sunday at home, alone," said Geoff, "did you do any baking?"

"My heart wasn't in it, Mr Mercer," sighed Kassie. "Maybe I'll be in a better mood next week."

"In that case, we won't keep you," said Kenneth. "The others will be waiting for their lunch."

Kassie collected the empty cups and plates, piled them onto her trolley, and headed for the door.

"Never mind, Geoff," said Gus. "Christine won't badger you about your weight this week. I'd better grab the murder file and drive back to the office. Then we can discuss the headlines and prepare the room for action."

"Try to leave something for DI Packenham to do next Monday," said Geoff with a grin.

"I hope you've reminded Freeman his new staff member isn't a junior officer," said Kenneth. "Ms Packenham won't be making coffees for you or running errands."

"We don't have anyone with us in that capacity now, sir," said Gus. "We're a team. Everyone pitches in regardless of rank. The others don't work *for* me; they work *with* me. It's how I've always operated."

"I'll try to forget that antiquated sentiment before reaching the PCC's office, Freeman," said Kenneth. "Careless talk costs lives."

Gus and Geoff left Kenneth standing by the window, staring into the middle distance.

"I shouldn't need to remind you not to antagonise Grace," said Geoff. "Kenneth's right, she is a DI, the same rank you achieved, and in the PCC's world, she would run the show, not a relic like you."

"A relic? That's harsh," said Gus. "I've got forty years' experience under my belt. Grace has a degree and has been in the job for five minutes, and she's already made Inspector. Times have changed, and not necessarily for the better."

"Your team's on a roll, Gus," said Geoff. "It would be a shame if the PCC put the brakes on."

"Suzie will say the same tonight," said Gus. "I'll be reminded every morning as we walk from the bungalow to the cars. Don't let Grace get under your skin. It's only three months."

Kenneth whistled a tune in his office as he gathered his things for the afternoon meeting.

♫ *There may be trouble ahead, but while there's moonlight and music and love and romance; let's face the music and dance*♫

As Kenneth tried to remember the rest of the lyrics and prayed it wasn't a sign of what lay ahead, Gus had left the car park and eased the Focus into early afternoon traffic on London Road.

A murder without a motive. Gus wondered how Amazing Grace would cope with that for her first-ever murder case.

Gus hoped he was leaving Devizes early enough to miss the school run. He was in luck, and progress was swift. He spotted the two council workers again as he passed the junction leading to the new custody suite on Crook's Way. They stood beside their vehicle, looking towards the town.

A flashing red warning sign attracted Gus's attention. It informed him that his Focus was capable of travelling at thirty-four miles an hour. So that was what they were up to earlier. However, he still couldn't fathom why the task needed two people or why they were admiring their handiwork two hours later.

Gus would have loved to continue driving safely into the town centre, but as usual, there were obstacles. Delivery vans left wherever it was most inconvenient—pedestrians crossing the road where it suited them rather than using the zebra crossing. Yet the council spent money adding to the already mammoth signage at the roadside. It made you proud to be British.

As he pulled into the car park behind the Old Police Station, Gus wondered whether getting a job as a traffic warden was still possible. Or had the role been consigned to history like a saggar maker's bottom knocker? A million cars in the country are driven without insurance. If they could get on top of that problem, there might be enough money in the kitty to employ a warden in every town.

Gus thought it better than wasting money on signs suggesting you slowed as you came into town. Why not change the message? Slow-moving traffic ahead - as usual.

When he reached the first-floor office, the team was eager to hear what lay in store this week.

"The Chief Constable has handed us the murder file for Katherine Alford, a forty-four-year-old mother and grandmother. Katherine was strangled in her car in the countryside near Marlborough ten years ago. The years following the initial investigation saw detectives follow up several lines of enquiry without success. The case was featured on a regional TV crime show and was covered extensively in the local press. Both initiatives yielded nothing. Katherine's daughter, Emily, remains hopeful her mother's killer will be brought to justice. Her comments from the TV programme showed how painful her mother's unsolved murder was to her and her family."

Gus pinned Emily Alford's comments to a noticeboard. Then he handed a copy of the headlines from the murder file to each team member.

"Read, mark, and inwardly digest," said Gus. "Coffee, anyone?"

Nobody offered to go in his place, so Gus left them trawling through the details of the murder and subsequent investigation and joined the Gaggia in the restroom. Fifteen minutes later, everyone was refreshed and ready to continue.

"We should keep these comments of Emily's in mind as we review this case," said Gus. "We need to bring closure for Emily, her younger brother, Paul, and her daughter, Sophia. It was a tragic and frustrating crime as the Marlborough detectives opened leads that showed such promise. As with every murder, the victim's life is examined in minute detail. Often that's the shortest route to determine any plausible motive or compile a list of suspects. DI Wayne Barnett and DS Anna Cromwell scrutinised Katherine's life in great detail but never found a motive for someone wanting to kill her."

"Is that ACC Cromwell, guv?" asked Neil Davis.

"The very same, Neil," said Gus.

"Her reputation suggests she doesn't miss much, guv," said Neil.

"We'll need to find something the team missed," said Alex Hardy.

"Or someone," said Lydia Logan Barre.

"The murder file tells us Katherine's family described her as a caring, loving person with no enemies. Police enquiries couldn't shake that view. Indeed, they decided Katherine was never involved in drugs or any illegal activity. Moreover, they found no evidence of a romantic relationship after her marriage ended in 2000."

"Why would anyone want to murder someone like her?" asked Blessing Umeh. "She sounds a saint."

"We can't discount the possibility Katherine was in a relationship," said Gus. "It may have had to be kept secret, or at least well-hidden. The telephone call she received on the night she was murdered was important enough for her to go out, despite having a ten-year-old son upstairs in bed. A report in the local paper said Katherine told her neighbour she was meeting her brother. That neighbour, Lily Faulkner, was asked to babysit Paul while she popped out. Katherine didn't have a brother, so that was a lie."

"It could be an error in reporting," said Alex. "It has happened."

"Or an excuse to hide the true reason for leaving home in a hurry," said Neil.

"I can't wait to delve into that murder file," said Lydia.

"Well, the whiteboards and the walls have been cleared," said Gus. "Now would be a good time to get a map of Marlborough and the surrounding district in position. Also, the crime scene photos and lists of people interviewed. Then, Alex, you can contact the family and eyewitnesses. Finally, speak to DCI Trefor Davies at Marlborough. He'll remember the case well. It was DI Barnett's first murder case, but Trefor looked over his shoulder."

"Which makes it less likely they missed the obvious, guv," said Alex. "DCI Davies is an old hand."

"Experienced," said Gus. "He's younger than me and doesn't retire until next year."

"Sorry, guv," said Alex.

"Your first comment was fair, Alex," said Gus. "If the motive had been obvious, they would have seen it. Whoever called Katherine and persuaded her to drop everything to meet them must have been someone she knew well. The murder occurred around midnight, meaning she was away from the house for two and a half hours instead of the ten minutes she promised Lily Faulkner. She would have organised a babysitter beforehand if it were a pre-arranged meeting. She wouldn't have dashed out to her car with just her keys if it were a date. Katherine didn't take a handbag or purse. She had applied no makeup. It points to the phone call catching her on the hop."

"There's no mention of a mobile phone, guv," said Lydia.

"Katherine didn't own one. Money was tight," said Gus. "The call came through on Katherine's landline, but the caller withheld their number. The police decided the caller lived close to Marlborough, or in the town, because of the arrangements."

"Why would the caller hide their number, guv?" asked Alex. "Katherine had been single for eight years. There was no husband at home, and she knew the person on the other end of the line, anyway."

"Katherine's number could have been in the telephone directory," said Neil. "Perhaps it was the return call they wished to avoid if the caller was married."

"The phone call was one mystery the detectives never solved," said Lydia.

"It wasn't the only one. They couldn't prove Katherine was the woman seen at the pub, guv," said Blessing. "The distance from her house to the pub made it sound plausible, but did Lily Faulkner see which way Katherine drove when she dashed out of the house? Perhaps she drove in the opposite direction."

"What about the man who said he recognised Katherine's red car?" asked Neil.

"Bert Harris?" asked Lydia. "He left home at half-past ten with his dog and walked from the Purlyn Acre estate towards Coldharbour Lane. Looking at the map on the wall, he was on the return journey when Katherine's car passed him. Did that mean he saw her through the rear window or was the car heading towards him?"

"We'll need to go through each witness statement with a fine-toothed comb," said Alex.

"The barmaid the police spoke with didn't recognise Katherine," said Neil. "Blessing could be right. Maybe Katherine and her killer were never near the pub. As for the women who stood outside, Charlotte and Jasmine, it's clear they didn't study the couple closely. The descriptions are vague, and there's no mention of a red car parked nearby."

"We're trained observers," said Blessing. "I suppose we would have noticed if the couple were close, holding hands, kissing—something to show their relationship. There was no mention of the women hearing the couple laughing, joking, or arguing. Nobody could confirm when they left. The detectives used the sighting of the car to figure that out. If the car were heading towards the pub when Mr Harris saw it, that would disrupt the later timings. If it was Katherine's red car, they must have just left The Roebuck and were driving back to the estate where she lived."

"Look at the street map," said Alex. "It's not the quickest route to West Woods, but the road Bert Harris saw them on isn't a direct route to Purlyn Acre estate. Instead of going right, they could turn left at the end of Coldharbour Lane and head towards the town centre. The A4 Bath Road out of Marlborough would be a fast route to the road leading to West Woods. The same road the two cyclists were using the next morning."

"If they were at The Roebuck, why not go straight to West Woods instead of driving around the estates?" asked Lydia. "I would have taken George Lane to Granham Hill. That goes through Clench Common, where the Doctor and his wife lived. Katherine would have got there quicker than going via Bath Road."

"We don't know she wanted to go there," Blessing said. "Perhaps the argument started in the car, whether or not they were at the pub, and they forced Katherine to drive around aimlessly until her killer convinced her to visit the remote beauty spot."

"Two things strike me about the eye-witnesses outside The Roebuck, guv," said Neil. "Had they been drinking all night? How reliable were those statements from Charlotte Ovens and Jasmine Park? The other thing the file headlines didn't clarify was their relationship. Both ladies were in their early thirties and engaged to be married. What did that mean?"

"The Chief Constable told me the murder file confirms that each person interviewed was alive and living at the same address as in 2008, Neil. However, Charlotte and Jasmine couldn't marry until 2014, and it will be pot luck which you interview first when you land on their doorstep."

"Right, guv," said Neil. "They were living together. That must be hidden in the murder file."

"I think that's enough discussion for today," said Gus. "We'll start our first round of interviews in the morning. I'll take Lydia with me to Marlborough to meet with Trefor

Davies and Wayne Barnett if you could make the arrangements, please, Alex."

"Already on it, guv," said Alex.

"Who's going to speak to ACC Anna Cromwell, guv," asked Neil.

"Let's see what we learn from Marlborough first," said Gus. "Dorchester's a long trip."

"I've got everything worthwhile on the whiteboards, guv," said Lydia. "The original witness statements are in piles on that table at the back of the office."

"Well done," said Gus. "Remember to bring both statements from the detectives with you in the morning."

"Trefor Davies will be available at ten-fifteen, guv," said Alex.

"That's fine. Have you got hold of anyone else yet?"

"Emily Alford can see us after she returns from the school run, guv."

"Neil, perhaps you and Blessing could handle that one," said Gus.

"Emily's daughter, Sophia, would be sixteen now, Alex," said Blessing. "Why is Emily still doing the school run?"

"Aiden Fowler now lives with Emily in West Manton, Blessing," said Alex. "They have two boys, aged seven and five, who attend the local primary school. Sophia goes to St John's school and has just started studying A-levels."

"How old is Fowler?" asked Neil.

"Two years older than Emily," said Alex.

"What happened to the brother, Paul?" asked Lydia.

"Paul Alford is twenty," said Alex. "He left school at sixteen and started working with a South Marston Industrial Estate company. They manufacture electrical components. He moved out of the family home and now lives in a one-bedroomed flat on Copse Avenue. That's a three-mile drive from his place of work."

"Paul would be at the bottom of my list of people I'd wish to see," said Lydia. "He was asleep upstairs when his mother left the house."

"Paul was ten years old," said Gus. "He could perfectly understand overheard telephone conversations or recognise people his mother knew that his sister didn't. We don't yet appreciate the family dynamic. What sparked the divorce in 2000? Was it Paul's arrival two years earlier? A gap of fourteen years between births isn't unknown, but was it planned? Did it cause friction? Emily was seventeen when she fell pregnant with Sophia. They described Emily as a single mother throughout the investigation. Who was Sophia's father? What happened to him? When did Emily leave home? We might learn it was the ex-husband, Matravers, behind that decision. I don't think we can discount anyone at this stage. We don't know much about the Matravers family between 1982 and 2000 and the Alford family in the eight years that followed."

"You could add Paul to the list of imponderables, guv," said Blessing. "Did he find a place of his own because of his sister's partner? Or had Paul fallen out with Emily? How have relations been between the family in the ten years since the murder?"

"We've got to speak to Daniel Matravers, too," said Gus.

"He's on the list for Thursday, guv," said Alex.

"Keep adding appointments, Alex. The more, the merrier."

"We won't have many people left to see by Monday, guv," said Blessing.

"DS Mercer and the Chief Constable urged me to leave something for DI Packenham to do," said Gus.

"We could send her to Dorchester, guv," said Neil. "It would get her out of the way for the best part of a day."

"I don't want Grace to travel alone, Neil. She may speak the same language as Anna Cromwell, but this is her first murder investigation. I can't have her asking the wrong questions or coming away from Dorset Police HQ without getting the right answers."

"Will I have to go with Amazing Grace, guv?" asked Neil.

"Alex is staffing the office now Luke has left us," said Lydia. "Perhaps one of us girls should accompany her. I can dress for the occasion, I promise."

Gus doubted Lydia had anything in her wardrobe that wouldn't give Grace Packenham and Anna Cromwell palpitations but decided now wasn't the time to mention it.

"Food for thought," he said.

"If we're interviewing someone as senior as an Assistant Chief Constable, shouldn't you go with DI Packenham, guv?" asked Blessing.

"Is that the time? I'd better get home and start cooking. I'll see you in the morning."

Gus headed for the lift. Alex and Lydia waited until the lift door closed.

"I bet the Chief Constable told Gus to send Grace to Dorchester," said Lydia.

"Kenneth Truelove's a wily old fox," said Alex. "Grace is a high-flyer on the same track Anna Cromwell took. If he shows Dorchester what an asset she could be...."

"Grace could get transferred before the end of the year," said Neil. "That's not wily; it's genius. I wonder if Gus realises?"

"You could be wrong, Alex," said Blessing.

"Maybe working with Grace won't be that bad," said Lydia.

"Let's follow Gus's lead and go home," said Neil.

Blessing cleared her desk and stopped by the notice-board on her way to the lift. She wanted to read what Emily Alford had said on the TV programme where they appealed for new information several months after her mother's murder.

'I want the killer to come forward. It would be good if they did. My daughter, Sophia, often asks about her Nana. We look at her picture and remember the times we spent together. She was six when Mum died, and I told her Nana was in heaven, but Sophia thought it was somewhere we could visit. It doesn't get any easier.'

Blessing called the lift and made her way to the car park. For the first time in a long while, she was looking forward to hearing her mother's voice when Maryam made her weekly call tomorrow evening.

As Blessing edged the Nissan into traffic and started her journey to the Ferris farm outside Worton, Gus passed the junction to Crook's Way. The council workers had gone home. He glanced in his rear-view mirror and allowed himself a brief smile as he saw the flare of rapidly applied brake lights.

Gus was standing in the kitchen, deciding what he could rustle up for a quick meal, when Suzie breezed through the front door.

"Hello, darling," she cried. "Have you had a good day?"

"Hard to tell," said Gus. "Kenneth handed us the Katherine Alford case, and Kassie Trotter didn't have any sticky buns to hand around this lunchtime. If there were positives, I can't recall them. Oh yes, we're having an evening at the Waggon & Horses on Friday."

"That will be fun. We haven't been there in ages."

"If you can call a farewell drink for Luke Sherman, fun," said Gus.

"Oh, the team will be there, too. Okay, I'll drive us to the pub. Who else can make it?"

"My team, plus Melody and Jamie-BT. Lydia thinks Luke might like to bring a mate. While I was at London Road, before I met with Kenneth, I invited Vera, too. I don't know what I thought, but she accepted the invitation and will bring Divya Yadav."

"Quite a crowd," said Suzie. "There shouldn't be a shortage of things to talk about."

Gus smiled.

"What? Did I say something funny?" asked Suzie.

"No, I was just wondering what Amazing Grace does on a Friday evening."

"You didn't mention her by name," said Suzie, "but I assumed Grace would get an invitation when you said the team would be there."

"Neil thought as it was a farewell to Luke, plus a reward for several jobs well done in the past few weeks, Grace's presence wasn't required."

"I don't suppose you put up much resistance either, Gus Freeman."

"Kenneth reminded me Grace is a DI, the same rank as you," said Gus. "I have to show her respect."

"Not in the same way you have with me, I hope?" said Suzie, wrapping Gus in a bear hug.

"Don't be silly," said Gus. "Shall I continue planning our meal, or do you have something else in mind?"

"You cook. I'll shower and change," said Suzie. "After we've eaten, you can remind me about the Katherine Alford case."

They were sitting in the lounge by seven o'clock with a

mug of coffee each. Suzie snuggled up to Gus on the settee and listened as he outlined the details of Katherine's murder.

"A secret lover could explain why her family and friends insisted Katherine wasn't in a relationship," said Suzie when Gus had finished. "Why keep it a secret, though? She'd been single for several years. Would it have caused trouble or even shame?"

"What are you suggesting?" asked Gus. "It wouldn't have been a shock if the relationship was with another woman. Times had changed by 2008. It wouldn't have caused a front-page scandal. I can see an affair with a much younger man causing trouble. The boy's mother could have been Katherine's friend or neighbour. Barnett and Cromwell unearthed nothing of that nature, no matter how deep they dug."

"The phone call prompted the spur-of-the-moment request to meet up," said Suzie. "Which supports a theory it wasn't always easy for the caller to see Katherine. But hang on, you've only got the neighbour's word that the caller made the request. What if Katherine insisted they met face-to-face?"

"What, and misled Lily Faulkner, just as she did by telling her she had to meet her brother? I suppose it's possible. This case baffles me. Everything in the murder file is open to interpretation."

"Was there a pub closer to Katherine's home than The Roebuck?"

"I don't remember seeing one on the map," said Gus.

"If they wanted a clandestine meeting, the caller would hardly suggest a place where Katherine's friends and neighbours might gather. Of course, the man with his dog wasn't at the pub, but it wouldn't be wise to drive around an estate close to home if you didn't want to be seen."

"That's bothered me from the outset," said Gus. "Katherine left home at around nine forty-five. If we accept they used The Roebuck for their urgent conversation, did Katherine drive straight there to meet the caller? Were they outside the pub for fifty minutes before driving towards her home? Katherine insisted she'd only be gone for ten minutes. So Lily Faulkner was sitting in the house alone."

"I don't remember you telling me what happened later that night," said Suzie. "Did the neighbour ring Emily? When did they call the police?"

Gus scratched his head.

"That information didn't make the headline report. I should have read Lily Faulkner's statement in full. She could have left Paul asleep upstairs, trusting that he wouldn't wake before morning. Lily may have thought Katherine would be home in the early hours. Wayne Barnett checked whether Katherine had a record. She was never involved in drugs or reported for neglecting her children. They knew a patrol car was scheduled to cruise past the car park at West Woods to scare off would-be courting couples. Would it even get logged if Marlborough Police received a call at eleven or midnight saying a mother hadn't returned home as agreed? They wouldn't have treated Katherine as a missing person. She had only been away from her house for a couple of hours."

"If an officer took a call like that, I would hope they would speak up when they heard a body had been found eight hours later," said Suzie.

"True, but I would have called Emily first," said Gus. "She could have collected Paul. Although Emily didn't drive at the time, according to the file, she could have got a taxi from West Manton to her mother's house to take him home until the morning. Why didn't that register when Kenneth gave me the background of the case?"

"It's another aspect that needs clarification," said Suzie. "You won't solve this one in a matter of days, Gus."

"Blessing asked what the couple could have found to talk about for so long," said Gus.

"The time of death was midnight, or thereabouts," said Suzie. "I can see where Blessing's coming from. So after chatting at the pub, they drove around for a while and headed for West Woods. They couldn't have arrived before eleven, or the patrol car would have spotted them. So who chose the destination, and why, I wonder?"

"That had to be the killer, surely?"

"So the guy was local, and the beauty spot was well known to them. It was a place with which he was familiar. Maybe he'd been there with someone else."

"I wonder whether those patrols ever caught anyone in the act? Perhaps they took names. That might be worth a check."

"Maybe the killer and Katherine had visited the spot before," said Suzie.

"Why did the police rule out the possibility the killer drove to West Wood in their car?" asked Gus.

"So. you're back to that again. Was it Katherine at the pub? Was anyone in the red car with her when the dog walker saw her?"

"We'll keep going back over it until something makes sense," said Gus. "Kenneth asked a reasonable question earlier today. He asked how did the killer get home after he'd strangled Katherine? The attack occurred in the car around midnight, according to the post-mortem report. The body hadn't been moved since she slumped over the steering wheel. Therefore, if Katherine drove to the car park, the assumption was that a passenger was her killer. How about this for a theory? When they left The Roebuck, she drove towards Purlyn Acre because that was where he had parked his car."

"The mystery caller was close to her house when he phoned, watched her dash next door to arrange a babysitter, and Katherine picked him up for the short drive to the pub. They made the return journey, and he then drove his car to West Woods."

"Why didn't they use his car throughout?" asked Gus.

Suzie had to think for a moment.

"We don't know who the mystery person was. Perhaps his car was too well-known. Or there could have been a simpler explanation."

"I wish," sighed Gus.

"Well, what if her companion lived out of town? Somewhere that made the A4 Bath Road the best route home? That makes sense. They could visit West Woods, have sex, and then go separate ways."

"The detectives didn't believe there was a sexual motive for Katherine's murder," said Gus. "She was fully clothed, and there was no evidence of her having had intercourse that Saturday. But, as Blessing remarked, they did a lot of talking between eleven and midnight. There must have been an argument, and the killer struck in the heat of the moment."

"Perhaps Katherine refused to have sex," said Suzie.

"Why spend two hours chatting and driving around Marlborough, then? Why not drive straight home after the conversation at the pub? Why not drop the guy at his car rather than go to a remote spot with a reputation for being frequented by courting couples? Katherine must have understood what was likely to happen. No, I think she wanted the relationship brought into the open. Your point about his car being well-known adds to that. Katherine wasn't content with being a bit on the side."

"I always enjoy evenings like this when we wrestle with the problems you're facing with a case," said Suzie. "We may have opened a couple of new lines of enquiry. However, there's just one thing that bothers me."

"What's that?" asked Gus.

"How on earth do you explain the gloves?" asked Suzie.

Chapter Three

Wednesday, 26 September 2018

GUS WOKE EARLY, rolled out of bed, and headed for the shower. He'd had a disturbed night. A psychiatrist might judge him as disturbed at any rate. In a recurring dream, he was chased by a mayor with a severe case of eczema.

Suzie found him in the kitchen twenty minutes later.

"Sorry if I threw a spanner in the works last night, sweetheart."

"No, we'll need to explain those cotton gloves before putting this case to bed."

"As well as clarify those loose ends we identified," said Suzie. "I thought Trefor Davies was a solid copper. How could he have left so many questions unanswered?"

"I remember one person told me Trefor was a solid copper," said Gus, "but another qualified that statement by saying he was solid from the neck up."

"The apparent gaps in the murder file don't reflect well on ACC Cromwell's first murder case," said Suzie.

"Anna rose through the ranks so quickly I doubt she's ever handled another murder," said Gus. "They're not that common in the county, thank goodness."

"I echo that sentiment," said Suzie. "If they were, you'd never get to retire."

"Kenneth told me yesterday he wouldn't let me go until I cleared the files in his drawer," said Gus. "He didn't promise that he wouldn't add to the list. His biggest concern seemed to be a clash of personalities between myself and Amazing Grace. If she went running to HR, and word reached the PCC's ear, I'd be on garden duty at the allotments within minutes."

"You need to count to ten and hold your tongue," said Suzie.

"I don't think that would work," said Gus. "I'd sound like a Scottish Nationalist politician."

"We should get breakfast," said Suzie, "or we'll be late."

"Waffles?" asked Gus.

"Coffee and toast," she replied.

They left the bungalow at twenty-five minutes to nine.

"I'm taking Lydia to Marlborough this morning," said Gus. "Trefor Davies hasn't many months left before retirement beckons. Maybe she can encourage him to spill a few secrets."

"I hope you didn't encourage Lydia to wear an ultra-short skirt, Gus. I've warned you about that tactic before."

"With Amazing Grace at London Road this week, this could be Lydia's last chance for extravagance. Would you like a meal at The Lamb this evening?" asked Gus.

"Don't change the subject," said Suzie. "The Lamb sounds great. It would be a shame to spend our Wednesday evenings anywhere else."

Suzie's Golf led the way along London Road, and she

turned into the Police HQ car park with a minute to spare. Gus knew he wouldn't reach the office before half-past nine, but Grace wouldn't be tutting her disapproval this week, and he and Lydia weren't due in Marlborough until a quarter past ten.

Gus slowed to twenty-nine miles an hour as he passed Crook's Way, and a flashing green sign was his reward. It's incredible the difference several minutes can make in the mornings. His trip to the town centre was smooth and uninterrupted. Lydia was waiting for him by the Crime Review Team parking bays with a grey folder. Everything else was bold and brightly coloured. No change there.

"Good girl," said Gus, nodding at the folder. "Suzie and I were later than usual leaving the bungalow. Jump in, and we'll head straight to Marlborough."

"I'd prefer to take my Mini, guv," said Lydia, "but I'll slum it, just this once. DCI Davies is still at the old police station in George Lane, isn't he?"

"That's the place," said Gus. "Complete with its secure cells built to hold suspect terrorists. Geoff Mercer told me they're hanging on until Trefor retires before selling the building. The other officers will soon be housed in a smaller unit near the town centre."

Forty minutes later, they turned off George Lane into the car park.

"When was this station built, guv?" asked Lydia.

"Around fifty years ago, I guess," said Gus. "One-third red brick and two-thirds glass tend to pigeonhole a building in a decade that architecture would prefer to forget."

Gus parked the Focus as close to the main door as possible, and Trefor Davies met them in the Reception area. The clock on the wall ticked around to fourteen minutes past ten.

"Thanks for seeing us this morning, Trefor," said Gus. "My colleague DS Hardy told you what we were after, I hope?"

"The Katherine Alford case from June 2008," said Trefor. "Who do we have here, Gus?"

"Lydia Logan Barre, sir," said Lydia.

"Beautiful one," said DCI Davies. "Your parents named you well."

Trefor Davies led the way to his office. There was no doubt where their host came from. A Welsh flag hung on the wall above his chair, and an autographed rugby ball sat on a cradle beneath.

"Did you play, sir?" asked Lydia.

"Until I was forty," said Trefor. "I played outside half."

Gus was none the wiser. It made sense that they would play a ball game outside, but it was a mystery where the half came into it.

"Are there any famous names on the ball?" asked Lydia.

"I won it in a charity raffle," said Trefor. "It's signed by the Six Nations squad that won the match at Twickenham in February 2008. The first time Wales had beaten England at home in twenty years. I was there."

"The murder we're here to discuss occurred four months later," said Gus. "I hope you didn't take your eye off the ball."

"Very droll, Gus," said Trefor. "No, I didn't win the rugby ball until December. A Christmas raffle at my old club in Pontypridd."

"Talk us through the events following the discovery of Katherine Alford's body," said Gus. "When did the police receive the first call?"

Trefor Davies went to a filing cabinet to retrieve a folder.

"I must admit I needed to refresh my memory on this one after Alex Hardy rang me," said Trefor. "My wife tells me my memory is selective, but I fear it goes deeper. Over the past couple of years, I have been looking forward to retirement. I'm sure you had similar longings, Gus. Nothing of the force we joined as young men has survived, but now retirement's almost upon me. I'm dreading what lies ahead."

"At least you and your officers followed procedure ten years ago and recorded everything," said Gus. "We would be in a mess if we went to court and didn't have our note-book to refresh our memory."

"The transcripts from the notebooks are in this folder," said Trefor. "I hadn't read them for a decade, and I haven't had time to get through them. So forgive me if I need to refer to the folder from time to time."

"You know how I work," said Gus. "It's only a few months since we were here before. This isn't a witch-hunt attempting to smear the reputation of detectives who handled the Alford case. We seek the truth, nothing more. Whatever we learn today will get added to the knowledge we gather over the coming days. I hope we'll find Katherine's killer, but whatever happens, no blame will fall on the shoulders of those involved in the initial investigation."

"I understand, Gus," said Trefor. "Let me see now. The first call came from Dr Dominic Gray on Sunday morning. We logged the call at four minutes past seven."

"Do you have the details of that call?" asked Lydia.

"Dr Gray said he had spotted what he thought was an abandoned car in the car park out at West Woods. His wife, Amy, was with him, and they were cycling from their home in Clench Common towards the Bath Road. While he approached the car, she stayed on the roadside with their two bicycles. Dr Gray was using his mobile phone to photograph the back of the car to capture the number plate when he realised someone was inside. The passenger door was unlocked, and Dr Gray leaned into the car and checked for signs of life. Then, after telling his wife to stay where she was, he called the police. He told the officer who took the call that the female driver had been dead for several hours and suspected someone had strangled her. Dr Gray then attached the photo of the number plate to an SMS and sent it to us. We soon identified the owner of the vehicle. When the first uniformed officers arrived at the murder scene, they cordoned off the area, took statements from Dr Gray and his wife, who then cycled home."

"It must have been a shock," said Lydia.

"More of a shock for Amy Gray," said Trefor Davies. "Dominic Gray's work at Savernake Hospital would have prepared him for what he discovered. Dr Gray told the uniformed officers he used a cloth from his cycle kit to avoid leaving fingerprints on the door handle. The only time he touched the body was to check for a pulse. The subsequent post-mortem confirmed his initial cause of death. Someone had strangled Katherine sometime around midnight."

"There was no record of a call late on Saturday night?" asked Lydia.

Trefor referred to the folder.

"We logged calls late on Saturday evening regarding a fight outside the Royal Oak. A concerned resident from Savernake also complained that boy racers were shattering the quiet on a road where they lived. Why, what were you expecting?"

"Katherine left home in a hurry," said Lydia, "leaving Lily Faulkner to babysit young Paul. Katherine was supposed to be home by ten o'clock. So why didn't Lily raise the alarm?"

"Mrs Faulkner told us she was watching television and fell asleep," said Trefor, rechecking the folder. "When she woke up, it was two o'clock. She checked outside the front door, but Katherine's car hadn't returned, and she assumed whatever was wrong with Katherine's brother meant she was unlikely to get back before morning."

"So, she stayed downstairs until Paul woke up?" asked Lydia.

"That's what she told us," said Trefor. "Mrs Faulkner told Paul his mother had been called away when he came downstairs at half-past eight. It was an emergency, but he wasn't to worry. Lily got his breakfast and told Paul she would look after him until his mother got home."

"When did the police reach the Purlyn Acre estate?" asked Gus.

"A little after nine-thirty," said Trefor. "Mrs Faulkner opened the door and immediately guessed something dreadful had happened. The boy ran outside looking for his mother."

"How awful for the poor lad," said Lydia.

"It's never a pleasant experience," said Trefor. "I'm sure Gus has had to notify hundreds of relatives of a sudden death over the years."

"I lost count," said Gus. "Did the officers know who lived at the address?"

"The number plate check had come back for a 1998 Peugeot 306 owned by Katherine Alford. The electoral roll showed Katherine lived at the address with her ten-year-old son, Paul. After speaking with Mrs Faulkner and finding out who she was and why she was in the house, the officers learned Katherine also had a daughter. Emily, who lived in

West Manton. She left home aged eighteen in 2002. As Emily was Katherine's next of kin, they visited her straight after leaving Purlyn Acre."

"What about Paul Alford?" asked Gus.

"The news the officers delivered didn't register at first. Finally, Lily Faulkner agreed to take care of the boy until they could make other arrangements."

"Who went to inform the family?" asked Lydia.

"DS Anna Cromwell and DC Callum Brady," said Trefor. "Callum left us in 2009. One of those that fell by the wayside."

"How did Lily Faulkner describe her relationship with Katherine Alford?" asked Gus. "Were they good friends?"

"They'd been neighbours for ages," said Trefor. "Katherine was well-liked on the estate; nobody had a bad word to say. Mrs Faulkner had lost her husband to a heart attack six years before the murder. Her only son had emigrated to New Zealand before that, so Lily was lonely and always ready to chat over coffee. Katherine spent a lot of time with Lily. They got on well enough, even before her marriage ended."

"Katherine didn't have a full-time job then?" asked Lydia.

"It was a bone of contention between Katherine and her ex-husband, Daniel Matravers," said Trefor. "He thought her place was in the home. So Katherine worked until she was seven months pregnant with Emily, and then she stayed home beyond her statutory maternity leave."

"That must have caused financial hardship when the marriage ended," said Gus.

"Lily Faulkner told our officers Katherine's mother died in 2002," said Trefor, referring to the folder for confirmation. "Mary Alford lived in a smaller property on the same estate. She'd been widowed when Katherine was in her early twenties. I imagine monies from her mother's estate allowed Katherine to cope with most of her ex-husband's income loss."

"It's clear Lily Faulkner was close to Katherine," said Lydia. "The phone call Katherine received didn't leave her with time to arrange something with her daughter on the other side of town. Katherine didn't give the matter a second thought and soon knocked on her door."

"And Lily didn't refuse," said Gus. "She agreed straight away. Had Lily stayed at Katherine's house babysitting Paul before that night?"

"According to her statement, it was the first time," said Trefor.

"DI Barnett and his colleagues could never find evidence of Katherine being in a relationship," said Gus. "Did Lily Faulkner have a closer insight on such matters? If they were good friends, perhaps Katherine would have confided in her. Did Lily hold something back from the police, I wonder?"

"No matter who Wayne and Anna spoke to, they couldn't find evidence Katherine was seeing anyone," said Trefor Davies. "The first person they asked was Emily, the daughter. She insisted her mother was happier since her father walked out. The last three years of the marriage had been hell. Since then, Katherine had avoided the subject of relationships. Emily believed her mother was unwilling to risk getting hurt again."

"Emily moved out around the time her grandmother died, and her brother, Paul, was just four years old," said Gus. "Did that seem odd to you or your detectives?"

"Daniel Matravers had walked out two years earlier," said Trefor. "According to Lily Faulkner, Katherine told her

Emily was a handful as a teenager. Lily could well believe it, with young men in cars dropping Emily off late at night every weekend. She told Katherine it would end in tears, and it did when Emily discovered she was pregnant."

"What happened to the father?" asked Lydia. "She was a single mother for several years."

"Emily couldn't be sure who Sophia's father was," said Trefor. "Katherine was upset and angry. There were problems in the marriage, and her mother was ill. As you know, Mary Alford died later in the same year. Meanwhile, Emily left to forge a life with her daughter, Sophia. Lily's opinion was that the age gap between Paul and Emily had resulted in Katherine lavishing more attention on the young boy. Emily feared her mother would favour Sophia over her, and she'd get relegated to third place in her affections."

"The fourteen years difference caused ructions," said Gus. "Emily had been an only child for a long period. So when did her parents start to argue, I wonder? Perhaps Emily was spoiled, having both parents' attention and no dramas on the horizon, and suddenly there was friction with another person in the house. Was Paul a mistake? Did his birth cause the final rift in the marriage?"

"That's where Wayne and Anna hit a brick wall," said Trefor. "Emily was in West Manton and had brief contact with her old neighbour. Unfortunately, Lily couldn't get Katherine to reveal what was going on between her and Matravers."

"Any signs of physical abuse?" asked Gus.

"Raised voices," said Trefor, "but no obvious signs Matravers ever struck Katherine."

"Let's forget Lily Faulkner for now," said Gus. "What did Cromwell and Brady find when they visited Emily Alford?"

"Emily lived in rented accommodation in West Manton with her daughter, Sophia. It had been decorated to a high spec, and the youngster looked healthy and well-dressed, as did her mother. Anna Cromwell didn't record any concerns for Social Services. Emily's circumstances meant they lived a simple life. Anna checked with Sophia's primary school, and there were no issues with non-attendance or signs of neglect."

"Did Emily rely on benefits alone to keep them both?" asked Lydia.

"Emily worked three hours a day, Monday to Friday, during term time," said Trefor. "That was at a small supermarket in town. She travelled to and from work on public transport. During the holidays, that proved more difficult, but Emily had made friends with other mothers in the village. Emily and her friends could access their kids' school holiday activities and play schemes. Emily kept Sophia occupied for a few hours at those places, which allowed her to cover an occasional shift. Some days, she had two or three other children at her home to amuse and vice versa. Paying for childcare was out of the question."

"How did she take the news of her mother's death?" asked Gus.

"It devastated her, of course," said Trefor Davies.

"There's no, of course, about it," said Gus. "Emily was a rebellious teenager who gave her parents four worrying years. Then, as Lily Faulkner warned, her lifestyle ended in tears, and she joined the ranks of teenage mothers. At a time when you might expect Emily to cling to her mother's apron strings for help in adjusting to her new circumstances, she leaves home."

"When you add in the failing marriage and her grand-mother's worsening health, it suggests the move was acrimonious," said Lydia. "Katherine needed Emily's support, but she still made the break."

"Anna and Callum recorded the same response in their notebook," said Trefor. "Emily answered the door. Sophia followed her mother from the kitchen and stood beside her, clutching a soft toy. Anna said it would be better if they came inside. Emily knew the news was bad, cried, and took them into the living room. Callum offered to take Sophia to a neighbour while they spoke with her, but Emily refused. She wanted her daughter close. Anna told Emily that Katherine had been found in her car that morning. Emily couldn't understand what her mother was doing at West Woods. It wasn't somewhere Katherine would visit at night. Emily had gone there with Sophia to walk amongst the bluebells in springtime. The beauty spot was two miles south of Emily's house."

"When was the last time Emily had spoken to her mother?" asked Gus.

"Two weeks earlier," said Trefor. "Emily called to wish Paul a happy tenth birthday."

"What about the last time Katherine visited Emily in West Manton, or Emily took Sophia to visit her grandmother?" asked Gus. "When Kenneth Truelove gave me the background to this case, Katherine was described as a devoted mother of two. It sounds like one-way traffic to me. Emily put distance between herself and her mother for a reason. I'm not hearing what that reason was yet."

"Anna and Callum didn't sense a breakdown in communications between them," said Trefor, rechecking the folder. "Katherine drove to West Manton with Paul at least once a month to visit her daughter and granddaughter. Callum Brady's notebook showed Emily had photos in the living room of the two children in the garden with Katherine. Everyone was happy and smiling."

"Did Emily take the bus to her old home, too?" asked Lydia.

"On occasion," said Trefor. "They didn't live in one another's pockets. That's not uncommon these days."

"Could Lily Faulkner confirm Emily kept in regular touch with her mother?" asked Gus.

"I'm not sure they asked," said Trefor. He flicked through the folder once more. "Emily said the bus service was less reliable for a trip of that nature. It was easier to call her mother and meet in town. Emily admitted to Callum that her mother always paid for snacks or drinks, which helped with her tight budget. So, Lily Faulkner might not have known they were meeting."

"Unless I'm mistaken, they missed something," said Gus.

"I don't follow," said Trefor.

"I do, guv," said Lydia. "When she was married, Katherine's husband insisted she was a stay-at-home mum. Katherine was always on hand for a coffee and a chat with Lily after her husband died. Why didn't Emily ask her mother to help with childcare during the school holidays if she wasn't working? Paul would have been company for Sophia, too."

Trefor searched the folder for an answer with no luck.

"What does it mean, though, Gus?" he said.

"I don't know yet," said Gus. "It's just another annoying question mark hanging over this case. Katherine and Lily were good friends, according to Lily. Yet, on the night she died, Katherine lied to her. She said she was meeting her brother. Don't make me laugh. For years, they were neighbours, and Lily knew Katherine's mother lived on the same estate. Consider the hours they spent together after Lily's husband died. Then, when Daniel Matravers walked away from the marriage, abandoning his two children, they got thrown together more often. Is it feasible that Lily hadn't learned Katherine was an only child?"

"You need to speak with Wayne Barnett," said Trefor. "I haven't read every detail in this folder to put my finger on the answer to your questions."

"I think you've taken us as far as you can, Trefor," said Gus. "When can we talk to DI Barnett? Is he here today?"

"I'm expecting Wayne back from Didcot at lunchtime," said Trefor. "He's interviewing a suspect in a fine arts fraud. I've warned him you're in Marlborough today. Can we say two o'clock?"

"That sounds good," said Gus. "I'll take Lydia on a tour of the town and surrounding areas. I'm not familiar with the layout. That will help me understand how the significant places in the case fit together."

"Wayne's office is next door," said Trefor. "He'll be there at two. I'm sorry if I've muddied the waters for you, Gus. It wasn't my intention."

"Several statements in the murder file are open to inter-pretation," said Gus. "If Barnett and Cromwell didn't double-check to get absolute clarification, then every step they took after that could have led them further from the killer, not closer."

"It was Anna Cromwell's first murder case," said Lydia.

"That goes for Wayne Barnett, too," said Trefor Davies. "He'd taken the lead in an armed robbery case six months earlier and made a decent fist of that. I thought he was ready."

"Wayne's still here, Trefor," said Gus. "He hasn't kicked on, unlike Anna Cromwell. You lost young Callum Brady too. Not everyone fulfils their early promise. It can't be helped. I'm sure you did your best."

"I hope so," sighed Trefor.

Gus and Lydia left Trefor Davies in his office.

"Right," said Gus as they reached the Focus. "You're my navigator. How do we get to the murder site from here?"

"The shortest route from here is along the A4," said Lydia. "Then turn left onto the road Dr Gray and his wife wanted to cycle. The quickest route is to go back along George Lane to the roundabout at this time of day. Take the first exit onto Granham Hill and drive through Clench Common. We turn right at the junction that leads to a caravan site and West Woods. The trip is four miles, and the last leg from the junction is one mile. We'll be there in ten minutes, tops."

"That sounds like the scenic route," said Gus. "On this occasion, I'm happy to oblige as we travel through Clench Common. DS Mercer and his wife are on the verge of buying their dream retirement cottage there. I don't know the address, however."

"Did you recognise these directions, guv?" asked Lydia. "It's how I suggested I would have travelled when we discussed the case yesterday afternoon."

"Yes, Katherine's car would have been on George Lane and passed the police station to reach this roundabout."

Gus followed Lydia's directions, and they were soon on Granham Hill.

"We wondered why Katherine's car was heading from the pub towards her house," said Gus. "As Alex pointed out, they might not have intended to turn towards Katherine's estate. This road would take them to Lovers' Lane in eight minutes."

"Clench Common is pretty, guv," said Lydia as they entered the village.

"A fair old drive to the nearest pub, though, Lydia," said Gus.

"Not everybody drinks, guv."

"Find me a country pub that doesn't serve food," said Gus. "The nearest takeaway would be in town. So no, this place wouldn't suit me. Not that I could afford the house prices."

"Especially with a family," said Lydia.

"There's the signpost to West Woods," said Gus. "It didn't take long to get here, did it?"

Gus turned off the lane and parked the Focus next to a Honda Jazz.

"Someone must be walking the trails and enjoying the late September sunshine," he said.

"Too early for anything else," said Lydia.

Chapter Four

"I CAN SEE the attraction of a quiet lane, late at night, with a willing partner," said Gus. "If you didn't have a place to be alone together. But if there were enough visitors for the local police to set up regular patrols, I'd find somewhere else, wouldn't you?"

"There wouldn't be much privacy, guv," said Lydia.

They sat and thought about Katherine Alford. Why had she driven someone here that night? Who could it have been?

Two ladies emerged from the trees and walked to the Honda Jazz. They got in and left the car park in a hurry.

"Did you see the look they gave us, guv?" asked Lydia.

"They didn't hang about, did they? She reversed and rattled along the lane towards Clench Common in double-quick time."

"Do you think they suspected we were here for a lunchtime quickie, guv?"

"Cheeky. I suppose it is almost lunchtime," said Gus.

"Why don't we drive back to Marlborough via West Manton and grab a bite to eat?"

"Follow the lane towards the Bath Road, guv," said Lydia. "Turn right onto Manton Road, and there's a pub called The Oddfellows that looks inviting, despite the name. We can drive through West Manton on our way."

"If there's a Manton, West Manton can't be huge. How many people live there?"

"Both villages only have a few hundred residents, guv," said Lydia.

"We'll check at the pub," said Gus. "If Geoff Mercer's moving to Clench Common, it has to be quiet and reserved."

"Lots of retired folk, guv."

"Exactly," said Gus. "Manton is closer to the main road. But perhaps, those two villages have a broader mix. Otherwise, why would an eighteen-year-old mother choose to live there?"

"There's a primary school, guv," said Lydia. "Isn't that where her two boys go to school now? I expect Sophia went there too."

"Aiden Fowler may have moved in soon after Katherine died," said Gus. "Their eldest son is seven, isn't he?"

Gus drove them along Manton Road, taking a spin around West Manton.

"We won't dally here," said Gus. "Neil and Blessing will visit Emily later. While we have lunch, we must decide which questions we should add to Neil's list."

The car park at The Oddfellows reminded Gus of the area behind the Old Police Station, where they were constantly trying to fit a quart into a pint pot.

"I'd better park on the roadside," he said. "It will be

practice for Friday night at the Waggon & Horses. A busy pub is always reassuring."

"I thought you feared your old Focus would look out of place, guv," said Lydia. "Everyone eating here is driving an upmarket model on new plates. You know what that means."

"We might not be able to afford more than a sandwich?"

"Mmm," said Lydia. "I don't mind if we have a coffee and a packet of crisps, guv, honest."

Gus opened the door and walked inside. It wasn't as bad as he'd feared. Strangers in remote village pubs often experienced a chill as every pair of eyes in the room turned their way. Outsiders weren't welcome, but today the buzz of conversation continued unabated.

Five minutes later, Gus and Lydia had found an empty table and were sipping their soft drinks. Two bacon and brie sandwiches, with salad and coleslaw, would be with them soon.

"Did you see who beat us here by several minutes, guv?" asked Lydia.

"Our two lady friends from West Woods," said Gus. "There must be another road from Clench Common, or we missed them while touring West Manton. Are they still tutting?"

"It's too noisy here to hear, guv," Lydia said.

"Ignore them," said Gus. "Right. What do we need Neil to ask Emily Alford?"

"Why didn't Katherine look after Sophia during the school holidays?"

"Anything else?"

"I would push her for the exact date she started seeing Aiden Fowler, guv," said Lydia. "We think he may have moved in not long after Katherine died, but when did the relationship begin?"

"Maybe that's important," said Gus. "I can't see why at present. Nothing I've read in the murder file and the supporting evidence Trefor Davies quoted from the notebooks tallies with the subsequent events leading to a murder."

"A witness must have lied, guv," said Lydia.

A junior member of staff delivered the sandwiches to their table. Gus realised it would restrict conversation for at least ten minutes. As they ate in silence, he considered Lydia's comment and wondered if everyone they had spoken to had been economical with the truth.

"Call Alex and tell him we're returning to George Lane," said Gus. "Get him to ask Neil to add those two questions to his list. If he hadn't already covered them in his preparations this morning."

"Got it, guv," said Lydia.

They left The Oddfellows and stood beside the Focus as a Honda Jazz left the car park and headed in the opposite direction.

"We can relax, guv," said Lydia. "They don't intend to tail us to the office."

"As we're driving to the local Police Station, I wish they would," said Gus. "I feel duty-bound to warn Geoff and Christine Mercer what narrow-minded neighbours they'll have in the village."

"Where did Jane Marple live, guv? Those reminded me of characters from the Agatha Christie books."

"St Mary Mead, I believe. That village wasn't in Wiltshire, though. Some things don't change. Rural communities can have more than their fair share of nosy parkers and bigots. The further they are from the towns and cities, the better. They can do less damage."

"Marlborough's a small town, guv, surrounded by dozens of rural communities. Could that have influenced the Katherine Alford case in any way?"

"I'm not seeing it yet, Lydia," said Gus. "We must keep a clear head, listen to what Wayne Barnett says, and try to separate fact from fiction."

They were soon back at George Lane. Lunch at The Oddfellows had done its job. They were fed, watered, and more aware of the distances they believed the red Peugeot had travelled.

The clock in Reception told them it was two minutes to two. The officer on the desk confirmed DI Barnett was in the building. After the young woman made the call, Wayne collected them.

"Trefor told me who you were, Mr Freeman," said Wayne. "You're a legend."

"Did he tell you about me, too?" asked Lydia.

"He mentioned you were too attractive to be a copper, miss," said Wayne.

Gus and Lydia followed Wayne along the corridor, past Trefor's office. Lydia spotted the rugby ball on the plinth behind Trefor's vacant desk.

"Take a pew," said Wayne as they entered his office.

"Is Trefor still at lunch?" asked Lydia.

"Wednesday is his day for choir practice," said Wayne. "He's Welsh, and they can't stop telling people they can sing. Trefor joined the chapel choir when he first arrived in Marlborough. Now he's also a leading light with the community choir. Roll on when he retires. Then, I won't have to listen to him practising next door."

"What did Trefor say?" asked Gus.

"He said you were a hot-shot detective at Bourne Hill in Salisbury for years. Then they pensioned you off because your face didn't fit the new regime. Trefor queried why they dragged you out of retirement when the Dennis Gates murder was up for review. He soon revised his opinion when he watched you at work."

"The old ways are often the best," said Gus. "Katherine Alford was your first murder case, wasn't it? Your name never cropped up while we were here earlier this year. So how come you didn't play a role in the Gates case?"

"I must have screwed things up big time," said Wayne. "I'm stuck here while her ladyship is climbing rapidly to the top."

"Anna Cromwell," said Gus. "Did you two not gel as a team?"

"Anna was never in a team," said Wayne. "She only ever looked after number one."

"We'll send a team member to speak to Anna next week," said Gus. "Let's return to 2008 and the hours following that early morning phone call from Dr Dominic Gray. When did you get the message?"

"Gray called here just after seven," said Wayne. "I wasn't supposed to be working that weekend. So, I had a few more beers than usual on Saturday night. Well, I am telling a lie. I started drinking at lunchtime. I wasn't feeling great when I had a call from this place telling me to get out to West Woods."

"When the proverbial hits the fan, everyone has to pitch in," said Lydia.

"Did you drive to West Woods?" asked Gus.

"Don't be daft. I couldn't have driven to the end of the road. I told the DC who rang me I needed a lift because I was over the limit. He told me Trefor wanted Anna

59

Cromwell to team up with me on this case. He added that Anna was on her way to collect me, and I needed to be ready in ten minutes."

"What happened then?" asked Gus.

"I hit the shower, threw up, thought I was going to die, you know how it is," said Wayne, staring at Lydia.

"Not really," said Lydia.

"Well, Anna was soon banging on my door and shouting that we needed to hurry. It took me another ten minutes to get dressed, drink a mug of black coffee, and stop seeing double."

"So, Anna drove you both to the murder scene," asked Gus. "Who did what when you got there?"

"When we arrived at the car park in West Woods, the uniformed officers had everything under control," said Wayne. "They had finished taking statements from Dr Gray and his wife. They cordoned off the murder scene and had traffic cones at either end of the only access road to keep people away. Anna was here when the call came in, so she knew Dr Gray had photographed the car's number plate. We didn't have anyone else to question at the scene, so Anna looked at the body. I let her get on with it. My stomach was already doing somersaults."

"You can't describe the inside of the Peugeot?" asked Gus. "Yet both of your notebooks stated there were signs of a struggle."

"I stood at the back of the car while Anna told me what she saw," said Wayne. "The forensic guys took a hundred photos anyway, so what's the difference? As you would expect, Katherine put up a fight when the guy strangled her. Anna said there didn't appear to have been any sex, consensual or otherwise."

"What made Anna think there had been a struggle?"

asked Lydia. "The killer left no discernible DNA, and Katherine didn't take a thing with her when she dashed out of the house. It's far different if an attack takes place in the home. Glasses can get smashed. Chairs get knocked over. In the confines of a small car…."

"Anna said Katherine had bruises on her left cheek and both upper arms and had broken a couple of nails. In addition, Katherine kicked out while being strangled and broke a big toe on one of the pedals."

"How soon after you reached West Woods did the cavalry arrive?" asked Gus.

"Forty minutes to an hour," said Wayne. "I can't remember now, but Anna and the CSO would have recorded the exact time. Anna checked in with Trefor, who had to miss chapel that morning. He wasn't happy. DC Callum Brady was following up on the car registration. When Anna learned who the car belonged to, she suggested I return here."

"You were neither use nor ornament in your state," said Gus.

"I wasn't supposed to be working, was I? I was single and in my late twenties. You need a life away from this job. So, Anna dropped me here, picked up Callum Brady, and they went to notify the next of kin. Trefor reminded me we patrolled West Woods most Saturday nights to scare away randy courting couples. I had another black coffee, checked the logs, and found a car had visited the murder scene at twenty to eleven. Nobody was in sight, which meant the Peugeot must have arrived after they left."

"Which way did the patrol car approach West Woods?" asked Gus.

"From the Bath Road," said Wayne. "They vary the route they take. If the boy racers, fly-tippers, and lovers knew the exact time we'd visit their favourite spots, there wouldn't be much point, would there? That Saturday night, the patrol car started near Savernake, cruised the town centre, drove out to Fyfield, and then pottered along the lane without headlights, hoping to catch someone *in flagrante*, but nothing doing. They doubled back to Bath Road after reports of a fight outside the Royal Oak. Officers were attending but needed backup."

"Was there anything useful on the dashcam?" asked Lydia.

"Evidence of cuts and bruises, mostly. Although, the fight started after a punter broke a bottle over the head of one of the door staff. He needed several stitches."

"I meant the journey between West Woods and the Royal Oak," said Lydia.

"Did you look for the red Peugeot on the dashcam of the patrol vehicle?" asked Gus. "What about the crew that responded to the fight? They could have caught Katherine's car on their camera if she had driven into town. You needed to pinpoint where Katherine was and at what time. A good image could have confirmed the identity of her killer. What were you thinking?"

"It's all very well having a go at me now, ten years after the event," said Wayne. "I hadn't headed up an investigation that important before. In theory, I knew how things went, and Trefor was supposed to be mentoring me. That was the deal. He collared me when I reached the station. Anna was looking for someone sensible to ride with her and found Callum. They went to Purlyn Acre, and Trefor told me he was giving me the reins."

"You hadn't discussed it before that morning?" asked Gus.

"Not really," said Wayne. "I thought I'd done okay on

an armed robbery case six months earlier. Trefor had told me jobs like that impressed the people that matter. He promised to give me a chance on another big case if it materialised."

"Murder isn't an everyday occurrence in Marlborough," said Lydia.

"Thank goodness," said Wayne. "I'd had a lousy start to the day, getting woken up six hours earlier than planned. I didn't cover myself with glory at the murder scene, and then Anna ran to the boss to say she wanted to ride with someone else when she notified the victim's family. When Trefor called me into his office, I thought I'd get a rollicking. Instead, he told me I was running the show with his guidance."

"What did Trefor tell you to do next?" asked Lydia.

"Get breakfast," said Wayne. "There wasn't much we could do until Anna and Callum returned from Purlyn Acre."

"We'll speak with ACC Cromwell next week," said Gus, "to hear her side of the story."

"Her ladyship won't say anything complimentary," said Wayne. "We didn't get on before that morning, and afterwards, she was pushing to get away from Marlborough."

"Onwards and upwards," said Gus. "I can imagine. When did you learn about the phone call that caused Katherine to dash out of the house?"

"After Anna and Callum got back. Anna looked daggers at Trefor when he announced I was leading the investigation. She was still only a DS, but she thought herself superior to me. Heck, she already thought Trefor was her junior. I felt sorry for Callum. He'd had to spend half a day getting pushed around like a pawn on a chessboard. No wonder he quit."

"Did you visit The Roebuck that afternoon?" asked Lydia.

"Anna had spoken to the neighbour," said Wayne. "She didn't know where Katherine had gone, but as she promised to be home in ten minutes, we visited the likely places within a five-minute drive. The local pub seemed as good a place as any to start."

"What did you learn there?" asked Gus. "Step me through what happened."

"Anna rode with me in the car," said Wayne. "She didn't have a choice as I was SIO. We got there at half-past five. Anna spoke to Belinda, the barmaid. It relegated me to asking punters in the beer garden or at the front of the pub if they were there the night before. Then I went to the side of the pub where the smokers congregate—the same story there. Either they weren't there, or they saw nothing. So I wandered indoors and asked to see the manager. I'd spotted the cameras outside and thought we'd get lucky. Instead, he told me they were only a deterrent. They used to work, but he couldn't afford to get them repaired with the state of the pub trade. So. we had nothing. Belinda hadn't been outside the bar all night, and she didn't recognise the photo of the victim Anna showed her."

"A waste of time," said Lydia.

"Not entirely," said Wayne, winking at her. "I got Belinda's phone number."

"When did the eye-witnesses come forward?" asked Gus.

"The two man-haters?" said Wayne. "I reckon that was on Tuesday. After the murder was featured on the regional television news on Monday night."

"Who did Charlotte Ovens and Jasmine Park speak to?" asked Lydia.

"One of them called the station, and the duty officer left me a message. I was attending the post-mortem with Anna. When we returned to the office, Anna called back and invited them to chat."

"What happened at that meeting?" asked Gus.

"I left Anna to handle them," said Wayne. "She had more in common with them than I did. Anna asked Callum to join them. The women said they were at The Roebuck from eight until closing time. It was their local, and they visited the pub two or three nights a week. On a warm June night, almost as many people were outside as inside the bar. Ovens and Park took their drinks outside just after ten o'clock to get some fresh air."

"Did they notice a couple arrive in the red Peugeot?" asked Gus.

"Cars were coming and going all the time," said Wayne. "It's a busy road. But they never mentioned seeing a car."

"Why did they remember the man and woman when they heard about the murder on TV?" asked Lydia.

"The news report showed a photograph of Katherine Alford," said Wayne. "We wanted to hear from anyone who knew where she was on Saturday night after a quarter to ten when she left home."

"Why were they certain it was Katherine?" asked Gus. "She didn't drink in The Roebuck. Did they recognise her as a familiar face from the Purlyn Acre estate?"

"They hadn't seen the woman before, but her clothes matched our TV description. So when they saw the photo, they thought it was the woman outside the pub."

"How did they describe the man they saw that night?" asked Gus.

"They could only offer a vague description," said Wayne. "He wore casual clothes and was of average height and weight. Anna asked if he had any distinguishing features, but he had his back to them, a dead end."

"Did either of them go inside the pub at any time?" asked Gus.

"Not that Ovens and Park noticed. Why?"

"Katherine agreed to meet someone. We can only guess it was at The Roebuck. Why stop there if they had no intention of buying a drink?"

"Katherine was only supposed to be out of the house for ten minutes," said Wayne. "I thought she was wary of being alone with the guy for any length of time. So she agreed to meet outside a busy pub, where she could get help if things kicked off."

"I could see that being the case if Katherine had driven straight there and he was waiting for her," said Gus. "Charlotte and Jasmine told you the conversation occurred forty-five minutes after she left home."

"And we believe a man was in the car with her ten minutes later," said Lydia, "when Bert Harris saw the red Peugeot."

"Anna thought the killer had changed his plans. He waved Katherine down as she left her estate, and they drove around for a while. Maybe they argued. We thought they were lovers initially, and Katherine wanted more from the relationship. Maybe the guy tried to persuade her things were fine as they were. Callum suggested the guy had calmed Katherine, and they stopped at The Roebuck, intending to get a drink, and then he'd drop her at home later. The mood changed again, and we know what happened instead."

"Were they arguing and drawing attention to themselves?" asked Gus. "Something that caused Charlotte and Jasmine to take a closer interest."

"At that time on a Saturday night, every conversation is animated inside or outside a pub," said Wayne. "Those two women couldn't hear what they said with the background noise. They said they thought the man was doing most of the talking."

"They must have done more than take a passing glance," said Lydia.

"Which suggests Katherine's body language set off alarm bells," said Gus. "Was her companion pointing fingers and raising his voice?"

"Did Charlotte and Jasmine get the impression the man was stopping Katherine from leaving?" asked Lydia. "Did she seem afraid of him?"

"Anna never cottoned on to what you just said, miss," said Wayne. "Ovens and Park said the guy was hogging the conversation, which meant one of them watched for an extended period. Anna and Callum didn't pursue that line of enquiry."

"We'll ask Charlotte and Jasmine when we speak to them," said Gus.

"As well as ask Anna Cromwell why she overlooked the comment," said Lydia.

"Callum Brady left this station within twelve months," said Gus. "Does anyone know where he went?"

"Trefor might know," said Wayne. "Do you need me for much longer?"

"I think we're done for now. We will need to speak to you again," said Gus. "There was one thing you might help us with. This station carried out regular patrols at West Woods, and they must have had more successful trips than when Katherine Alford died. Therefore, somewhere, there's a record of the people they caught. Did you check those records? Could the killer have been there before?"

"Those records will still be here," said Wayne. "Trefor didn't nudge me in that direction. It was possible, I suppose, with the benefit of hindsight. It isn't always the bloke, though. Katherine Alford was driving. Why couldn't it have been her that was a regular visitor to West Woods? We found no evidence of her being in a steady relationship, but that didn't mean she wasn't sexually active on the sly. Her daughter wouldn't have known, living on the other side of town, if her mother was picking up guys now and then and taking them somewhere quiet."

"Did that notion just come to you?" asked Gus. "Or was it something that figured in your thinking ten years ago?"

"Trefor thought the simplest explanation was most likely," said Wayne. "Katherine had been in a secret relationship for months. Her lover called, wanting to chat. We wouldn't know how the conversation went until we got our man. Someone wanted the affair to end, and they argued back and forth, stopping at the pub and then driving to West Woods. The argument continued, and her lover snapped. That was the line we followed. Anna agreed with Trefor, and whatever I threw into the mix was never evaluated to any degree."

"Trefor's theory explained the sequence of events as you understood them," said Gus. "A theory that required you to accept Katherine and her companion were together from a quarter to ten until sometime between midnight and one."

"We interviewed Bert Harris," said Wayne. "He couldn't confirm whether there was anyone in the car with Katherine. Bert was adamant it was her car, though. He had lived on the same estate as Katherine for years and remembered she bought the Peugeot after her husband walked out."

"We'll speak to Bert ourselves," said Gus. "I've read your team's statements from Daniel Matravers and the

Alford family. We hope to meet with each of them in the coming days and ask the questions that you and Anna Cromwell didn't."

"Good luck with that," said Wayne. "Nobody we interviewed from that crowd was there that night. We checked their alibis. There was nobody with motive and no killer among the people Katherine knew."

Gus and Lydia made their way back along the corridor to Reception. Lydia grabbed Gus by the arm when they were outside in the car park.

"What if there were two men, guv?" said Lydia. "Wayne's got me thinking now. The phone call meeting didn't pan out the way the caller had hoped. Katherine spotted another guy as she passed the pub. Maybe, someone she'd been with before. They drove to West Woods, but she changed her mind. Katherine realised Lily would be worried, and Paul could wake up, but the guy she picked up wouldn't be messed about and flipped."

"Suzie would have a question for you if she were here," said Gus. "Wayne's theory is a plausible explanation for the sequence of events. However, he would have needed to prove there was another man. How could he do that? Where to start? Trefor Davies allowed Wayne to lead the investigation, but he steered Wayne's thinking towards the most likely scenario."

"So you think Trefor Davies was right, guv?"

"Too early to tell, Lydia," said Gus.

"What question would Suzie ask, guv?" asked Lydia.

"How do you explain the light cotton gloves?" said Gus.

Chapter Five

MEANWHILE, Blessing Umeh looked nervously at the clock on the wall in the office.

"Are you ready to leave, Neil?" she asked.

"Don't panic, Blessing," said Neil. "I'll drive. We've got plenty of time. Emily will appreciate five minutes of extra time to quieten her sons. I don't want to walk into a room full of hyperactive kids."

"You'll have one of your own in a few months," said Alex.

"Melody will endure the screaming and tantrums," said Blessing.

"I won't be that bad," said Neil with a grin. "Come on then, let's go."

They rode in the lift, and Neil soon headed out of town on the Devizes road.

"You wouldn't have reversed your Micra out of the parking bay yet, Blessing," said Neil.

"Cheeky," said Blessing. "Do you feel you've got a handle on this case yet, Neil?"

"It sounds like Gus and Lydia found a few fresh lines of enquiry," said Neil. "Whether they'll lead us anywhere, I can't tell. Why? Have you cracked this one already?"

"Don't be daft," said Blessing.

Neil turned off the A4 Bath Road and followed Gus and Lydia's earlier route.

"Country roads must confuse visitors," said Blessing, checking the map on her phone. "We're on Manton Road, and the village is dead ahead. When we reach the next junction, we turn right to West Manton, but we're on High Street if we drive straight on. So why change the name?"

"To confuse the enemy," said Neil.

He turned right at the junction and looked for Emily Alford's address.

"There we are," said Blessing. "No car on the drive. That means Aiden Fowler is at work."

"Sophia won't get home for another half hour," said Neil. "She needs to get a bus from St John's in Marlborough."

"That's good," said Blessing. "You can get a clear run at Emily while I keep the boys occupied."

"That sounds like a plan," said Neil as he parked the car.

Emily Alford opened the door before they got halfway up the garden path.

"Are you the police?" she asked.

"We are," said Neil. "I'm DS Davis, and this young lady is DC Umeh. Our colleague, DS Hardy, will have told you we're taking a fresh look into your mother's murder. It may be ten years, but no case is ever closed. We hope to ask different questions to those the detectives asked at the time, and your answers might unlock the mystery of who was responsible."

"Come in," said Emily.

Blessing spotted two faces peering at her from the top of the stairs.

"What are your two sons called?"

"Benedict and Harvey," said Emily. "I told them to stay in their rooms until you left."

"I'll sit with them, if I may," said Blessing.

"Okay," said Emily, "you won't need to question them, too, will you?"

"Heavens, no," said Neil. "Although, we would appreciate a chat with your daughter, Sophia, in a while. You can sit with her for that. What time does your partner get home?"

"Aiden wouldn't know anything," said Emily. "He never met Mum."

Neil followed Emily into the family room, which boasted double-seater settees on three walls and a massive TV screen. He'd already spotted the modern kitchen at the end of the hallway.

"I can tell what you're thinking," said Emily. "How can we afford this place?"

"Aiden's not here, so I imagine he's working," said Neil. "We'll check, of course."

"Life wasn't always this good. When I fell for Sophia, it was all I could do to make ends meet."

"Can we start there, Emily?" asked Neil. "We've read the statement given by Mrs Faulkner, your next-door neighbour."

"Lily didn't like me," said Emily. "She told the police I was a wild child. I saw the curtain twitch when I got home at night."

"Did you cause your parents a few sleepless nights?" asked Neil.

72

"I could ask you the same question, DS Davis. There's only, what, five years between us?"

"Was there no possibility of marrying or getting together with Sophia's father?"

Emily clasped her hands in her lap and stared at the floor.

"I wasn't certain who the father was," said Emily. "Lily Faulkner interpreted that as me being with a different boy every night. That wasn't true. I went out with one boy for two months, and then we split up within a couple of days of having sex for the first time. Straight after that, I met someone, and we had a one-night stand. That was a mistake. Then I missed my next period."

The door opened, and Blessing appeared with the two boys.

"I've been told there's a programme starting the boys never miss," she said. "Their homework's done for school in the morning. We could move into the kitchen while they watch TV for a while if you wish."

"Okay," said Emily. "I'll get them a drink. Do you want a coffee?"

"White, one sugar, please," said Neil, following Emily to the kitchen.

"White, no sugar for me," said Blessing.

"Thank you, miss," said Benedict and Harvey in unison.

Blessing gave them the thumbs-up and joined Neil and Emily.

Emily made the coffee and then took soft drinks to the boys.

"Where was I?" she said when she returned.

"You were telling me about the early weeks of your pregnancy," said Neil. "When did you tell your mother?"

"As soon as I missed my second period. Mum was angry

at first. Then, after we'd been to the doctor, she just said she knew it was bound to happen."

"The late nights and different boyfriends," said Blessing. "Lily Faulkner didn't miss much, did she? Did your parents not want you to take precautions? If you were sexually active, it would have been wise to go on the pill."

"Dad was strict," said Emily. "He sat me down when I wasn't much older than twelve and gave me the third degree. Don't do this, don't do that. Dad thought contraception was a free pass. He was dead against it. He thought it encouraged kids to over-indulge."

"Your Dad had left two years before you fell pregnant with Sophia," said Neil. "Did that mean you were closer to your mother?"

"I suppose," said Emily.

"We've read the comments you made on the TV appeal, Emily," said Blessing. "They struck a chord with me, and I'm sure they did with many viewers. However, they don't tell the entire story, do they?"

"I don't know what you mean," said Emily.

"You said it would be good if the killer came forward," said Blessing. "Sophia often asked about her Nana, you said. There were no photos of Katherine in your daughter's room when I was upstairs. When detectives spoke to you after the murder, they spotted photos in the living room of Katherine, with you and Sophia, happy and smiling in the garden. I looked out of the boy's bedroom window upstairs. Those photos weren't taken here. Who took them, and where?"

"Paul took them," said Emily. "He was eight or nine then. We were in the back garden at home. He had a couple of tries before he kept the camera still."

"When I read those words about how you would sit and look at that photo together and recall happier times, it brought a tear to my eye. But it wasn't like that, was it?"

"It was a dreadful time in our lives," said Emily, looking tearful. "You have no idea."

"There are photos of the boys in the living room and Sophia," said Blessing. "You and Aiden make a good couple, judging by the photos on show, but nothing remains of your parents or your brother."

Neil realised Blessing had hit a raw nerve. He returned to the theme of his earlier remark.

"When I suggested you were closer to your mother after your father left, you said you supposed that was true. Were there problems between you and your mother before your father left?"

"She had Paul to care for," said Emily. "I didn't get a look-in."

"The last couple of years of your parent's marriage must have hurt all of you," said Blessing.

"Mum and Dad weren't fighting," said Emily. "They just stopped communicating after Paul was born."

"Why do you think that was, Emily?" asked Neil.

"You would have to ask my father," she replied.

"You must see how things that happened even years before your mother died could be relevant," said Blessing. "Our colleagues from Marlborough searched for several weeks for a motive to explain why someone murdered Katherine. They delved deep into the lives of anyone and everyone who came into contact with her. They found nothing, whether they were family members, friends, or neighbours."

"One reason was that someone didn't tell the truth

75

during the first investigation," said Neil. "Paul was born in 1998, and nobody mentioned anything about a breakdown in the relationship between Katherine and Daniel Matravers."

"Lily Faulkner told detectives Katherine maintained the split was because of irreconcilable differences," said Blessing.

"Which suggests there was no one else involved," said Neil.

"Mum wasn't seeing anyone else," said Emily. "I would have known. When it was just the three of us, life was great. Even though Dad was strict with us, we still got on well. We went on family holidays. Mum and Dad came to my school concerts."

"Your father wasn't just strict with you. Is that what you're implying?" asked Neil. "Your mother had to be wary of what she said or did in case he lost his temper."

"Dad never hit Mum," said Emily. "It was only words. Dad was particular about mealtimes, keeping the place tidy, and not spending too much time gossiping with neighbours. Mum would avoid seeing Mrs Faulkner in the evenings and at weekends. I had to do my homework before I could watch television. As you discovered upstairs, I continue his lead and insist on that with my children. A little discipline is beneficial in young people's lives. The things important to Dad might sound annoying and petty to most people, but that was Dad's way. He didn't lash out at anyone if they couldn't maintain the high standards he demanded. He just got exasperated and went into the garden or sat in the living room with a book alone."

"When did the mood change?" asked Neil. "Was that around the time your mother found out she was expecting Paul?"

"Everything changed from the minute Mum came home from the doctor. It was a weekday evening, and I sat at the dining table doing my homework. Dad was in the lounge watching the evening news. He'd sat with me for five minutes, asking me what we were studying, and suggested how to handle the project I'd brought home. It was the last time I can remember being happy."

"The pregnancy wasn't planned," said Neil.

"It was the last thing we needed," said Emily.

"In what way?" asked Blessing.

"We weren't well off," said Emily. "Dad had a well-paid job but wouldn't let Mum work. So instead, he insisted her place was at home, looking after me and keeping the house tidy."

"A somewhat old-fashioned view these days," said Neil.

"It wasn't a popular view ten years ago," said Emily.

"Yet your mother didn't complain?" asked Blessing.

"Not within my hearing," said Emily.

"Perhaps Katherine enjoyed her marriage the way it was for the first fifteen years," said Blessing. "Then, when you were older and more independent, she needed someone who relied on her for everything again. Katherine was only in her early thirties when she got pregnant. The long gap between the births was unusual, but perhaps she felt a child was necessary for her well-being."

"That's when things went south between you, wasn't it?" said Neil.

"Between my parents, you mean," said Emily.

"That too," said Blessing. "You had been the centre of attention. Now a baby threatened that, and you weren't happy. Let's talk about your father first. You insist your mother wasn't having an affair. That tallies with what Lily Faulkner told the police. They couldn't find anyone on the

Purlyn Acre estate with a bad word to say about her. Katherine was a good wife and mother, by all accounts. If anyone had suggested Paul wasn't Daniel's child, they would have been ridiculed."

"Can you see where DC Umeh is going with this line of questioning?" asked Neil.

Emily shook her head.

"We asked why your parents hadn't insisted you went on the pill," said Neil. "You told us your father was against that course of action. How did your mother avoid getting pregnant after you were born? Didn't that ever cross your mind? After her murder, a post-mortem was carried out to confirm the cause of death, and one thing recorded in the notes didn't get acted upon by detectives. I can understand why not, given the major thrust of their investigation. Katherine didn't get pregnant because she had had a coil fitted. The post-mortem report showed it was due for replacement based on the age of the device. When he discussed the matter with her GP, he learned Katherine had her first device fitted in the mid-Eighties. However, in 1998, she had asked for the coil to be removed. The coil identified during the post-mortem had been fitted in 2000 after Paul was born."

"You're saying Mum was due to have an old device replaced, and she deliberately chose to have it removed," said Emily. It was clear this was news to her. "She didn't tell Dad she might get pregnant. She didn't care how it would affect us."

"We won't know her reasons for certain," said Blessing, "unless your father knows the answer. Katherine may have yearned for another child for years, but your father had decided one child was enough. Your financial situation could have had a bearing. Did you ever have any contact with your father after he left?"

"Never," said Emily. "He hasn't attempted to contact me, and I never forgave him for leaving."

"Do you know where he lives?" asked Neil.

"In Salisbury," said Emily. "Where he lived as a child. We heard he married again."

"Ironic, isn't it?" said Neil. "We got the impression the last thing he wanted when he left Marlborough was to be married, and yet within a year or two of leaving your mother, he found someone else."

"What do you want me to say?" said Emily. "I can only tell you what my eyes and ears told me about how things were between them. The three of us were happy until Mum told Dad she was expecting. He switched off completely from then on. We stopped going on holiday. He stopped attending my school functions. Mum was getting bigger, and after Paul arrived, she spent all her time with him. I didn't have anyone to turn to. Grandma was ill, and we couldn't visit her like we used to. So I went out with my mates from school, desperate for attention. In the end, I got more attention from a couple of older boys than I had bargained for. I was screwing around because I thought they loved me, and you know how that turned out. Sophia's a lovely girl, but she wishes she knew her father. Aiden does his best, but he'll be nothing more than a stepdad."

"What prompted you to move away from Purlyn Acre?" asked Neil.

"I told you," said Emily. "Mum said my getting pregnant was bound to happen. I needed her to help me with Sophia, but she devoted her attention to Paul. There were problems during my pregnancy with high blood pressure. Then, when Sophia arrived ten days early, I was in labour for sixteen hours. Mum collected us from the Great Western Hospital in Swindon, and we lived under the same roof, but after Dad had left, nothing was ever the same between us."

"You left home at eighteen," said Blessing. "Was there a specific event that brought matters to a head, or was it just a gradual deterioration in your relationship?"

"How long was that after you brought Sophia home from the hospital?" asked Neil.

"Six months, maybe," said Emily. "It was soon after Paul's fourth birthday. That was the final straw. I was a single mother, claiming benefits, but Mum kept reminding me it could be worse. At least I had a roof over my head. Mum took most of the money I received to help feed Sophia and me. Then Grandma died. Mum was an only child and inherited the house and what little money Gran had. I couldn't believe the money Mum splashed out on Paul's birthday party and presents. There were never any extras for Sophia and me."

"When your father left, that must have made things difficult for your mother financially," said Neil. "I can't imagine she had much spare cash in the first two years, even if your father made the correct maintenance payments for Paul. She hadn't worked since two months before you were born. Her mother's death was yet another blow to withstand. Mary Alford's estate would have helped her offset the problems caused by the divorce, but you can't measure the loss of your mother in monetary terms."

"You believed your mother would always favour Paul over you," said Blessing. "So, despite her suffering from losing her mother, you packed your bags and walked out."

"That can't have been easy to arrange at short notice," said Neil. "How did you secure a house as good as this?"

"It belongs to the father of a boy I went out with before

I had Sophia," said Emily. "Kane's dad was rolling in it and bought him a flash sports car when he reached eighteen. That's what attracted me to him. He was twenty-two when we met and always had cash to burn. Anyway, a few days after Paul's birthday, I bumped into Kane. We hadn't seen one another for three years. He hadn't lived at home since he was nineteen. Kane said his father had a house in West Manton he'd renovated that I could rent. This place was fully furnished. I told Kane I didn't have the money to afford something that good, but Kane said he'd convince his father to help keep me from being homeless. When I got on my feet, I could either pay the going rate or move somewhere I could afford."

"How old were you when you went out with Kane?" asked Blessing.

"Fifteen," said Emily.

"Kane couldn't have been Sophia's father," said Neil. "Unless you were seeing him towards the end of 2001."

"No, as I told you, we hadn't seen one another for three years."

"Did you remind Kane you were underage when you had sex with him?" asked Blessing.

"I might have mentioned it," said Emily. "I said a lot of things that day. Mum had wound me up so tight with how she treated Sophia and me. Kane was the first person I could unload my frustrations on."

"So, you moved here towards the end of 2002 and paid a peppercorn rent," said Neil.

"No, I paid everything I could afford, and Kane made up the difference. His father never knew."

"When did you meet Aiden Fowler?" asked Neil.

"Aiden works for Kane's father, renovating properties in and around Marlborough. He dropped by one weekend, around four years after I moved in, to fix a problem with the shower in the en-suite bathroom. I'd called Kane, and he said he'd send someone over. I'd never seen Aiden before. He'd moved from Hungerford eighteen months earlier, and Sophia took to him straight away. She sat on the floor watching him work. I made him a coffee and a sandwich, and we chatted for an hour after he'd fixed the shower. That's how it started. He called in for a coffee the following weekend and asked me out. He moved in later that summer."

"When did you adjust the rental arrangement?" asked Neil.

"As soon as Kane heard that Aiden had moved in. We still don't pay full whack because Aiden's on the company payroll. But Kane's dad pays his staff top dollar, and they also get perks."

"Does Kane work for his father?" asked Blessing.

"He doesn't graft like Aiden," said Emily. "Kane searches out the properties, attends auctions, and manages the renovation projects. He doesn't come anywhere near me these days."

"Does that mean he used to visit?" asked Neil.

"Kane only came indoors if I needed maintenance on the house. Every month, he'd drop the cash through the letterbox for the rent, but Kane had just married when Aiden arrived on the scene. It wasn't so easy to drive over from Savernake to West Manton without an excuse."

"Kane didn't want his wife suspecting there was another woman," said Blessing.

"It wasn't like that," said Emily. "We never picked up from where we left off."

"When your mother was murdered, the detectives came here on Sunday morning to notify you," said Neil. "Where was Aiden? There's no mention of him in their statements. So you didn't tell them you were in a relationship?"

"None of their business," said Emily. "Aiden had nothing to do with Mum's murder."

"We know Lily Faulkner was looking after Paul while the detectives visited you," said Neil. "When was it decided Paul would come here to live?"

"Aiden thought we should. I wasn't keen," said Emily.

"Relations between you and Paul were still frosty," said Neil.

"Aiden reminded me we were brother and sister."

"Lily Faulkner told detectives Katherine drove here with Paul once a month to visit you and Sophia," said Blessing. "Isn't that true?"

"They came here," said Emily. "I got to Purlyn Acre as often as I could. But, although Kane covered much of the rent on this place, I still struggled. We had to take the bus across to Mum's house."

"So you met in Marlborough to save money," said Neil.

"I would call Mum and meet in a café in town when Paul and Sophia were at school. Mum always paid the bill, which helped make my cash last to the next benefit cheque."

"Did those trips stop when you met Aiden Fowler?" asked Blessing.

"They were less frequent," said Emily. "Aiden was with us for just under a year before Mum died."

"With neither you nor your mum working, I suppose it wasn't too difficult to fix a coffee date," said Neil. "Although it must have been harder in the school holidays."

"I was working at a supermarket," said Emily. "Only for the number of hours a week I could without it affecting my benefit. Term-time was never an issue, but holidays meant a lot of planning to fit in the occasional shift."

"Why didn't you just ask your mother to have Sophia?" asked Blessing. "Paul was home from school, too. They would have been company for one another."

"I asked, but Mum said it was inconvenient."

"Why was that?" asked Neil. "She could have brought Paul here in the car and stayed with Sophia while you went to work. Or they could have collected you both and dropped you off at work before driving to her home. She could have taken the kids out for the day in the summer."

"Are you sure your mother didn't have a job to go to?" asked Blessing. "Something part-time, with hours that varied from week to week. It would explain why taking care of Sophia throughout the holiday wasn't possible."

"But if Katherine worked somewhere, she needed someone to look after Paul," said Neil. "Lily Faulkner would have known about it and undoubtedly be the first person Katherine would have asked to take Paul for a couple of hours."

"We weren't as close as before Paul was born," said Emily. "Mum came here once a month, and I made an effort to visit her at home or in town when I could. Apart from that, we didn't ring one another every day, so it's possible she was involved in something I knew nothing about. Heaven knows what it might have been. The police kept asking if she was in a relationship. How would I know? Would she have told me if she was?"

"Paul might know if there was something the detectives didn't discover," said Blessing.

"Do you know where he lives?" asked Emily.

"We do," said Neil. "What we'd like to know is why he left here?"

"I've been upstairs," said Blessing. "I know you could still accommodate him."

"Paul had nowhere else to go after Mum died," said Emily. "When he came here, he was ten and a half. Then after the summer holidays, Paul started at St John's, where Sophia is now. She was still at the junior school in Manton, and I walked her there every day. Paul travelled on the bus like Sophia. He was a quiet boy, withdrawn—no big surprise when you know what had happened in his life. Aiden had moved in the year before Mum died, and we were getting on great. Aiden and Sophia got on like a house on fire and still do. Paul never felt he belonged. That was partly my fault because I still resented him spoiling the good thing I had going before he was born."

"So Paul left school at sixteen and started working with an electrical component firm on the South Marston Industrial Estate. Did he travel there each day on the bus?"

"At first. I didn't mind because the commute added to Paul's time away from the house. On weekends, he spent most of the time in his room. But when I told Aiden and Sophia that I was expecting Benedict, that was it for Paul. He couldn't wait to find a room closer to work to get away."

"Benedict was born in 2011, is that right?" asked Neil.

"Yes," said Emily, "and Harvey arrived in 2013. Paul moved out before Christmas at the end of 2014. By then, he could afford to live on his own and rented a room in a house in South Marston."

"I see that your mother's estate took almost two years to clear probate," said Neil.

"For the first six months, nothing could happen because the police were still investigating the murder," said Emily. "We had to wait weeks for them to release the body, let alone get a solicitor organised. Then, the house was on the market for a year without an offer. Plenty of people viewed it, though."

"Had your mother made a will?" asked Blessing.

"At forty-four, she thought she had time," said Emily.

"The house finally sold in 2010, did it?" asked Blessing.

"In July, and I told Aiden about the baby soon after. Then, after the house sale, my and Paul's share of the money went into our bank accounts in early October. He used that money for a deposit when he found a one-bedroomed flat on Copse Avenue in 2016."

"There was a mortgage on the property in Purlyn Acre," said Neil. "Hang on. I'm confused. Your father walked out of the marriage, and your mother kept the house after the divorce. So she must have had to pay him something."

"They had been married for almost seventeen years," said Blessing. "Maybe Katherine secured a loan to reimburse Daniel Matravers and cleared a substantial portion of that with the money from her mother's estate in 2002. Then, when the house sold in 2010, the solicitor cleared the balance. Paul and Emily received half each."

"Katherine still had to make payments between the divorce and benefiting from her mother's estate," said Neil. "Yet she didn't get a job. We're missing something. How can someone earn a living without leaving home and nobody finding out?"

"Especially a nosy neighbour like Lily Faulkner," said Emily.

She collected glasses from the living room, took Neil and Blessing's empty cups and stacked them in the dishwasher.

"Sophia will be home in a minute," she said. "Can I have a word with her first? It will come as a shock talking to the police. She won't have done anything like it before."

"We only need a few minutes with her," said Neil. "Call her into the kitchen when she arrives, and we'll get underway."

"I can keep the boys happy for another ten minutes," said Blessing.

Emily Alford shrugged her shoulders. She knew when she was beaten.

Chapter Six

TWO MINUTES LATER, the front door opened, and Sophia Alford burst into the house.

"Whose car is that outside, Mum?" she called. Neil heard her climbing the stairs.

Emily walked into the hallway and called out to her daughter.

"Get changed and come to the kitchen, Sophia, please."

Neil heard a bedroom door slam. Then, five minutes later, the stairs took another hammering as the sixteen-year-old girl made the return journey.

"What?" asked Sophia.

"Take a seat, please, Sophia," said Neil. "I'm DS Davis from Wiltshire Police. My colleague, DC Umeh, will sit with your brothers while we chat."

"I have done nothing wrong," said Sophia. She slumped into a chair next to her mother and watched Blessing disappear into the next room.

Neil could see the family resemblance. Sophia was five foot six inches tall, with long fair hair, and good-looking, just like her mother and her late grandmother. But, like most teenagers, Sophia disguised her figure with a baggy sweat-shirt and loose-fitting tracksuit bottoms.

"There's nothing wrong," said Neil. "We came to talk with your mother because we're re-investigating your grand-mother's murder. All we want is for you to tell us what you can remember of events. You were only six, but you might remember a detail that meant nothing to anyone else. Something that seemed odd to a six-year-old and stuck in your memory. It might have been irrelevant to a grown-up, so they dismissed it and forgot it."

"Like what?" asked Sophia.

Neil felt this was going to be like pulling teeth.

"What can you tell us about the day when the police arrived to speak to Mum?"

"Aiden had left for work at eight. We'd had breakfast together, the three of us. A car drew up and parked on the road. The same spot yours is in now. A man and a woman walked to the front door. Mum told me to stay in the living room and keep quiet."

"Quiet about what?" asked Neil.

"I wasn't to mention Aiden," said Sophia. "Mum didn't want people knowing he lived here."

Emily coughed and gave a nervous half-smile at Neil. He wondered whether she had always claimed the correct benefits. She wouldn't be the first not to tell the authorities her circumstances had altered.

"Mum learned her mother's body had been found in her car at West Woods. You knew that spot, didn't you?"

"We'd visited with Nana when the bluebells were at their best, but I never went back."

"Was it somewhere Nana might have visited without you, do you think?"

"I don't know. There's plenty to do there all year round," said Sophia. "She could have taken Uncle Paul to West Woods after we moved here. But, of course, we wouldn't know."

"Paul came here to live after Nana died, didn't he? So, how did you two get on?"

"It was odd having him here every day. We didn't see Uncle Paul that often while Nana was alive. We got on okay, but he's four years older than me. Of course, that's nothing for people your age, but the gap meant we could do nothing together while he lived here."

"Did Paul get on with Aiden?" asked Neil.

"He was quiet and didn't have the same interests as Aiden. Although he wasn't the brightest student, Uncle Paul studied hard at school. Aiden loves working with his hands. He's clever in a different way. I used to sit and watch him doing things around the house. Uncle Paul spent a lot of time in his room reading books. He caused no trouble. He didn't have anywhere else to go."

"Yes," said Neil. "His father walked out, his grandmother died, and someone murdered his mother. Then, finally, his sister was the only person he had left in the world."

"I suppose," shrugged Sophia. "I lost my Nana too, and Grampy had left us. At least Uncle Paul knew his father. Mine wanted nothing to do with me."

"Come on, Sophia," said Emily. "I've told you before. Your father didn't abandon you."

"Have you had this conversation with your daughter?" asked Neil.

"When she was old enough to understand," said Emily. "Telling her what had happened wasn't my proudest moment."

"Right," sighed Sophia. "Of course, the police know everything. My Mum slept around when she was my age, and she didn't know who made her pregnant. If that doesn't mess with your head, I don't know what does."

Sophia pushed her chair back and stood.

"Are we done?"

"No, sit down," said Neil. "One more outburst, and we'll carry on this conversation at the police station. We're hunting a murderer, Sophia. My questions might upset you, but until I'm satisfied with the answers I get, I'll keep asking them. Now, why did Uncle Paul leave this house?"

Sophia sat in her chair again.

"He had inherited half of Nana's money. Uncle Paul never felt he belonged. It was best he found a place of his own."

"Who said it would be best?" asked Neil. "Your Mum or Aiden?"

"Neither of them. Uncle Paul wanted to make a clean break."

"Did Uncle Paul ever speak with you about his time at home with Nana?"

"What do you mean? Where did they go, or what did they do? Only in general terms. We didn't discuss things that often."

"We wondered why you didn't spend time in the holidays with them," said Neil. "Mum struggled to fit in shifts at the supermarket, with you at home and Aiden working. So why couldn't you have stayed with Nana?"

Sophia shrugged.

"Nobody ever told me. I used to spend a day with one of my friends from school. Their Mum looked after me until Mum finished work. Then, on another day, Poppy or Olivia came here, and we'd play games. Mum would get us lunch, and we'd have a party in the garden. Their Mum could go to work then."

"Did Uncle Paul ever mention anyone who visited Nana's house?"

"What, the man who reads the electricity meter?" said Sophia.

"Well, a meter reader might have turned up every three months in those days," said Neil. "I was thinking of someone who dropped by every week or more often."

"Uncle Paul didn't mention anyone," said Sophia. "He wouldn't have known, though, would he, not once he started playschool. I don't know what goes on here during the eight hours I'm away."

"Fair comment," said Neil. "Half-term is just around the corner, and you would notice, wouldn't you? If there was a regular visitor here, then."

"Which there isn't," said Emily. "But if there had been someone turning up at Mum's house every few days, Paul would have seen them during the holidays unless they stayed away to avoid being seen. Why would they do that? We're going around in circles. The police never found evidence Mum was having a relationship with anyone."

"Why did it have to be a relationship?" asked Sophia.

"Who else could it have been?" asked Emily. "Don't be silly, Sophia. Mum knew her killer well. If she hadn't, why rush out to meet them?"

"I'm rushing out after dinner to walk to the park with Polly," said Sophia. "We're mates, and I can assure you we're not in a relationship."

Neil wanted to get back to the office. It had been a long afternoon.

Blessing came through from the living room. Neil heard the boys thumping up the stairs.

"Programme over?" he asked.

"That finished a while ago," said Blessing. "We were playing cards. Harvey spotted Aiden's van outside. I told the boys to make themselves scarce until Mum gave them a shout for dinner."

"Thank you," said Emily. "Aiden usually hits the shower as soon as he gets home. Do you still want to speak to him today?"

"It will keep," said Neil. "We'll say hello on our way out and arrange to see him again. Sorry if I was tough on you, Sophia, but we did hear something worthwhile."

Sophia looked puzzled, as did her mother.

Blessing stood back as Sophia dashed into the hallway to run upstairs.

Emily walked with Neil and Blessing to the door. Aiden was removing equipment from the van and locking it in a tool store at the side of the house. Neil noticed the security camera and proximity lighting.

"Busy, Mr Fowler?"

"Always," said Aiden. "I'm on a different renovation project tomorrow, so I won't need to carry this kit around. Have you finished speaking with Em?"

"For today," said Neil. "We had a brief word with Sophia, too. Perhaps you could make yourself available on Friday afternoon? Only for thirty minutes. Pop into the police station at George Lane, and we will be there to meet you."

"Do I have a choice?" grinned Aiden.

"Always," said Neil. "Two o'clock or three o'clock?"

Neil slipped into the driver's seat of his car.

"What did you learn, Neil?" asked Blessing.

"Families can weave a tangled web," said Neil.

"Is it necessary to speak to Aiden Fowler, Neil?"

"I think the benefits people might want a word with Emily," said Neil. "As for Aiden, he's just two years older than Emily and lived in Hungerford until 2005. So it's unlikely he knew Katherine Alford."

"The boys didn't have a bad word to say about their father," said Blessing. "Or their mother, if it comes to that."

"How do they get on with Sophia?" asked Neil.

"She can be temperamental," said Blessing. "I remember feeling the same way in my early teens, but I didn't have a couple of younger brothers. I didn't sense any ill feeling there."

"No, it's Emily who still carries a grudge from childhood. She blames Paul for spoiling the happy times she shared with her parents. Paul moved from West Manton over two years ago. I don't think they're in touch. We'll find out when someone speaks with him."

"There won't be time for a debrief when we get back to the office," said Blessing.

"Gus and Lydia will have got their reports into the files by now," said Neil. "Alex will have arranged tomorrow's meetings. Someone will be off to Salisbury to speak with Danny Matravers. Maybe we'll get another trip to Marlborough to visit Lily Faulkner or Bert Harris."

"This line of traffic ahead suggests there's been an accident," said Blessing.

"In that case, we won't see anyone until the morning."

Neil dropped Blessing next to her Nissan Micra forty minutes later. As she left the car park, he was riding to the office in the lift. He knew everyone had gone home fifteen minutes earlier but wondered whether Gus or Alex had left a note.

Alex had added a list of Thursday appointments to the whiteboard closest to his desk. As Neil had thought, he and

Blessing were returning to Marlborough in the morning. Gus was taking Lydia to Salisbury.

Neil called Melody to tell her he was leaving and was heading for the lift when the phone rang.

"Crime Review Team office, DS Davis speaking."

"I guess everyone's gone home?"

"Luke? How are you? Will we see you tomorrow night?"

"I'm planning on being there," said Luke. "I've spent the past couple of days at Portishead. You wouldn't credit the number of incidents where Larcombe Manor played a significant role. I found it hard to accept the view they were criminals."

"We can't have vigilantes running riot around the country sorting problems the police don't have the resources to tackle," said Neil.

"You sound like the ACC I've been listening to, Neil," said Luke. "Then I look at names of people who no longer threaten decent law-abiding citizens and realise how much worse things would be if they were still alive."

"Not a topic of conversation for Friday night, mate," said Neil. "Gus wants a light-hearted get-together to thank you for your contribution to the team."

"Don't worry, Neil," said Luke. "I'll behave."

"Friday night at nine. Don't be late," said Neil.

Neil wondered how Luke would cope with his new role as he rode to the car park.

Thursday, 27 September 2018

"SEE you at the usual time tonight, then," said Suzie.

"I'll try to be better company than last night, I prom-ise," said Gus.

They had joined Brett and Clemency in The Lamb for a meal and drinks last night. Bert and Irene were having a quiet night at home, watching another of the documen-taries they were so keen on. Gus heard conversation around him and contributed with something he hoped was appro-priate from time to time. He couldn't stop mulling over the Alford case.

Gus was concerned about Trefor Davies. The senior detective had a reputation for being solid, reliable, and organized, yet when they spoke this morning, Gus felt things were slipping.

The constant need to refer to the folder for information was a concern. Was he too hard on the man? Could he recall specific details from a case he handled in Salisbury a decade ago? Gus reckoned that given a couple of minutes to refresh his memory; he'd have the salient points at his fingertips.

Trefor wasn't at George Lane when the call came through from Dr Gray. He was the senior officer. Why call a detective who wasn't scheduled to be at work? The detective constable who took Dr Gray's call had told Anna Cromwell Trefor wanted Wayne Barnett to take control.

Gus had realised the officer who took that call must have rung Trefor first. The DCI had then passed the ball swiftly to Wayne Barnett and asked the DC to tell Anna Cromwell she would be Wayne's second-in-command. Was Sunday morning chapel more important to Trefor than what might be a high-profile murder case? Trefor was only months away from retirement now, but back then, a successful outcome could have worked wonders for his chances of promotion.

Something didn't add up. When Wayne recalled how the investigation had gone, there was little evidence of Trefor mentoring his protégé. The suggestion there had been two men with Katherine that night wasn't something to be dismissed out of hand. So why didn't Trefor insist they continue with every line of enquiry they uncovered?

As he approached the Old Police Station car park, he spotted Blessing Umeh chatting with Neil Davis. Gus was keen to hear what they had learned from Emily Alford yesterday afternoon.

"Good morning, each," he said as he hopped from the Focus.

"Morning, guv," said Neil. "We got back at a quarter past five last night, and I popped upstairs to check where we were today."

"Alex has you booked to see Lily Faulkner at ten o'clock, I believe? We've got fifteen minutes before you need to leave. Let's have a quick chat before you go. I need to drive to Salisbury with Lydia at nine-fifteen too."

"Alex and Lydia are upstairs already, guv," said Blessing. "She hopes to persuade you to let her drive today."

"We'll see," said Gus.

"Luke Sherman called the office last night, guv," said Neil.

"He must have known we'd have gone home. Is he okay?"

"Not sure, guv. Luke's had a couple of tough days at Portishead."

"I'll have a quiet word tomorrow night," said Gus.

They travelled up in the lift and debriefed the previous day's meetings.

"We won't have time to get our reports into the Freeman Files this morning, guv," said Blessing.

"Crack on with that this afternoon after you've spoken to Lily Faulkner and Bert Harris," said Gus. "I expect to return from Salisbury by one o'clock at the latest."

"If I'm driving, it shouldn't be a problem, guv," said Lydia.

"Here we go again. I'm ready when you are," said Gus.

Neil and Blessing drew up outside Lily Faulkner's house in Purlyn Acre at one minute to ten.

"I wonder who lives next door?" asked Blessing.

"We know from what Emily told us yesterday the house stayed empty for two years," said Neil. "We can ask Lily if they're friendly."

Lily Faulkner answered the doorbell within seconds. Neil knew she was sixty-six years old, but her eyes were bright, although her hair was snowy-white.

"You must be the police officers I'm expecting," she said. "Come in. I suppose you'd like a cup of tea or coffee; you've had a long drive."

"I wouldn't say no, Mrs Faulkner," said Neil. "Two coffees, one with one sugar for me, please."

Lily showed them through to the lounge while she went to the kitchen. Neil thought once you'd seen one front room belonging to an older person, you'd seen the lot. Too many pieces of furniture, dozens of trinkets, and photographs, she must spend the day dusting. Her television was lost in the corner of the room. She hadn't followed the trend of filling a wall with a wide-screen version.

"Will there be biscuits?" asked Blessing.

"I'd bet on it," said Neil.

Minutes later, Lily wheeled a trolley through the door with three coffees and a plate of biscuits.

"There we are, my dear," said Lily, handing a mug to Blessing. "White, no sugar."

"Thank you, Mrs Faulkner," said Blessing.

Neil made the introductions and explained once more why they were there.

"Where do you want me to start?" asked Lily.

"Were you living here when Katherine and Daniel moved in?" asked Neil.

"Yes, dear. My husband was still alive then, of course."

"What did you make of them?" asked Neil.

"A perfectly normal young couple," said Lily. "In love, starting married life in a home of their own. It's so much more difficult for youngsters today, isn't it? The prices of everything have shot up."

"Their daughter, Emily, was born in 1984," said Blessing. "That couldn't have been long after they moved in."

"Emily was a honeymoon baby," said Lily. "Don't worry. I did the sums. Katherine wasn't expecting when she walked up the aisle."

"Can you remember where Katherine worked?" asked Neil. "We believe she stopped working around two months before the birth."

"We didn't talk to one another as much in those early years. Our son was living at home then, and Doug was here too in the evenings and weekends. Katherine and I spoke if we saw one another in the garden or at the front of the house, but nothing more. I saw Katherine leave for work in the mornings and come home at night. Where she went and what she was doing, I never knew. Daniel had a good job, though. An accountant, something of that nature."

"He earned enough for them not to need his wife's wages," said Blessing.

"I didn't go back to work after we had Guy," said Lily. "It was more common back then."

"We understood Katherine would have preferred to be working," said Neil.

"Daniel had strong opinions about women, DS Davis," said Lily. "I don't hold with some changes over the past fifty years, but I can't help but think his attitude caused the break up in the marriage. Daniel wouldn't bend. It was his way or nothing. Not that he ever got violent, don't get me wrong. He was an odd character."

"Did it surprise you when you noticed Katherine was pregnant again after so long?" asked Blessing.

"I'll say," said Lily. "You could have knocked me down with a feather. Guy had just told us he was emigrating to New Zealand. Everything seemed to happen at once. Young Emily was developing if you get my drift. Teenage boys soon notice that, don't they?"

"You didn't talk to Katherine about the baby?" asked Neil.

"Not my place to, my dear," said Lily. "What year was that? Let's see; it must have been 1997. Paul was born in 1998. Guy flew to Christchurch a month later. Doug had his first heart attack a week before Christmas, and Emily didn't get home until three o'clock on Christmas Eve."

"A young man driving a sports car dropped her off," said Blessing.

"How did you guess, my dear?" laughed Lily. "That sort are like flies around a jam pot."

"The marriage deteriorated after Paul's arrival," said Neil. "What did you see or hear of that?"

"A few conversations with raised voices," said Lily. "A

slammed door now and then. I can't swear it was always Daniel and Katherine. It could have been an argument over Emily's wanton behaviour."

"When did you lose your husband, Mrs Faulkner?" asked Blessing.

"After his third heart attack sixteen years ago, my dear. Married for twenty-six years and alone for sixteen."

"So, you and Katherine got closer after your husband died?" asked Neil.

"Katherine was a treasure. She popped in to sit with me. We relied on one another through our time of grief. She lost her mother less than a year after Doug passed, and Emily became pregnant. Well, what did the young girl expect? You can't keep rolling the dice and win every time, can you?"

"Emily moved out when Paul was four," said Neil. "Did Katherine ever give a reason for that?"

"Emily doted on her father," said Lily. "When Paul was born, it was obvious Katherine needed to devote her attention to her new baby, but Emily had been an only child for too long and resented the intrusion. Things got worse after Daniel walked out. Emily moved to West Manton, and as far as I know, she's still there."

"She is. We spoke to her and her family yesterday afternoon," said Blessing.

"More children, how lovely. Is she married this time?" asked Lily.

"Not yet," said Blessing. "They're happy as they are for now."

"We've read your account of what happened the night Katherine died," said Neil. "Today, you've confirmed that after you lost your husband, the two of you spent more time together. Living next door, you were well-placed to see people coming and going. Was there nobody who visited between the day Daniel Matravers left and the night of the murder?"

"You make it sound as if I did nothing but stare out the window," said Lily. "There are always people walking up and down our paths. People deliver the post; youngsters hand out flyers for takeaways. Then there are the chaps who come to read the meters. Don't you think I didn't rack my brains ten years ago when the police asked me that question? If I'd seen a strange face, it would have registered. I would have known if she had a friend or relative who dropped by regularly. I'd hope Katherine would have mentioned them, anyway."

"That leads me to something that bothered us," said Neil. "When Katherine ran here that night to ask you to babysit Paul. Who did she say she had to go to meet?"

"Katherine was agitated," said Lily. "She made little sense. I thought she said she was meeting her brother. So that's what I told the police."

"Had Katherine ever mentioned a brother before?" asked Blessing.

"No, dear," said Lily. "We had spoken about Mary, her mother, and losing her father when she was in her early twenties. When Doug and I married, Mary was already living on the other side of the estate. I was certain Katherine was an only child."

"Why didn't you tell the police that?" asked Neil.

"I told them she was agitated and not making sense. I was flustered, too, with the shock of learning she'd been murdered. They needed to let Emily know, and I kept an eye on Paul until someone came back to collect him."

"It must be hard to stop thinking about things like that," said Blessing.

"I still think about that night now, my dear," said Lily.

"Katherine said 'brother', of that I'm positive. Years ago, I decided I had misheard her, and it might have been like a brother or something similar. I knew I should tell the police, but I couldn't see how it would help. There was no brother, and there was nobody close to her. The police would have found them, wouldn't they?"

"The police always believed Katherine knew her killer well," said Neil. "She wanted to meet him. Katherine wouldn't have run to you for help otherwise. So despite the time that's passed, there has to be a person still around that everyone's missed."

"Maybe Daniel Matravers can tell our boss who that might be," said Blessing. "He's with Daniel now."

"What did you do when Katherine left in such a hurry?" asked Neil.

"I sat and watched television, with the sound turned low, to hear Paul if he awoke."

"Did Katherine leave you in the living room and dash out? Did you see which way she went?"

"Katherine ran here and asked me to sit with Paul. I followed her next door, and she collected her car keys from the table in the hallway. I stood by the door as she reversed off the drive, waved, and closed the door. Where she went after that, I couldn't tell; she was out of sight in seconds."

"There's always been a question about where Katherine drove between leaving here and the sighting at The Roebuck at half-past ten," said Neil.

"I don't drive, DS Davis," said Lily, "but once Katherine was a few hundred yards from here, she would have joined Herd Street until she reached London Road. That route would have taken her past The Roebuck. Even with my old legs, I could walk there in twenty-five minutes. Katherine would have reached the pub in her car in four minutes."

"Katherine hoped to be there and back in ten minutes," said Blessing. "Perhaps she didn't intend to go as far as the pub. The meeting point could have been closer, possibly?"

"When I told the police Katherine had promised to get back in ten minutes, the lady detective said, well, that's what people say. Ten minutes isn't an exact time; it's another way of saying you won't be long. So I might have refused to do as she asked if Katherine had told me she'd be gone for an hour."

"That's not true, though, is it?" said Neil.

"No, but that's what the lady detective thought," said Lily. "She said Katherine said what I wanted to hear, that she was just popping out for a short while."

"Could there have been another spot where Katherine might have met someone?" asked Neil.

"Dozens," said Lily. "Where would anyone start? She could have been on Kingsbury Street or Port Hill in minutes. The first has shops and offices on either side, and the other has a large field where people park on the grass opposite their properties. If you knew Marlborough well, you would know plenty of places someone could stop for a chat, and nobody would pay any attention. That was all it was supposed to be. That's what Katherine told me. I need to pop out for ten minutes to talk to him. He's been like a brother to me."

Blessing saw Lily was upset. Perhaps that caused her to recall Katherine's exact words.

"Just calm down, Mrs Faulkner," said Neil. "Think carefully. Could that have been what Katherine said to you that night? She said it was a man like a brother to her?"

"I couldn't swear to it in court," said Lily. "I wanted to help the detectives when they came here to tell me Katherine was dead, but I couldn't remember her exact words. So I said she was meeting her brother. If I'd not been flustered and had tried harder to remember every word Katherine said, they might have found her killer. It's my fault he's still at large."

"You mustn't blame yourself," said Blessing. "I don't have a friend who's like a brother to me, but I would expect my friends and family to know him if I did. But, unfortunately, nobody ever came up with a name."

"We can always come back if we think there's something else you can help us with, Mrs Faulkner," said Neil. "We're sorry to have stirred unpleasant memories. Thanks for the coffee and biscuits. They were lovely."

"Where are you off to next, DS Davis?" asked Lily.

"One of your neighbours, Mr Harris," said Neil as Lily came with them to the front door.

"Old Bert Harris, who lives on the other side of the estate?" said Lily. "Let's hope you catch him on a good day."

"Moody?" asked Neil.

"Senile," said Lily. "Goodbye to you both. You're welcome to drop by whenever you're passing. But, sadly, few do these days."

Neil and Blessing returned to the car.

"That was useful," said Neil.

"It would be if Lily recalled Katherine's exact words," Blessing said. "The trouble is Lily may have gone over it so many times in her head she found a pattern of words that pointed the finger at a mystery man. But, on the other hand, it helped ease her conscience."

"I wonder whether I should call Gus to tell him what we've learned?" asked Neil.

"Let's visit Mr Harris first," said Blessing. "We might not be with him long."

Chapter Seven

IN SALISBURY, Gus and Lydia were sitting in the offices of a chartered accountancy firm in the Clarendon Centre on Southampton Road.

"You have a view across the fields to the River Avon, I see," said Gus. "That's something I never enjoyed while I worked in Salisbury."

"You were lucky to catch me," said Daniel Matravers. "I retire at the end of October when I reach fifty-seven. Of course, I could stay in the rat race until I'm sixty, but France beckons, and a view of the Garonne near Bordeaux has more appeal."

"Our colleague, DS Hardy, explained why we needed to speak to you," said Gus.

"He thought I could help solve my ex-wife's murder."

"I've read the file," said Gus. "I know the questions DI Barnett, and DS Cromwell asked. However, we want to pursue a different line of enquiry."

"Fire away," said Daniel. "It won't change the facts. I left Marlborough eight years before Katherine's murder. We exchanged unpleasantries during the divorce proceedings. Apart from that, I never returned to the town and had no contact with the woman."

"Or your children," said Lydia.

"I should have known *you* would ask that question," said Matravers. "The sisterhood must stick together."

"Did you love your wife when you married?" asked Gus.

"Of course I did—what a foolish question. We clearly understood our different roles. I was the breadwinner, and Katherine, the homemaker."

"Your daughter was born a year after the wedding. Is that right?" asked Gus.

"Emily was the perfect baby. We named her after my mother. Our family was complete."

"You never wanted a big family?" asked Gus.

"One child was enough," said Matravers. "I hoped Emily would have a brief career, then make a good marriage. Katherine and I could then retire when I reached fifty. It was how I'd planned it ever since we met."

"You insisted Katherine had a coil fitted," said Lydia.

"We agreed there would be no more children," said Matravers. "I left it to Katherine to decide which method she should adopt."

"Celibacy wasn't an option, I assume?" said Lydia.

"Of course not, and neither was the contraceptive pill."

"We learned yesterday that you were adamant Emily shouldn't go on the pill despite being sexually active."

"Emily was still a child, even at fifteen. I had sat her down aged twelve and told her very firmly how I expected her to behave. Self-control is vital in those teenage years. Girls who take the pill can rapidly become promiscuous. Young lads they meet don't care what damage they're doing to the child's emotions. They soon realise they can have sex whenever they like, with no consequences. Not that way in my parents' day. One careless moment and two people's lives were ruined."

"Were you aware Emily was sleeping with boys while underage?" asked Gus.

"Emily didn't share that knowledge with me," said Matravers. "I suspected as much, but Emily had become moody and defiant. A typical teenager. If Katherine had helped me, we could have brought Emily into line, but then Katherine did something unforgivable."

"Katherine ditched the coil and let nature take its course," said Gus.

"Without a word to me," said Matravers.

"Emily told us after Katherine received confirmation she was pregnant, she returned home and told you both. After that, nothing was ever the same."

"How could it be? I knew I was losing my daughter. She was no longer the little girl I loved spending time with, and suddenly, I was handed a fait accompli. My wife made a unilateral decision to have a baby, which meant our early retirement plans went out of the window."

"So, two years later, you walked away from the marriage," said Lydia. "What took you so long?"

"I needed time to re-adjust my plans," said Matravers. "I continued working as a chartered accountant in Marlborough, working overtime rather than going home. Weekends were the worst, especially after Paul was born. I never knew when Emily would get home either, which kept me awake half the night. Finally, I couldn't take it any longer. I had to leave."

"Did you return here to Salisbury?" asked Gus.

"I moved back in with my parents," said Matravers.

"Were you surprised Katherine didn't return to work after the divorce?" asked Gus.

"It didn't interest me," said Matravers. "Whatever situation she was in, she'd brought on herself. I learned that her mother died a couple of years later, which would have helped Katherine out of a financial jam. As for Emily, she sent a photograph of her daughter, Sophia, to my parents. She had asked for it to be passed on. I didn't respond. Why she thought I'd be interested, heaven knows. When I gave her the talk, I warned Emily an unmarried mother wasn't something I would accept in the family."

"Did Katherine leave school at sixteen?" asked Gus.

"She did. Her exam results meant any further academic progress was futile. I met Katherine when I was twenty, and she was eighteen. We married a month after I'd left university, and Emily was born one year later. I had two more years before becoming a fully-fledged chartered accountant."

Lydia smiled to herself, which wasn't missed by Daniel Matravers.

"What did you find amusing?" he snapped.

"Did you ever watch the TV character, Mrs Merton, when she asked Debbie McGhee what first attracted her to the millionaire, Paul Daniels? If Katherine was such a dunce, how did the two of you get together in the first place?"

"My colleague may have a non-standard approach to an interview," said Gus, "but her point is valid. It offended you when we asked if you were in love with Katherine when you married. Perhaps it was a marriage of convenience."

Daniel Matravers leaned back in his chair.

"I don't wish to continue this conversation," he said. "The

detectives who took my statement in 2008 were happy to accept I had nothing to do with my ex-wife's murder. I've never returned to Marlborough since 2000 and haven't contacted either of my children. On the night Katherine died, I was at a concert at the City Hall with a party of sixteen people. We had a meal together, attended the concert, and went for drinks afterwards. Detectives checked that bullet-proof alibi. I will need my solicitor present if you wish to ask further questions. Your current line of questioning borders on harassment and could play no part in helping you find Katherine's killer."

"As you wish," said Gus. "We'll continue to probe for answers from other witnesses and people connected to Katherine. I'm not satisfied we've heard the truth from everyone so far. If I believe you're hiding something that would offer us a positive outcome, we'll arrange a meeting at Bourne Hill. I've noted that you plan to emigrate at the end of October. There are frequent flights from Bordeaux to Southampton or Bristol International."

Gus and Lydia left Daniel Matravers's office and returned to the car park.

"Well, that was unexpected," said Lydia.

"You provoked him," said Gus. "Who was this, Mrs Merton, anyway? I don't remember watching that series."

"It was a 90s classic," said Lydia. "No doubt you were involved with cases at Bourne Hill. A relaxed evening at home watching television never rated highly in your marriage with Tess, did it?"

"I found it killed conversation and distracted my thoughts," said Gus. "I prefer listening to music when analysing witness statements and zero distractions when trying to talk to someone. I learned the hard way. Tess once asked which towels I would prefer in the bathroom. I was listening to a reporter on TV outside the Old Bailey and said the dry ones. Tess was standing in the doorway with two samples she'd brought home. I didn't have to worry about distractions for a week. After that, she didn't speak to me."

"We'd better return to the office," said Lydia. "I'll put the radio on, keep quiet, and let you work out what Daniel Matravers is hiding."

NEIL AND BLESSING had driven from Lily Faulkner's home and found Bert Harris's house on a road parallel to Purlyn Acre.

"I'm not surprised Bert Harris recognised Katherine Alford's car," said Neil. "As Lily said, it was a short drive from her place to Herd Street, and Bert lived near the junction. So if he was walking his dog in the vicinity, he could have seen Katherine often."

"Let's hope he remembers," said Blessing.

Neil rang the doorbell.

Blessing heard the bolt slide back and the key turn in the lock.

Bert Harris opened the door enough to see who was on his doorstep.

"We're the police, Mr Harris," said Neil. "Do you remember someone calling you?"

"Of course I do," said Bert. "How do I know you're the police?"

Neil and Blessing produced their warrant cards, and the seventy-four-year-old studied them closely.

"You had better come in," said Bert. "Sorry for the mess. The cleaner hasn't been today."

Bert dragged open the door. The hallway was crammed with newspapers, cardboard boxes, unopened rolls of wallpaper, an old bicycle, and a washing machine. Bert closed the entrance to the lounge. Neil also spotted a similar hoarding in that room.

"The kitchen will be best," said Bert.

Neil and Blessing followed him through the narrow channel to the kitchen door. Every square inch of storage space was filled with cans and cartons, but Bert had spared the kitchen table and two chairs.

"Do you want a cuppa?" asked Bert.

"We're fine, thanks," said Neil.

Blessing hoped they wouldn't be long. No way was she going to ask to use the bathroom.

"Do you live alone, Mr Harris?" she asked.

"Since the wife died, miss," Bert replied. "I've let things go in the last eight years. Sit yourself down."

Blessing looked at the nearest chair and decided it didn't look too bad.

Bert disappeared next door, and Neil heard several dozen books hitting the floor.

"Here you are, son," said Bert. "You can take the weight off. I've got three more chairs in there somewhere."

When all three were seated, Neil asked Bert if he could remember what he was doing on the night of Katherine Alford's murder.

"Katherine? That was the lady who lived over the road, wasn't it?" said Bert. "She drove a red car, and a foreign make it was. She didn't have a car before that. Her husband always had a posh motor. A stuck-up bloke who always thought he was better than the rest of us."

"A chartered accountant," said Neil. "Daniel Matravers walked out of the marriage in 2000 and moved back to Salisbury."

"Did he? I wouldn't know. My wife, Betty, knew Mary

Alford, Katherine's mother. After Mary died, Katherine had a bit of money. That was when she bought the car. She'd had to scrimp and save after that fellow of hers left them. How can anyone walk out on two kids?"

"You remember things clearly, Mr Harris," said Blessing.

"The newspapers help, miss," said Bert. "I know where to put my hand on the daily papers, the weekend supplements, and the local rag. After your chap called me, I found the ones with reports on the murder. I was reading them just before you got here. I've got a job to remember what I had for dinner last night or if I had a bath last Friday without writing things on paper."

Blessing wondered whether Bert ever lost those scraps of paper. Perhaps he knew where to put his hand on them, the same as the newspapers.

"Do you still own a dog, Mr Harris?" asked Neil.

"Not now, son. After I had to have Biggles put to sleep, I decided not to get another dog. I don't get out of the house much these days. It wouldn't be fair not being able to give the dog the right exercise."

"What time did you leave home with Biggles that night?" asked Neil.

"As soon as Betty went upstairs to bed. It was a warm night. I put the dog on the lead and went out in just a shirt and slacks. I slipped a poo bag into my pocket, and we made for Coldharbour Lane, our usual route. Biggles did his business; I dropped the bag in the bin at the bottom of the Lane, and we turned around to walk home."

"You told detectives that walk took you around twenty minutes," said Neil.

"I couldn't do it in twenty minutes now, son," laughed

Bert. "That was about right, though, twenty minutes, there and back."

"So, where were you when Katherine's car passed you?"

"Almost at the top of Coldharbour Lane. Her red car went past the junction. I wasn't mistaken. It was definitely Katherine."

"Was she alone?" asked Neil.

"She was past the end of the road before I could see," said Bert.

"Hang on, when you told detectives her car passed you, their report suggested she was on Coldharbour Lane. We wanted to ask whether you saw the front of the Peugeot as it came towards you or the back of the car as it passed."

"That French car wasn't on Coldharbour Lane, son," said Bert. "As sure as I'm sitting here. It went from left to right. It must have come from the junction with Herd Street, and she was gone when I crossed the road again. I thought she'd gone home."

Neil stopped to think. The girls at the pub reckoned it was around half-past ten when they spotted a man and woman talking. They had come outside with their drinks at around ten because it was too warm indoors. Could they have been mistaken, and it was five or ten minutes earlier? Even if it was half past ten, it was possible the couple stopped talking, got into the car and returned to the estate.

"How far were you from home when you saw the red car, Mr Harris?" asked Blessing.

"What, to cross the road and walk to the top of the road, miss? A couple of minutes. Biggles stopped for a sniff and a scratch every few yards, but I was indoors by ten to eleven. I didn't check the clock, though."

"One last thing before we go, Mr Harris," said Neil. "Did you walk the same route with Biggles every night?"

"Some nights, we'd walk along The Thorns. Biggles had plenty of trees and bushes at the side of the road there. So I'd let him off the lead for a run. Why?"

"I wondered whether you ever walked past Katherine Alford's house."

"A bit out of my way," said Bert. "Sorry."

"No matter," said Neil. "We can't identify a regular visitor to Katherine's house."

"Do you think she was seeing someone while she was married?" asked Bert. "That doesn't sound like Katherine."

"Everyone spoke highly of her," said Blessing. "There had to be someone the police missed ten years ago. A tradesperson or a professional who called door-to-door."

"The vicar came here for a visit after Betty died," said Bert. "I haven't seen him since. I don't answer the door to cold callers, but they leave leaflets for double-glazing, solar panels, or a conservatory. They're in a pile behind the door in the front room if you want to look. As for builders and the like, I doubt Katherine needed much done while her husband was there. He handled the general maintenance. But, no, I can't put a finger on the person you're looking for."

Neil had to agree. He hoped Gus and Lydia had more luck in Salisbury.

"We'll be off, Mr Harris," said Neil. "Thanks for your help. You've cleared up one mystery."

"Have I, son?" asked Bert. "What happens now? Will I need to go to court to testify?"

"We've caught no one yet, Mr Harris," said Neil. "If we do, we'll cross that bridge when we come to it."

Bert followed them as they retraced their steps through the piles of rubbish.

"You should get someone to help remove this," said Blessing.

"What would I do if it got taken away, miss?" asked Bert. "I wouldn't have anything to remind me where I used to work, that I was married, and that Friday night's bath night. You've still got your memories in your young head. I can't always remember things clearly, but if I can look at the newspaper with a picture of me being presented with a carriage clock on the day I retired, I'm back on track."

Bert closed the door behind them, locked it, and Blessing heard the bolt slide across with a firm clunk.

"That was spooky," she said.

"We could tell the authorities," said Neil. "But Bert might be worse off if they got involved. I wonder why Barnett and Cromwell didn't check the road layout to see whether Bert's statement stood up?"

"What he told us makes perfect sense since we drove along those particular roads," said Blessing. "You queried whether Charlotte and Jasmine were outside for a shorter time than they thought before seeing that couple. If we accept Katherine and her friend were talking outside The Roebuck at ten-thirty, they could have left at twenty to eleven and driven to her estate by ten-forty-five. Lily told us it was only a four-minute drive."

"I guess the timing fits," said Neil. "It still doesn't feel right, does it? Katherine left Lily on the doorstep at nine forty-five. Charlotte and Jasmine saw her forty-five minutes later, long after she was due home. Now, Bert tells us, her car whizzed by the end of Coldharbour Lane and drove past his house. He was indoors by ten to eleven. Katherine was ten seconds from the turning into Purlyn Acre."

"Why didn't she just drive home?" asked Blessing.

"Not only that, where was Katherine between leaving

home and being seen at The Roebuck? We solve one mystery and get left with a bigger one."

"Where next?" asked Blessing.

"Back to the office," said Neil. "Gus reckoned they would get there by one o'clock. We need to update him on what we learned from Lily Faulkner and Bert Harris. All is not lost. We haven't spoken to Paul Alford yet. He may remember someone his mother often spoke to on the phone when he was young. A name, that's what we need. We can work out where it was she met the guy later."

"I wonder who will go to Dorchester with DI Packenham next week?" asked Blessing.

"You can volunteer if you wish," said Neil.

"I hope Gus picks Alex," said Blessing.

"We don't get to pick and choose, Blessing," said Neil. "If either of us gets the short straw, we'll have to grin and bear it."

They drove back to the car park behind the Old Police Station office.

"There's Lydia's Mini," said Blessing. "They got back quicker than they thought."

"All will be revealed," shrugged Neil.

Blessing called the lift, and two minutes later, they joined their colleagues.

"Ah, good to see you back," said Gus. "How did it go in Marlborough, Neil?"

"Lily Faulkner and Bert Harris modified the statements they gave to the police ten years ago," said Neil. "In some ways, the new information answered a couple of our questions, but they also threw up fresh ones."

"We got shown the door by Daniel Matravers," said Lydia.

"Lydia annoyed him," said Gus. "Which can often be a

useful ploy. Matravers wanted us to accept that as he had a cast-iron alibi for the night of the murder, we shouldn't ask him questions at all."

"Was it possible he paid someone to murder Katherine?" asked Blessing.

"What would have been his motive?" asked Alex. "No, that's not the reason he shut you down."

"Look, everyone has reports to complete from yesterday and today," said Gus. "I propose we spend the rest of the afternoon updating our files. What time did you arrange for us to speak to Paul Alford, Alex?"

"After nine tomorrow morning, guv," said Alex. "Paul's taking a half-day holiday but will need to leave for work by a quarter to one."

"If you collect me from home in the morning, Neil, we'll see Paul Alford at his place in Copse Avenue together."

"Got it, guv," said Neil. "I'll be at the bungalow at half-past eight."

"When Neil and I return, we'll recap everything we've learned this week," said Gus. "I don't want a late finish tomorrow."

"Someone must visit George Lane to talk with Aiden Fowler, guv. He's agreed to get there at two o'clock."

"I've pencilled in Charlotte Ovens and Jasmine Park for tomorrow, guv," said Alex. "They work together in Marlborough and agreed to take an extended lunch break. So Lydia and I could cover that meeting if you wish."

"Call the ladies and confirm you'll see them between twelve and two," said Gus. "Neil and I may return from Swindon before you need to leave. We can pass on any new information or add it to your list of questions. As for Aiden Fowler, it would make more sense if you and Blessing carried on from where you left off, Neil."

"No problem, guv," said Neil.

"That just leaves ACC Cromwell to interview," said Blessing.

"Ah, but does it?" asked Gus. "What about Callum Brady? What can he add to our knowledge? Are we happy Dr Gray and his wife can't throw light on the dark corners of this case? We haven't pooled our latest information yet to see whether it points us in another direction. Let's park those matters, update our files, and regroup sometime tomorrow. I want a clear idea of where we are and how we will proceed next week."

"Amazing Grace will be with us then," said Lydia.

"Which is why I want clarity," said Gus. "Grace will pick up on any muddled thinking and missed opportunities."

"How do we find Callum Brady, guv?" asked Neil.

"Alex can call Trefor Davies," said Gus. "He'll know where Brady went after he left George Lane. Wayne Barnett didn't seem to remember. We can't afford to hang about until Grace Packenham has a cosy chat with Anna Cromwell next week. I want Grace to drop a subtle hint we're checking Anna didn't make a mess of her only murder case."

Gus watched as Neil and Blessing entered details of the various interviews they'd attended into the files. He would love to tell them what he'd learned in Salisbury and hear what they'd uncovered in West Manton and the Purlyn Acre estate.

Experience told him it was best to get those reports done while things were still fresh in his mind. He'd wasted too many hours trying to interpret what he'd scribbled in his notebook when he finally listened to repeated requests from his superiors to submit his paperwork.

Enough reminiscing, he told himself. It was time to get the gist of this morning's meeting into the computer. Then he remembered he still hadn't dealt with reports of the long day he'd spent with Lydia yesterday. Gus looked at the clock on the wall. He might finish by five o'clock if he could make sense of his scribbled notes.

"Goodnight, guv," said Alex as he and Lydia were about to leave.

"Heck, is it that time already?" said Gus.

"We'll see you when you return from seeing Paul Alford," Lydia said.

"Okay. Just putting the finishing touches to my final report," said Gus.

Gus heard the lift doors close as Alex and Lydia followed Neil and Blessing to the car park.

Five minutes later, he was in the Focus and leaving town. Suzie might make it home before him tonight, which was no big deal. They had planned a quiet night in.

He slowed as he passed the gateway to the allotments by the church, but he didn't spot Bert Penman or The Reverend. Gus struggled to recall when he'd last spent more than five minutes on his patch of land. In the past week, there had been precious little spare time.

He spotted Bert ahead as he negotiated the last hundred yards of the lane before turning into the driveway. He sounded the horn. What a terrible sound it made.

Bert waved his new walking stick and turned back to meet Gus by the gateway.

"Miss Suzie beat you home tonight, then, Mr Freeman?"

"Almost, Bert," said Gus. "You'll get there."

"Happen I will," said Bert, "happen I won't. It's difficult to change the habits of a lifetime."

"Have the bruises faded?" asked Gus.

"Everything's a lot better, thank you," said Bert. "Irene's still fussing, but I'm getting out of the house for a little longer each day. I hope to see you this weekend. Your patch of land could do with some tender loving care. Haven't you got a tricky case you can ponder and slip away for a few hours? I can sneak four cans of cider out in my trug if you need something to stimulate those grey cells. What do you say?"

"I could have done with that offer last weekend, Bert," said Gus. "Suzie and I are going to the Waggon & Horses tomorrow night, a farewell drink for a colleague. I might prefer a flask of black coffee at the allotments on Saturday."

"That could be arranged," said Bert. "I'll amend my list. Two cans and a flask, it is. Is something about this case you're working on giving you a hard time, Mr Freeman?"

Gus laughed.

"Not some of it, all of it," he said.

"I have every confidence you'll sort it out, Mr Freeman," said Bert. "However, you had better get indoors. Miss Suzie is giving me the stare from the front doorstep."

Bert waved his stick with a flourish, and Suzie waved back. Gus parked the Focus under the trailing roses and joined Suzie to watch Bert making his way steadily up the lane.

"He's back in the old routine," said Suzie. "How about you?"

"Let's eat first and then dissect the Katherine Alford case."

Chapter Eight

Friday, 28 September 2018

GUS WAS first out of bed in the morning. As he padded towards the bedroom door, he noticed Suzie stirring and knew she would go straight to the kitchen to prepare breakfast.

Neil was rarely late, so Gus needed to be ready at half-past eight.

When he reached the kitchen, he was in for a surprise—boiled egg and soldiers. Gus sat at the table, sipped his black coffee, and prepared to strike the top of the sizeable free-range egg. Suzie kissed the top of his head as she headed for the bathroom.

"We trawled through your interviews with Trefor Davies and Wayne Barnett last night," she said. "I understand your concerns. If you like, I could ask around at London Road."

"Be careful what you ask," said Gus. "It's impossible to get the lid back on something of this nature. Trefor doesn't have long left."

"I'll be as vague as I can, I promise," said Suzie.

While Suzie showered, Gus buttered another piece of toast.

"I can hear a car outside," said Suzie as she walked through from the bedroom. She was suited and booted, ready for work. But, before leaving, Gus needed to find a clean shirt, drag a comb through his unruly hair, and search for his shoes.

Suzie was outside chatting with Neil when he finally emerged from the bungalow.

"Ready, guv?" asked Neil.

"Yes, I can't wait to hear what young Master Alford says," said Gus.

Neil stood to one side as Suzie drove towards the gateway with the usual spray of gravel. Neil checked the boot of his car.

"A few chips in the paintwork, Neil?" asked Gus. "I expect they were there already."

"A couple more won't matter then," said Neil. "I thought we'd take the Beckhampton Road, guv, and drive through Avebury and Swindon. It shouldn't take longer than an hour at this time of the morning."

"I assume Alex convinced Paul Alford to get out of bed in time?" asked Gus. "I don't want to stand on the doorstep while you throw stones at the window."

"Paul Alford told Alex we could see him after nine, guv," said Neil.

"Alford has lived in Copse Avenue for two years," said Gus. "I wonder what attracted him to the area?".

"Copse Avenue is near the football ground, guv," said Neil.

"How did Emily describe her brother, Neil?"

"Quiet and withdrawn, guv," said Neil. "Maybe that

was because of what he'd been through, or he may have felt uncomfortable with Aiden Fowler living there."

"No, if Paul was quiet and withdrawn when he moved to live with Emily aged ten, he'd been that way since he was a child. He will be the same person today; you mark my words. I doubt he's interested in football."

Neil soon found Copse Avenue, and Gus checked house numbers as they weaved through the estate.

"Liquorice all-sorts," said Gus. "The developer opted for a mix of one, two, and three-bedroomed properties to maximise the number they could fit into the space available. So here we are, on our left."

Neil parked on the road and hoped a fire engine didn't need to pass.

Gus was ringing the doorbell when Neil locked his car.

Paul Alford answered the door. He seemed wide awake, if not pleased to see them.

"Come in," he said.

Gus and Neil followed the twenty-year-old through to the small living room.

Neil noticed Paul was taller than Emily and her daughter Sophia. His hair was darker, too. However, as he hadn't met Daniel Matravers, he didn't know whether the lad took after his father.

"Freeman's the name," said Gus. He wondered what Neil was doing. He was away with the fairies. Gus wanted to get on with it. The sooner they were out of here, the better.

"I'm Detective Sergeant Davis," said Neil. "We thought you might help us."

"Why?" asked Paul.

"Your mother's murder was never solved," said Gus. "That doesn't sit right with me. So we're going over everything again, trying to discover what somebody missed ten years ago."

"Sounds boring," said Paul.

"What can you remember of that Saturday?" asked Gus.

"The day she died do you mean?" asked Paul.

"Humour me," said Gus. "Did you do anything differently during the day?"

"I could tell you it was a normal Saturday, but you wouldn't understand. Nothing was what most kids call normal. My Dad walked out when I was two. It might have been better if he'd left before I was born."

"Your mother compensated for that, though, didn't she?" asked Neil.

"I couldn't have asked for a better mother."

"Let's concentrate on the day in question," said Gus. "Did anyone visit the house? Can you recall your mother speaking to someone on the phone?"

Paul Alford shrugged his shoulders.

"If the phone rang, it was never for me anyway," said Paul. "Why would I know who called Mum or why? Now and then, the doorbell rang while I was watching TV or in my room reading. I didn't rush out to see if it was someone from school wanting to ask if I could come out to play."

"Did that happen often?" asked Neil.

"Never," said Paul. "I didn't give anyone my number."

"Had Lily Faulkner ever visited the house before that night?" asked Gus.

"Not in the evenings," said Paul. "Mrs Faulkner dropped in for a coffee during the school holidays. I wouldn't know if she did that while I was at school. She enjoyed a chat, and she missed her son, Guy. He'd emigrated to New Zealand the year I was born."

Gus sat up straighter in his chair, but Neil nodded to confirm that he and Blessing had heard that yesterday.

"Lily Faulkner told us it was the first time she'd been asked to babysit you," said Gus. "Is that correct?"

"Mum hadn't been on a night out for years," said Paul. "I didn't know she'd left home that night anyway."

"You didn't wake until half-past eight the following morning," said Neil.

"When I got downstairs, Mrs Faulkner told me what had happened. Mum received a call, had to go out in the car for ten minutes, but still wasn't back."

"Then the police arrived," said Neil.

"I ran outside thinking Mum was in the police car. While the man and woman spoke to Mrs Faulkner, I looked at the gadgets in the car. I was hoping they'd let me play with the lights and sirens, but suddenly, Mrs Faulkner was crying and called me back indoors."

"Did she tell you what had happened?" asked Gus.

"It didn't sink in," said Paul. "I was in a daze."

"Did you go to your sister Emily's house that day?" asked Neil.

"Yes. Mrs Faulkner said I couldn't stay at home, and she couldn't look after me. So I had to live with Emily."

"How did you feel about that?" asked Gus.

"Gutted. Emily hated me."

"Did you never get on?"

"Did you have a younger brother or sister?" asked Paul.

"No," said Gus. "I was an only child."

"I realised when I went to live with Emily that I'd been a mistake. I mean, who waits fourteen years to have another baby?"

"You were too young to understand why your father

walked away from the marriage," said Gus. "Did your mother try to explain the reasons as you grew older?"

"Kids at school made comments," said Paul. "They weren't nice. I had weird ideas, but Mum always fobbed me off with the excuse that they just didn't get on anymore after sixteen years. It was no one's fault. She told me I mustn't blame myself."

"Irreconcilable differences," said Gus.

"That's it," said Paul, "in a nutshell."

"What do you remember of the time when Emily left home? How old were you?" asked Neil.

"I was only four and a half, so I don't remember much," said Paul. "When Emily lived with us, she was always rowing with Mum. I hid in my room when that happened. There was a lot of shouting, doors slamming, and Emily crying next door in her room. I didn't understand. Kids at school called her a slut. I'd heard that word at home when Mum lost her temper."

"We spoke to your father yesterday morning," said Gus. "He's retiring and will live in France after the end of next month. Did you know?"

Paul shook his head.

"He turned his back on me eighteen years ago. I never knew him. Mum told me he'd gone home to Salisbury. When I was living with Emily, she told me she'd sent a photo of Sophia to our grandparents, but nobody wrote back. They didn't care about us either. They're probably dead now."

"Why do you think you and Emily never got on?" asked Neil.

"Emily was so much older than me. It was just Mum and me at home when Emily was at school. Maybe I got spoiled, and my sister was jealous. Emily never hit me or anything like that. She just ignored me. Then she had Sophia, which made things worse between her and Mum. In the end, Emily moved out. There were no more rows, and Mum and I got on great. They were the happiest days of my life."

"During those five years, did your mother ever work?" asked Gus.

"She couldn't go to work with me at home, could she? Mum was always there when I came home, unlike the kids I heard talking at school. She looked after me every day during the holidays. Sometimes, we went to see Emily and Sophia, or they came to see us."

"So, had your mother and Emily resolved their differences?" asked Gus. "They weren't arguing as they were when she lived with you?"

"Mum would say Emily had made her bed, and she had to lie on it, which made little sense to me when I was eight. But no, they didn't argue as they had before."

"Who visited your mother in the evenings, at weekends, or in the school holidays?" asked Gus.

"I don't remember seeing anyone," said Paul. "Although, after I'd gone to bed and fallen asleep, I suppose someone could have been downstairs. How would I know? Who do you mean, anyway?"

"We don't know, Paul," said Gus. "Nobody ever came forward to say they were a friend of hers when the police made an appeal on television. So when Mum dashed out of the house that night, she had to be going to meet someone she knew well."

"What about places you went with your mother?" asked Neil.

"What, apart from school activities or visiting Emily?"

"Anything that comes to mind," said Neil.

"Mum took me with her when she went shopping. I sat and watched as she had her hair done at a salon in town. When Mum went to the dentist or the doctor, I sat and read a comic or a book while waiting. Then, when it was my turn to visit those places, Mum came too. We went to the park to play, and Mum taught me how to swim at the indoor pool. It felt great doing normal stuff with her, but one day, I woke up, and it was over. Mrs Faulkner told me I had to live with my sister. Emily didn't want me there, you know," said Paul. "Although she and Mum had buried the hatchet, things weren't any different. Finally, Aiden, her boyfriend, persuaded Emily I should move in."

"Things didn't change after you went to live in West Manton?" asked Gus. "How did you get on with Sophia?"

"Nothing changed," said Paul. "Sophia was okay, but she was four years younger than me…. and a girl. The only thing we had in common was that we didn't know our fathers. I didn't belong in that house. Aiden and Emily wanted a family, and after I moved there, that's what they did. I was never close to my nephews; they probably didn't miss me. So, as soon as our old house sold and the money went into my bank account, I started planning to move out. I couldn't leave before I was sixteen, but I found a place in South Marston to rent. Then I spotted this house for sale. It's perfect. Close to work, nobody bothers me, and I don't have to have anything to do with my family."

"Everybody needs someone, Paul," said Neil. "Why not give Mrs Faulkner a ring? She would love the company, and who better to tell you about your mother? Everything I've heard tells me she loved you very much. That's something worth holding onto."

Gus wondered whether Paul Alford had anything useful

to add. Perhaps it was time to leave. He might follow Neil's suggestion if they left him to ponder matters.

"We'll let you get on with your day, Paul," said Gus. "I know you need to get ready for work. We'll get in touch if we think of something we've missed. If you think of anyone your mother spoke to regularly, either by phone or on the doorstep, don't hesitate to let us know."

"Okay," said Paul.

Neil gave a deep sigh when they were standing on the pavement outside.

"He's still only twenty, and the poor lad had plenty to put up with, guv. Is it any wonder he's bitter and twisted?"

"I haven't read every report yet, but I sense we heard more of the same from Paul Alford," said Gus. "I just wish one of these interviews threw light on the case."

"Maybe one of us has heard something that will solve the mystery, but we don't realise it yet."

"That's why our 1 debrief this afternoon is so important," said Gus. "Let's get back to the office.

"I'VE FINISHED," said Lydia. "How long before you're ready to head for Marlborough, Alex?"

"I didn't have any reports to write," said Alex. "No wonder Luke was so keen on taking control of the scheduling. He needed to be on top of the reports you entered into the Freeman Files but didn't have the slog of translating his notebook."

"My files are up-to-date, too," said Blessing. "Neil and I aren't seeing Aiden Fowler until two o'clock. Does anyone fancy a coffee?"

Alex heard the lift descending to the ground floor.

"That sounds like Gus and Neil spent next to no time with Paul Alford."

Gus and Neil exited the lift, and Blessing soon delivered five cups of coffee.

"Just what the doctor ordered," said Neil. "Paul Alford didn't offer to make us a cuppa."

"Did you learn anything?" asked Lydia.

"More of the same," said Neil.

"Get your head down, Neil," said Gus. "We need to get these reports done. Then we can compare notes. Maybe we'll spot a discrepancy when we sift through the different versions of the same events."

"A golden nugget amongst the gravel," said Blessing.

"Lydia and I need to leave in fifteen minutes, guv," said Alex. "Charlotte and Jasmine will be available at noon."

"Whatever Aiden Fowler has to say to Neil and Blessing at two o'clock shouldn't take long," said Gus. "We need to aim for three o'clock for our get-together. I want everyone to spend the final two hours of the week reviewing the information we've gleaned so far."

"Got it, guv," said Alex.

"We'll get back as soon as possible, guv," said Neil.

Gus and Neil began updating their files. Alex and Lydia were soon en route to Marlborough, and Blessing collected the empty cups and returned them to the restroom.

As she was drying the last cup and stacking it on the shelf, Blessing wondered whether Amazing Grace thought this was beneath her. Teamwork got results, thought Blessing. If they were going to find a breakthrough in this latest mystery, this afternoon would be where it happened.

"DO YOU MIND IF I DRIVE?" asked Alex when he and Lydia reached the car park. "I haven't been out of the office for days."

"Okay. You could park at the police station in George Lane," said Lydia. "The house where Charlotte and Jasmine run their reiki therapy business is a two-minute walk towards the A4 junction."

"I didn't tell Gus what they did," said Alex. "I'm not sure he's a fan of alternative therapy."

"It's been around for ages," said Lydia. "Reiki promotes relaxation and reduces stress and anxiety through gentle touch."

"There you are," said Alex. "If I told Gus that Charlotte and Jasmine use their hands to deliver energy to a client's body, he'd think we were back in Gentle Touch territory."

"Trust you, Alex Hardy," said Lydia. "Get your mind out of the gutter."

Alex drove them to George Lane, parked the car, and popped into Reception to tell a PCSO they were conducting an interview up the road.

"Okay?" asked Lydia when Alex caught her.

"I think he understood. But we could do with one of those 'On Call' cards that doctors leave on the front windscreen."

Lydia rang the bell when they reached the address in George Lane.

"Very soothing," said Alex. "That refrain is from Tubular Bells, isn't it?"

The sharp elbow in the ribs from Lydia left Alex wondering whether he might benefit from healing hands while they were here.

The front door opened, and two middle-aged ladies in white uniforms greeted them.

"Welcome. Please come in."

"I'm Lydia Logan Barre, and my colleague is Detective Sergeant Alex Hardy. We're from Wiltshire Police."

"I'm Charlotte, and we know why you're here," said the taller woman. "It's to do with the murder ten years ago."

"Our two treatment rooms and kitchen are on the ground floor," said Jasmine. "So, if you follow us upstairs, we can talk in our private accommodation."

"Have you been here long?" asked Lydia.

"We opened in 2006," said Jasmine.

"I worked in Swindon," said Charlotte. "Jasmine and I met in a club in Old Town. She worked a dead-end office job when we bought this house in 2005. We set up the business the following year and never regretted it."

When they were upstairs, Lydia noticed they had converted the third bedroom into an office. A family bathroom and bedroom were at the rear, and the main bedroom at the front was now the couple's living room.

"There's a tremendous demand for the services we supply," said Jasmine.

"I'm sure there is," said Alex.

"How can we help?" asked Charlotte.

"We'd like to hear what you remember of that Saturday night," said Alex. "I know you've been over it several times with the police, and no doubt some of your clients will have commented on the murder in the weeks and months that followed."

"Sometimes, we find memories alter with age," said Lydia.

"We were very clear about what we saw and heard," said Charlotte.

"We didn't embellish things to make it sound like we'd seen more than we did," added Jasmine.

"What time did you leave here?" asked Alex.

"A few minutes before eight," said Charlotte.

"We walked to The Roebuck," said Jasmine, "spoke to Belinda, got a drink, and sat by the window."

"The open window was our only hope of fresh air," said Charlotte.

"Was the bar busy?" asked Lydia.

"It always was on a Friday and Saturday night," said Jasmine. "More so in the summer. We were younger then and went there more often."

"There were loads of people inside and outside the pub," said Charlotte. "Everyone wanted a cold drink."

"Mostly regulars?" asked Alex. "Or did you see anyone you didn't recognise?"

"We were chatting, not people-watching," said Jasmine. "Friends would stop at our table for a catch-up, but it got too hot indoors. So I said to Charlotte, why don't we get another drink and go outside?"

"That was at ten o'clock," said Charlotte. "Give or take five minutes."

"So you stood outside with a drink and continued chatting," said Alex. "What was going on around you?"

"Several groups doing the same," said Charlotte. "Some sat under the huge umbrella that covered the six-seater picnic tables that were all the rage back then. Others gathered at the car park side of the pub, where they could smoke."

"We steered clear of that area," said Jasmine. "People were spilling out onto the pavement because it was so busy."

"You told the police you saw a couple in conversation close to where you were standing," said Alex. "That was at around ten-thirty. With so many others doing the same thing packed into a relatively small area, what made you notice them?"

"We've asked ourselves that question a thousand times since that night," said Jasmine.

"The woman was pretty," said Charlotte.

"A natural beauty," said Jasmine. "She hadn't brushed her hair or put on any make-up."

"What about the man?" asked Lydia.

"He had his back to us," said Charlotte.

"Did you see them arrive?" asked Alex.

Both women shook their heads.

"Were they holding glasses, sipping from their drinks?" asked Lydia.

"I don't think so," said Jasmine.

"So the couple hadn't been inside the bar before you came out?" asked Alex.

"It was busy. They might have been inside, finished their drinks and were chatting before they left."

"That can't be right, Jasmine," said Charlotte. "We spoke to Belinda the next time we went in the pub, and she couldn't remember serving them. Belinda said the police showed her a photo of the woman on Sunday. The woman was a stranger to Belinda. We saw the same photo on TV on Monday night, and we both said, didn't we?"

"Yes," said Jasmine. "We both said that was the woman we saw on Saturday night."

"Which of you watched the couple talking?" asked Lydia.

"I was facing their direction," said Jasmine. "Charlotte had turned away from the side of the pub because too many customers crowded the smoking area. So we moved further round the corner to escape the smell of smoke."

"What could you see from your new position?" asked Alex.

"The woman was listening, not speaking," said Jasmine. "The police asked me if she looked frightened or angry, but I thought she was more upset than anything else. Disappointed, if that makes sense."

"When did they leave?" asked Lydia.

"A crowd of young lads spilt out from the bar," said Charlotte. "Eugene, the landlord, followed them outside to ensure they didn't cause any trouble. But, unfortunately, they had all had too much to drink. So Eugene watched them head into the town centre, and then he returned inside. I don't remember seeing the couple after that."

"At that time, people were always leaving the pub," said Jasmine. "Some were on foot; others had booked a taxi. Few people drove to The Roebuck. The police asked if we saw a red Peugeot arrive or leave, but we didn't notice. We finished our drinks, said goodnight to Belinda and walked home. We were indoors by ten past eleven."

"You didn't see a red car as you walked home along George Lane?" asked Alex.

"Cars would have passed us, I suppose," said Charlotte. "But we didn't know what to look for, did we? It wasn't until we watched television on Monday night that we knew the woman had been driving a Peugeot. After that, we kept asking ourselves whether we could have done more. But we couldn't know that man would strangle her within a couple of hours of us seeing them together."

"Of course not," said Alex.

"Did the police ask any other questions when you saw them on Tuesday?" asked Lydia. "You saw DS Cromwell and DC Brady, didn't you?"

"I don't remember their names," said Charlotte.

"They wanted to know the same things as you. Did we see what the man looked like? Had they arrived by car? Did we see them leave? We couldn't tell them what we didn't see."

"The man had his back to you throughout?" asked Alex.

"Yes," said Jasmine. "Five feet six inches tall, and he wasn't overweight or muscular. I'd guess he weighed around eleven stones. Once, he spread his arms out, and his hands didn't look like a labourer's hands. I thought he might have worked in an office. The police asked about tattoos, piercings, facial hair, and glasses, but I couldn't be more helpful with a description than I've just said."

"His appearance was nondescript," said Charlotte. "The sort of person from the back that could be thirty or sixty, and you wouldn't know until they turned around."

"You said you don't visit The Roebuck as often these days," said Alex. "Any particular reason?"

"Eugene has gone. They've got a new landlord who wants to attract a younger crowd," said Jasmine.

"We're in our mid-forties now, and our clubbing days are behind us," said Charlotte.

"You're running a successful business; you're happy," said Lydia. "That's more important."

"True enough," said Jasmine. "Plus, we can get our booze cheaper from the supermarket."

"We don't have to hold our breath while walking through the smokers to get into the pub," said Charlotte.

"Or hear the snide remarks from the young lads when they see we're a married couple," said Jasmine.

"I hope we haven't taken up too much of your lunch break," said Alex. "We'll walk back to the police station to collect our car and be on our way. I don't think we'll need to bother you again."

"We're always happy to oblige the police," said Charlotte.

"It's been a long time," said Jasmine. "Do you think you'll ever find the killer?"

"We're a step closer," said Lydia. "Later today, we'll know how many steps we've taken since we started reviewing Katherine Alford's case. If they're still in Marlborough, the killer can't relax."

"Oh, you think they live in the town?" said Jasmine. "I won't sleep tonight now that you've said that."

"I don't think you need to worry," said Alex. "Everything we know about this case points to it being personal."

Alex and Lydia walked downstairs, followed by Charlotte and Jasmine. The two women stood on the doorstep and watched until they were out of sight on George Lane.

"They made a lovely couple, didn't they?" said Jasmine.

"Lydia was hot," said Charlotte. "Her colleague walks with a hint of a limp. He's hurt his ribs on the left-hand side in the past twenty-four hours. DS Hardy isn't my type, but he's a hundred times better than that homophobic dinosaur Barnett that was supposed to be in charge of that case."

"What possessed Belinda to give him her phone number?" asked Jasmine.

"I wonder what happened to Belinda after she left The Roebuck?" asked Charlotte.

"Perhaps we could drop in tonight, for old times' sake, to ask if anyone knows?"

"I bought a bottle of Prosecco for tonight. It's in the fridge."

"That's that sorted, then. Let's grab a sandwich before our two o'clock appointments arrive."

Chapter Nine

ALEX AND LYDIA returned to the car park and collected the car.

"Was it the hands that made you say we were a step closer?" asked Alex as they headed along the A4 towards Chippenham.

"If it wasn't an embellishment they'd added in the past ten years," said Lydia.

"They both seemed genuine," said Alex. "We'll add it to everything the team has gathered and see if it makes sense."

Neil and Blessing were leaving the lift en route to George Lane when Alex swung his car into the Old Police Station car park.

"Any luck?" asked Neil.

"Maybe," said Lydia. "Jasmine remembered a detail about the man at the pub that might help. We could have stayed in Marlborough to save you a trip."

"You didn't know how long your meeting would last," said Neil. "We spoke to Emily and Sophia. So, for continuity's sake, we should see Aiden Fowler."

"We won't get back until half past three," said Blessing.

"You won't miss the fun, Blessing," said Alex.

Neil disappeared into Church Street, and Alex and Lydia rode upstairs in the lift.

"How did it go?" asked Gus when they entered the office.

"Jasmine reckoned the man had soft hands, guv," said Lydia. "Not the hands of a labourer. So that rules out Aiden Fowler."

"He was never on my radar," said Gus. "But that snippet of information might point us towards our killer. Get your files updated. Please familiarise yourself with everything we've learned. I won't bother you for the next hour. We'll make a start at three o'clock and take a break when Neil and Blessing rejoin us."

NEIL AND BLESSING arrived at George Lane before two o'clock. Neil parked by the main door and spotted a van entering the car park.

"That's Aiden's van," he said. "We'll wait for him to park, walk him inside, and with luck, we can get through Reception quicker.

The PCSO Alex had spoken to earlier had left, but the desk sergeant who replaced him knew who they were and had booked an interview room. The system worked like clockwork, and they entered the room with Aiden Fowler at two minutes past two.

"I hope this won't take long," said Aiden. "I've got several quotes to do this afternoon. I need to be in Figgins Lane in twenty-five minutes."

"We'll do our best," said Neil. "When did you move to Marlborough?"

"At the end of 2002," said Aiden. "I was doing similar work with a firm in Hungerford and fancied a change of scenery."

"Did you know Kane Routledge?" asked Neil.

"Not Kane. I'd met his father. There are only ten miles between the two towns. We were renovating properties on the same housing estate more often than not. Kane doesn't get his hands dirty. He handles the auctions, plans the projects, and sources our building supplies."

"Did you know Kane knew Emily before you arrived on the scene?" asked Blessing.

"She explained how she came to live in such a nice place," said Aiden. "Not straight away; that was after we started seeing one another. She didn't want us to have any secrets."

"Did you ever wonder?" asked Neil.

"Whether Sophia was Kane's daughter? Never. Em told me they finished ages before she got pregnant. I believe her."

"It's difficult to take on another man's child," said Blessing.

"What can I say?" said Aiden. "Kane called to ask me to fix the shower at a place in West Manton. I did not know who lived there. So, I drove out, Em showed me to the bathroom, and then little Sophia sat and watched me work. Em asked me to stay for a while when I finished the job. I don't think they had many visitors. We had a coffee, chatted, and I knew I'd be back."

"You returned the following week to ask her out on a date," said Blessing.

"Yeah, and I moved in later that summer."

"That would be in 2007," said Neil.

"A year before Emily's mother died," said Blessing.

"I never met Katherine," said Aiden. "Em always ensured I was working if her mother paid a visit and removed any signs that she had someone living there. So, as far as I know, Katherine never knew I existed."

"The police didn't ask you where you were on Saturday night because they didn't know you lived with Katherine's daughter," said Neil.

"I was at home with Em," said Aiden. "I worked in Broad Hinton in the morning, arrived home at one o'clock, and we went shopping in the afternoon. Then we took Sophia to the cinema at Greenbridge Retail and Leisure Park. She wanted to see Kung Fu Panda. Before leaving, we stopped at McDonald's, drove back to West Manton, and ate our meals. Sophia went to bed at nine, and we followed two hours later. I was due back in Broad Hinton at half past eight in the morning. I left in my van just after eight. The police arrived on Em's doorstep around a quarter past ten."

"Had Emily tidied around in case her mother came calling?" asked Neil.

"I wouldn't have thought so," said Aiden. "Em's mum always rang before driving across to make sure Em wasn't working or going shopping."

"I wonder why the detectives didn't notice a third person was living at the address," said Blessing.

"Em said they asked to come inside," said Aiden. "They suggested Sophia go to her room, but Em wouldn't have it. So instead, she just wanted to learn what had happened."

"We noticed several photographs when we were there the other afternoon," said Blessing.

"We didn't have the boys ten years ago," said Aiden. "Em still had photos of her with her mum and Paul in the living room."

"There was no cause for the detectives to visit any other

room in the house," said Neil. "I suppose if you didn't leave shoes or clothes lying around, it wouldn't be obvious Emily had company."

"What happened next?" asked Blessing.

"After they'd told Em what had happened, she was in a state. Sophia was upset, too. Em called me as soon as they left. The lady detective told Em her brother was being cared for by the next-door neighbour. She reminded Em that she needed to act before social services got involved. Paul couldn't stay where he was, so if Em didn't take him in, he'd be taken into care. I told my gaffer I needed to get home, and I was with Em in twenty minutes."

"Emily wasn't keen on having her brother live with her, was she?" asked Neil.

"They didn't get on that well," said Aiden. "I didn't know the full story. You have to remember. Em had left home to make a life away from her family, and although Em saw her mum and Paul now and again, there had to be reasons she kept them at arm's length. But, when it came down to it, no matter what happened before her mother's murder, Paul was still Em's brother. So I thought she should take him in. The poor kid was only ten years old. So we drove over to collect him after lunch."

"Paul was never happy in West Manton, though, was he?" asked Blessing.

"They had an uneasy truce," said Aiden. "Paul wasn't an outgoing character, not like Sophia. He didn't take to me, and I must admit I made little effort. Em looked after her brother under sufferance, but there were never any stand-up fights. She loved Sophia and tolerated Paul. That was the size of it."

"You said there were no secrets between you," said

Blessing. "Yet you say you didn't know the full story of what had happened while Emily lived at home."

"I knew her father had walked out, but I meant things from our past when I said secrets. I had never been married, and there weren't any children running around. Em had played with fire and got burned. She had to grow up fast, and as soon as I met her, I could tell Em was a splendid mother to Sophia. You saw her with Benedict and Harvey the other day. No matter what happened at Purlyn Acre, Em's doing a grand job with our family."

"Life must have got easier after Paul left," said Blessing.

"It got better for both Paul and Em," said Aiden. "He must have felt the way Em did when she was his age. Paul was thirteen when Ben was born and fifteen when Harv arrived. No wonder Paul shot off to South Marston as soon as he turned sixteen. Those two boys were yelling day and night, plus Sophia's early teen tantrums. Em and I thrived on it. Paul hated it. After he'd gone, Em seemed to blossom even more. Maybe she felt she couldn't show how happy she was with her life while he was there? What do I know? I'm just a builder, not a psychologist."

"You had better make tracks if you want to make that Figgins Lane appointment," said Neil. "Thanks for sparing the time to meet us this afternoon. I can't say we won't need to speak with you or your family again, but we're happy for now."

"Em always wanted the police to find her mother's killer," said Aiden, "but as the years have passed, she's come to terms with the fact that it might never happen. Even if it did, it wouldn't change our lives. We're one big happy family."

Aiden Fowler got up and left the interview room.

"What did you make of that, Neil?" said Blessing.

"He's right," said Neil. "They're strong enough that nothing will knock them off-course. Emily Alford and Aiden Fowler had nothing to do with Katherine's death. Let's get back to the office."

"THREE O'CLOCK, GUV," said Lydia.

"Neil called to say he and Blessing left George Lane just before twenty-five past," said Alex.

"Short but sweet then," said Gus. "We can expect them here by three-fifteen."

"I'll get the coffees, guv," said Lydia.

The traffic lights were out of action at the Bumper's Farm roundabout, so it was closer to twenty-past-three when Gus heard the lift descend to the ground floor.

Blessing and Neil emerged two minutes later.

"Nothing dramatic, guv," said Neil. "Just a different perspective from Aiden Fowler on the Alford family's troubles."

"Aiden struck me as a decent, hard-working individual, guv," said Blessing.

"Good to know we're not the only ones," said Gus. "You two can get a coffee and then update your files while we dissect what we know. Chip in if you believe we've missed something or misinterpreted it."

"Got it, guv," said Neil.

Gus stood by a whiteboard with the appropriate marker pen at the ready. He double-checked to be sure.

"Let's start at the beginning," he said. "Why didn't the caller go to Katherine's house if he wanted to speak to her? She'd been single for eight years."

"What reasons were suggested by the detectives running the case?" asked Alex.

"The caller was married, and at that time of night at the end of June, someone would likely recognise them or their car," said Lydia.

"How do we know they were even in Marlborough at half-past nine?" asked Alex. "They could have been calling from somewhere a short drive away."

"Katherine told Lily Faulkner she would only be gone ten minutes," said Gus.

"True, but they could have been driving, using a hands-free phone," said Lydia. "Or they might have travelled into town by bus."

"They weren't on a train, that's for sure," said Gus. "The railway station closed over fifty years ago. We could check bus timetables to see when they could have arrived in Marlborough."

"Arriving by car makes little sense, guv," said Blessing. "Where was the killer's car?"

"Bert Harris saw Katherine's red Peugeot," said Alex, "but he couldn't say whether Katherine had a passenger."

"Do we believe Bert was right about what he saw?" asked Gus. "If he was, the killer must have been in the Peugeot. If she were alone, Katherine would have turned right at the top of the road where Bert lives and been chatting to Lily Faulkner inside two minutes."

"I believed Bert Harris, guv," said Neil.

"I'm inclined to believe him, too," said Gus. "There could have been another car, but the killer must have joined Katherine in the Peugeot soon after leaving the estate."

"Not necessarily, guv," said Lydia. "Maybe Anna Cromwell got it right. Ten minutes was always a loose description of how long it would take to sort matters out. Lily took it as gospel."

"You're suggesting Katherine drove somewhere to

collect the caller," said Gus. "Perhaps a place they knew well. So they started their conversation in the car and then made for The Roebuck."

"That could explain the forty-five-minute gap, guv," said Neil. "Or at least some of it."

"Where was that pick-up, though?" asked Gus. "I made a note in the murder file just after the Chief Constable handed it over. He asked how did the killer get home from West Woods?"

"The killer's car wasn't at West Woods, guv," said Lydia. "The patrol car would have seen it. They said the car park was empty at twenty to eleven."

"Back to the drawing board," said Gus. "Or, in this case, the whiteboard. I'm not writing many salient points here for us to follow up. What was another reason for the caller not visiting Katherine at home?"

"The person was a well-known figure in the town," said Alex. "That could mean a councillor, headteacher, or even a police officer."

"Our first case involved the local MP," said Lydia.

"Marlborough is in the Devizes constituency, Lydia," said Gus. "We can trust that lightning didn't strike twice on this occasion."

"What if they used to live on the Purlyn Acre estate, guv?" asked Blessing.

"That's a possibility," said Gus.

"Lily Faulkner would have recognised them," said Neil. "If they knew the estate, they'd know Lily's curtains would twitch as soon as they set foot on the driveway."

"Could the person we're looking for have been so frequent a visitor that nobody noticed?" asked Blessing.

"Someone delivering the daily pint of milk," said Gus, "the newspaper or the mail? That doesn't fit with what

Emily, Paul and Lily have told us. Don't forget what Daniel Matravers was like. He told Katherine not to waste time chatting with the neighbours and discourage cold callers. No doubt he included the frequent visits made by the people we're talking about. It's hard to see how Katherine could have established a close relationship with anyone in those occupations."

"We get a different person doing those deliveries every few months around our way, guv," said Neil. "You don't get the continuity to establish friendships as they did in the old days. I hoped we might uncover the name of someone who enabled Katherine to work from home. Everyone tells us she didn't return to work after she had Emily, but she must have needed money after Daniel Matravers walked out."

"It's hard to see how she covered the period between the divorce and when she benefited from her mother's estate," said Gus. "However, we haven't asked the forensic accountants at the Hub to dive into the records yet. They might learn Mary Alford transferred sufficient sums from her savings to keep Katherine's head above water. There, I have something to add to the board under the need to check the bus timetables."

"What sort of work could Katherine Alford have done from home, Neil?" asked Lydia. "Daniel Matravers told us she left school at sixteen and inferred Katherine was as thick as a brick."

"We only have his word for that," said Gus. "It's worth looking at her academic prowess."

"If it was manual work, there had to be regular deliveries and collections," said Neil. "Emily and Paul would have noticed boxes or trays when they came home from school or during the holidays.

"Lily Faulkner would have known about it," said Alex.

"Don't discount the theory," said Gus. "We need to check local businesses that employ part-time staff working from home. I recall a company that produced rubber milk liners paid outworkers to trim the flash that escaped the moulding process. Constant use of small pairs of sharp scissors resulted in a rash of repetitive strain injuries among the ladies they employed."

"Any work Katherine carried out couldn't have involved anything bulky or smelly," said Lydia. "The children would have noticed."

"Do we know where Katherine Alford worked before she married?" asked Blessing.

"I don't remember reading about it in the murder file," said Gus.

He added another item to his list.

"ACC Cromwell has questions to answer, guv," said Neil. "As does Wayne Barnett. We can't question Callum Brady yet, but he's just as guilty. Cromwell and Brady didn't discover Emily had Aiden Fowler living with her for almost a year before the murder. They arrived to notify her of her mother's death, and although they went into the living room, Cromwell didn't ask Brady to have a nose around. He could have gone to the kitchen to fetch a glass of water and popped upstairs to use the bathroom. Ten seconds and he would have known Emily and Sophia didn't live alone."

"There was no car on the drive, guv," said Blessing. "Emily told us she took the bus into town when she visited her mother. Emily did the same when she went to work at the supermarket. Yet the detectives left her in tears and drove to George Lane. Aiden returned from work to comfort his partner and then took them to Purlyn Acre to collect Paul. So why didn't the police take Emily into town?

A conversation between Emily and Paul, or Emily and Lily, could have opened new lines of enquiry."

"What about how the house looked, guv?" said Neil. "Why didn't it seem suspicious to Cromwell and Brady that a young unmarried mum could afford to live there? They didn't contact the landlord to confirm who was paying the rent. If they had spoken to Routledge Senior, they could have found that his son, Kane, was paying the lion's share. Again, a line of enquiry was missed. They left so many loose ends without bothering where they went."

"You said Wayne Barnett had questions to answer," said Gus. "Can you elaborate?"

"It was clear from your report in the Freeman Files that Barnett is homophobic. He refused to speak to Charlotte Ovens and Jasmine Park and handed the responsibility to Anna Cromwell and Callum Brady. Barnett suggested Cromwell had more in common with those two man-haters, as he called them. How can anyone with those views still be in the job, guv?"

"Why did Trefor Davies put Barnett in charge of the case in the first place, guv?" asked Blessing. "Barnett seemed more interested in getting the barmaid's phone number than finding clues that would lead them to the killer."

"I've asked myself that question, Blessing," said Gus.

"I think you told us earlier in the week that DCI Davies retires next year, guv," said Lydia.

"We could tell he was winding down to retirement when we visited George Lane, Lydia," said Gus.

"He kept apologising for being forgetful," said Lydia.

"We should move on," said Gus. "How did you and Alex get on with Charlotte and Jasmine this morning?"

"They added little to their statement ten years ago," said Alex.

"Apart from adding more colour to the period when Katherine and her companion were standing outside The Roebuck," said Lydia. "For instance, the smoking area at the side of the pub was more crowded than usual. That encouraged the women to move further around the corner to escape the smoke."

"They didn't mention that before," said Gus. "It gave them a different angle from which to view our couple. Yet they still couldn't see the man's face."

"If the man continued to have his back to them, it wouldn't have mattered, guv," said Alex. "They would have had a different view of Katherine's face."

"The way Charlotte and Jasmine described it, the warm night resulted in several groups of people surrounding them," said Lydia. "With only thirty minutes until closing time and other pubs in the town centre with a late licence, those groups of people were constantly on the move. The exodus started soon after twenty to eleven, and the landlord came outside to usher a noisy group of lads from the premises. Charlotte and Jasmine noticed the couple had disappeared after things had quietened down. They did not know whether they walked into town or drove away in a car."

"Jasmine remembered that the man's hands weren't hard and calloused like a labourer's," said Alex. "She described them as soft, something she associated with an office worker."

"When we discover where Katherine worked before she had Emily, that could prove important," said Gus. "Unless it related to the working from home angle."

"Lydia reminded the ladies that people's memories can

alter with age," said Alex, "but they were adamant they stuck to the truth throughout and didn't embellish their story to give it more importance than it merited."

"You reckon the soft hands are a genuine memory," said Gus. "Not added to the story they've told their friends and customers over the years?"

"We can't be one hundred percent certain, guv," said Lydia. "Our overall impression of the two women was that they were telling us what they saw. Why Jasmine didn't remember the guy's hands ten years ago, I don't know."

"We've already identified failings in the original investigation," said Neil. "Anna Cromwell and Callum Brady went to interview those two women. Those two were the only eye-witnesses apart from Bert Harris, yet Trefor Davies and Wayne Barnett never saw them."

"That's not how we operate, guv," said Blessing. "Our senior officers interview the key people identified in the murder file, and the rest of us handle those on the fringes."

"I involve everyone on the team with the key people at some point," said Gus. "At least, I try to. It's the best way to help each of you progress. Onwards and upwards."

"Cromwell and Brady ignored DI Barnett's idea there was a possibility of two men being with Katherine that night," said Neil. "Wayne thought Katherine could have met the person who called her, and they argued and split up. Then she picked up a friend who went with her to The Roebuck."

"It wouldn't have affected the interview with Ovens and Park," said Gus. "Yes, there was an outside chance the man with Katherine wasn't the man who called her at nine-thirty. On Tuesday, Ovens and Park contacted the police regarding the TV news item. They recognised the woman in the photograph. Bert Harris saw the red car at a time that fits with Katherine leaving The Roebuck during the melee outside the pub. We've got several pieces of the jigsaw, and we're putting them together to suit our supposed narrative. I worry we don't have all the pieces yet."

"And the picture on the front of the box belongs to another jigsaw," said Blessing.

"The youngest and least experienced among us has hit the nail on the head," said Gus.

Chapter Ten

THE MOOD in the Crime Review Team office was downbeat.

Gus couldn't recall when they had faced such a tough challenge. They appeared to be going around in circles. Everyone they spoke to had added a hitherto unrecorded fact, yet they were no closer to finding Katherine's killer.

"We still have over half an hour left today," he said. "Let's keep going. What else has anyone picked up from the reports?"

"I noticed something when I read Wayne Barnett's account of events at West Woods, guv," said Neil. "He reckoned everything was under control when they arrived. The uniforms had secured the crime scene, closed the approach roads, and were taking statements from the couple who found the body."

"Because Barnett was hungover, they were late getting to the murder scene," said Alex. "So Anna Cromwell had to drive him there."

"Barnett didn't know at that point Trefor Davies had decided to put him in charge," said Lydia.

"What's your point, Neil?" asked Gus.

"I wonder whether Barnett or Cromwell ever spoke to Dr Gray and his wife."

"Wasn't there a follow-up meeting?" asked Blessing.

"I can't recall seeing it in the murder file," said Alex.

"Why not?" asked Neil. "Surely they needed to be interviewed?"

"We do have the uniformed officer's statement, guv," said Neil. "I've found it in the file."

"Let's hear it then, Neil," said Gus. "We can ask Barnett why he decided no further action was required, but as his mentor, I'm surprised Trefor Davies didn't give him a nudge. A quiet word that it's always best to dot the i's and cross the t's."

"The constable collected the couple's preliminary details, guv," said Neil. "Name, address, and telephone number. Then he asked what had happened that morning. Dominic Gray said they had left their house in Clench Common and cycled towards the A4 Bath Road. They planned to cycle to the Roman city and back. It was a route they followed once a month. They cycled to different destinations each weekend whenever his job permitted. Each trip was between sixty and one hundred miles and took between six and eight hours."

"They were keen," said Lydia.

"Hence the lycra and safety helmets," said Alex.

"Dominic Gray told the constable that as they cycled past the entrance to the car park, he spotted a red car."

"He thought it had been abandoned, stopped, took out his mobile phone, and photographed the rear number plate. Yes, we know that much," said Gus.

"Sorry, guv," said Neil. "Gray took them through what he'd done once he realised someone was inside the car. He phoned George Lane police station and made his report, then sent through the photo of the number plate."

"Four minutes past seven," said Gus. "That was when the duty officer logged the call. The officer then called Trefor Davies, who didn't report for duty as expected but handed the case to an off-duty detective, Wayne Barnett."

"Barnett was in no fit state to run a raffle, let alone a murder case," said Alex. "After Barnett complained of having his weekend disturbed, the duty officer must have gone back to DCI Davies. As DS Cromwell was in the building, Trefor told the duty officer to tell her she would report to Wayne Barnett and should collect him from home en route to the murder site."

"What else did the constable ask the doctor, Neil?" asked Lydia.

"He asked where he had been the night before," said Neil, "purely for elimination purposes."

"The police hadn't identified the victim when this statement was taken," said Blessing. "So they couldn't be specific and ask where the doctor was between nine-thirty and one o'clock."

"They were following procedure. The constable asked the doctor whether he had heard anything—sounds of an argument. A screaming woman. Gray heard nothing."

"How did Dr Gray say he spent the day?" asked Gus.

"Dominic Gray had been at Savernake Hospital throughout the day, arriving home at around half-past four. His wife, Amy, cooked them a meal, and then they planned a quiet evening. They wanted an early night with the long cycle ride planned the next morning."

"They planned a quiet night in, Neil," said Gus. "What happened?"

"A patient Dr Gray had been treating earlier in the day had a sudden relapse. Dr Gray rushed to the hospital, but it was too late. His patient died."

"How long a journey is that?" asked Gus.

"Under four miles," said Neil. "A ten-minute drive."

"What time did the hospital call the doctor?" asked Lydia.

"Dr Gray told the constable he got the call at ten minutes to nine."

"When did Doctor Gray return home?" asked Gus.

"He couldn't be certain," said Neil. "The death was unexpected. His patient was recovering from an operation, and their vital signs were stable when he left the hospital. Dr Gray had been confident the patient would make a complete recovery. Instead, the dramatic turn of events made him question whether he'd missed something. As the attending doctor, he had to complete a Medical Certificate of Cause of Death. He remembers sitting in his office, poring over the patient's notes, trying to work out what went wrong."

"That must be a shock," said Blessing, "losing a patient that way."

"The constable then asked Amy Gray what had happened on Sunday morning," said Neil. "The same sequence of questions he'd asked her husband. Amy Gray had waited on the grass verge outside the car park while her husband went to the car. She held their two bikes while Dominic photographed the number plate and examined the body. Her husband rejoined her. He called the police, and they waited for them to arrive. Everything Amy Gray told the officer matched the information provided by her husband. When asked what she'd done during the day on Saturday, Amy said she went shopping in the morning and met a friend at The Oddfellows, where they had lunch. She then pottered in the garden in the afternoon until her husband returned from work at around half-past four. They ate together at around six-thirty, then spent thirty minutes in the garage checking that their bikes were ready to go in the morning. Amy said they finally relaxed at eight o'clock. The hospital rang several minutes before nine and told Dominic it was an emergency. He'd apologised and told her he needed to leave but would return as soon as possible. Amy said she went to bed at around eleven and had just started reading when she heard the front door. Dominic came upstairs, told her the news, and said he needed a drink before bed. He returned downstairs, and Amy said the alarm woke them at six the following morning."

"Mrs Gray couldn't confirm when her husband came to bed," said Lydia.

"If she was in bed at eleven, and Gray got home soon after, he wouldn't have been near West Woods to see the Peugeot," said Alex.

"Dr Gray would have followed the same route through Clench Common we did, guv," said Lydia. "When he reached home, he would have been over two miles from where our killer and Katherine were arguing."

"Did the constable add to the statements later?" asked Gus.

"He received confirmation from the hospital Dr Gray had been there, guv," said Neil. "A patient died from complications following surgery at seven forty-eight on Saturday evening."

"Any other possibilities?" asked Gus.

"What about Lily Faulkner's son, Guy?" asked Lydia.

"Does it seem odd that he flew to New Zealand in 1998, only weeks before Paul Alford was born?"

"What, you think it possible Guy Faulkner was Paul's father?" asked Blessing.

"Why not?" asked Lydia. "He lived next door to Katherine ever since she moved in. I haven't checked how old he was, but Katherine was attractive and only thirty-four when she had Paul."

"They must have kept the relationship very quiet," said Gus.

"I've just checked. Guy Faulkner was thirty when he flew to New Zealand, guv," said Neil. "His mother would have known if something had been going on."

"Maybe Lily Faulkner knew of the affair," said Gus, "but hoped to keep it hidden."

"I was thinking what Katherine said to Lily, guv," said Alex. "That the person who called her was like a brother to her. Could Guy fit that description? A next-door neighbour, a man only four years younger."

"An affair, I could accept," said Gus. "I think it unlikely Katherine would describe Guy as like a brother if they had been lovers. Would Guy fly home without telling his mother he was on his way? Why wait ten years to come back anyway if he had hoped a lasting relationship would result from the affair? As soon as Guy heard Daniel Matravers had walked away from the marriage, he'd be on the next flight if it was that serious. No, that doesn't feel like the explanation for our mystery."

"We should ask Lily whether Guy and Katherine were friends, guv," said Neil. "We don't want to make the same mistake as our colleagues. So let's eliminate the daft ideas and the sensible ones."

"I'll add it to the list, Neil," said Gus. "First thing

Monday morning, after welcoming Amazing Grace, we'll tackle the items on the whiteboard."

"Who do you want to go with DI Packenham on Tuesday, guv?" asked Alex.

"Ah, a volunteer," said Gus. "Just what we needed. Thanks, Alex."

Lydia giggled.

"You walked into that one, Alex," she said.

"I had one final thought, guv," said Blessing. "How closely did detectives in the original investigation look at Daniel Matravers? He had an unpleasant attitude toward marriage, children, and contraception. So what did he have to hide, I wonder?"

"I found Daniel Matravers objectionable, Blessing," said Lydia. "I put my foot in it by asking why he married Katherine. However, Lily Faulkner said they seemed very much in love when they first moved in next door as they started married life in their new home. Daniel doted on his daughter, Emily, too, as she confirmed. It takes all sorts, I suppose."

"Whichever officer checked his alibi. They couldn't shake it, Blessing," said Gus. "Daniel wasn't the man seen with Katherine that night. Before throwing us out of his office, he said something that might explain matters. When he warned Emily not to get involved with boys and allow things to go too far, he said one slip and two lives were ruined. Now we know that didn't refer to him and Katherine, so I suspect it was his parents who had to get married. If he was an only child, like Katherine, perhaps his father felt Daniel had prevented him from achieving his full potential. Who knows? Daniel could have suffered physical and mental abuse throughout his childhood."

"Did anyone check whether Daniel remarried after returning to Salisbury to live, guv?" asked Blessing.

"I doubt it," said Neil. "If he wasn't involved in Katherine's murder, what difference would it make?"

"Something doesn't feel right," said Blessing. "If Daniel doted on his daughter, why did he take against his son? I know we've heard he wanted no more children, but how many men would use the birth of a son to end a marriage? I'm an only child, and my father laments that another thread of the Umeh family name will die out when he's gone."

"Lily Faulkner said the idea Paul was another man's child was ludicrous," said Lydia. "Nobody thought Katherine was having an affair. She didn't appear to have a relationship with anyone eight years after Daniel left her. So why did nobody suspect someone else was Paul's father?"

"It still doesn't feel right," said Blessing. "Just because nobody saw anything to suggest another man in Katherine's life, that doesn't mean there wasn't. I believe Daniel Matravers walked out because he could tell the moment he set eyes on Paul he wasn't the boy's father."

"Tough to prove, Blessing," said Gus.

"We could ask him before he retires to France, guv," said Lydia.

"Let's draw a line under things for today," said Gus. "We'll have a few beers tonight, discuss the meaning of life, say farewell to Luke, and return refreshed on Monday morning."

Five minutes later, the Crime Review Team office was empty.

In the car park, Blessing Umeh sat in her Nissan Micra. As usual, she had waited for the others to leave because it simplified matters when nobody was parked next to her.

But, as she started the engine and headed for the Church Street exit, she wondered why Daniel Matravers hadn't done the obvious thing and had a vasectomy if he was adamant he didn't want more children.

Blessing stalled the car as she sat waiting for a break in traffic.

That could explain why Daniel walked out of the marriage if he had. He hadn't told Katherine he'd had the snip any more than she'd told him she'd had the coil removed. So that was something to consider.

GUS SLOWED as he passed the London Road car park. He couldn't see Suzie's Golf, so she must have already left. Gus wondered what they should have to eat before Suzie drove them to the Waggon & Horses.

He swung the Focus through the gateway and parked beside her car.

"I wondered whether you had forgotten we were out tonight and stayed in the office," said Suzie as he strolled into the kitchen.

"We wrapped things up at five," said Gus. "I can't be held responsible for the slow-moving traffic through Seend. You must have left on the dot of five to have got this far."

Suzie was ready to put a homemade chicken pie into the oven.

"I know you enjoy this," she said. "You need something substantial at your age if you intend to have a few drinks tonight,"

"Enough of the 'at my age' comments, young lady," said Gus, hugging Suzie. "How did you get on today?"

"I was careful not to point a finger," she replied, "and never mentioned your name."

"People will put two and two together," said Gus. "They'll still suspect I started the ball rolling if this comes out. I don't need to know who said what, but what was the consensus?"

"Trefor Davies seemed certain to achieve a higher rank," said Suzie, "but he has free-wheeled through the past ten years of his career. Like others before him, Trefor landed a job at a place where he felt he belonged. People I spoke to thought he was happy with his lot, loved the area and was content to stay where he was until retirement. Others hinted at him losing concentration, even forgetting to attend the odd meeting at London Road."

"Trefor was barely past his mid-forties when the Alford case landed on his desk," said Gus. "Yet he passed it on to Wayne Barnett, who was clearly unprepared for the responsibility. But then, Trefor didn't offer the promised guidance and support. When we dealt with him earlier in the year, I didn't notice any problems, but as soon as we sat with him this week, he was clearly losing it."

"You're afraid he has early onset dementia, aren't you?"

"Today, I am," said Gus. "I don't know how he could have hidden it for a decade."

"What else could it have been ten years ago?" asked Suzie

"Personal problems?" said Gus. "Is Trefor married? Did that crop up in the conversations you had today?"

"Trefor lost his first wife to cancer soon after moving to Marlborough from South Wales," said Suzie. "Megan died at least nine years before the Katherine Alford murder. They had no children. Trefor married Maureen, a local divorcee, two years after Megan's death. So, his cheerful outlook on life in Marlborough was interrupted, but Trefor and Maureen are a popular couple, especially in the choir community."

"If anything goes wrong at George Lane, Trefor can suggest the top brass look at Wayne. His work is sloppy, and he has all manner of prejudices that don't belong in the modern police force. They've been lucky for the past few years and haven't dealt with a major incident. Trefor can blame Wayne for the next cock-up, and keep his fingers crossed he can retire unscathed."

"He doesn't have much to look forward to, does he?" said Suzie.

"Nor does Maureen, but if Trefor's been fighting the fight for part of the last decade, he's desperate to make it to the finishing line. I'd be more concerned if he were asked to retire early. We lose too many retired officers to suicide who can't live without the job."

"Let's change the subject," said Suzie. "What are you wearing tonight?"

"A pale blue shirt, black trousers, no tie. Are we going to clash?"

"Not with that outfit, sweetheart," said Suzie. "I'm going for a loose-fitting colourful number, with flat, comfortable shoes. It's all the rage."

"It's only a little bump," said Gus.

"I don't want Melody to feel left out. She's a couple of months further along."

"That chicken pie smells good. So when do we eat?"

"After we've got out of our work clothes and showered," said Suzie. "You can prepare the remaining vegetables while I go first."

Gus did as instructed. He wanted time off for good behaviour tomorrow to escape to the allotment. So while he tackled the backlog of chores, he could work through the list of items he'd added to the whiteboard this afternoon.

He couldn't help thinking Grace Packenham would shake her head at their lack of progress this week.

Gus took his turn in the shower later, and they sat down to dinner at a quarter past seven.

The phone rang at twenty-past.

"Freeman residence. Who may I say is calling?"

"Gus, is that you?" It was Grace Packenham.

"Grace, this is a surprise. I wasn't expecting to hear your voice until Monday."

"I just wanted to know how you got on this week. My report on streamlining the administration area is on DS Mercer's desk. That phase of my career is behind me now. I'm eager to look forward. There's nothing worse than coming into a new squad room cold. Can you spare thirty minutes to update me on your progress?"

"We're off out in a few minutes," said Gus.

"Somewhere nice?" asked Grace.

"A noisy pub," said Gus. "Not your scene. I'll be in the field next to the church in Urchfont village tomorrow afternoon if you think it is necessary."

"Not shooting?" asked Grace, horrified.

"Heavens no, tending to my allotment. I need to harvest my butternut squash, kale, and leeks."

"An allotment? That's something you do when you're retired," said Grace.

"Gardening is an exercise that delivers homegrown products beneficial to your health. Like many younger people, DI Packenham, you've got much to learn. As much as I'd love to chat, we must dash. Good evening."

"I hope that's not a sign of things to come," said Suzie.

"Kenneth reminded me she's a Detective Inspector,"

said Gus. "If she wants to sit on an upturned box for thirty minutes listening to me tell her how few additional facts we've unearthed, that's her problem. I'm getting ready to leave."

"At least she didn't ask who else was going tonight."

"I doubt Grace Packenham has heard of the Waggon & Horses," said Gus. "Far too rural sounding for people who think allotments are for geriatrics. Grace would drink cocktails in the Green Vegan Lounge."

"Ouch," said Suzie. "Come on, finish your meal; I'll make us a coffee. Then we can sit and let the world go by until we need to drive to Harrington End."

They left the bungalow at twenty to nine, and Suzie rattled through the country lanes at breakneck speed in the Golf. Gus prayed they met nobody coming the other way.

The council had maintained nothing except significant thoroughfares in the county for years, and they did not design these lanes for motor vehicles. There were adequate passing points when two farm vehicles approached one another at a walking pace. They could edge past one another without losing too many bales of straw, but with high hedges restricting vision, you took your life in your hands when you ventured into the wild west country in a modern car.

Somehow, they emerged unharmed into the village's open spaces and began hunting for a parking space.

"That's reasonable," said Gus when Suzie had perched the VW on the grass verge. "Only a short walk to the pub and out of harm's way if a boy racer blazes around that bend ahead."

"That smart, sporty number belongs to Jamie, doesn't it?" asked Suzie. "Blessing and her dreamboat are here already."

"I can't see Lydia's Mini," said Gus. "Alex might be their designated driver tonight."

"Let's get indoors," said Suzie. "You're in the chair. Tell the young man behind the bar how much you're putting in the kitty, and don't be stingy."

"A pity Grace isn't here," said Gus. "As we're the same rank, we could split the bar bill fifty-fifty."

Suzie punched his upper arm. They walked to the quieter corner bar that had become the Crime Review Team's favourite drinking hole.

"Evening, guv," said Neil.

"Gus, tonight, Neil," said Suzie.

"Old habits," said Neil. "Melody grabbed a table on the right if you want to join her."

Suzie crossed the room and sat next to Melody.

"How's it going?" asked Suzie.

"Amazing how much trouble something the size of a banana can cause," said Melody. "I could do without the dizzy spells and heartburn, but it's for a good cause. Can we talk about something else now? I get it every day from the prospective grandmothers."

"Sorry," said Suzie. "I've been lucky so far. I'm working full-time, and my mother's busy at the farm. So I escape the third degree as long as I report in once a week. We thought we saw Jamie's car outside. Have you seen him and Blessing?"

"I've not seen Jamie before," said Melody. "What a hunk. He took Blessing into the other bar, where they have live music. They'll be back in five minutes. It looks like the others have arrived."

Suzie looked up to see Alex and Lydia join Gus and Neil at the bar. It was impossible to miss the red-haired Lydia. The moderation Gus attempted to impose at work had flown out of the window. Her hair was an explosion of corkscrew curls. The short leather skirt would qualify as a belt on a more generous-sized woman, while Lydia's blouse was a riot of autumn colours.

"She knows how to make an entrance," said Melody. "I wish I could hate her, but she's so nice. It's not fair."

"I couldn't carry off five-inch heels even before becoming pregnant," sighed Suzie.

"They must teach stilt-walking in Scottish schools," said Melody.

"As long as it means they can't play the bagpipes, I'm in favour," said Suzie.

Neil brought a tray of drinks across and sat down.

"Alex said he spotted Luke's car in the lane as they walked inside. So he'll be here presently."

Gus waited at the bar, sipping his pint of lager. There was still no sign of Vera Butler. Perhaps she had decided against joining them.

"Evening, Gus," said Luke. "Have you met Tom Spencer?"

"Our eyes have met across a crowded squad room at Gablecross," said Tom. "I worked with DI Raj Sengupta on a case you reviewed. Unfortunately, I didn't have the pleasure of seeing you at work. Luke tells me it's an education."

"It's good to see both of you," said Gus. "Gablecross has several promising young officers they can rely on in the coming years. Raj Sengupta will be fine if they keep him in the office. So how's the rising star I identified?"

"Travers?" asked Tom. "He's running rings around Jake Latimer. I reckon it will be a race to see who makes DI first."

"Get yourselves a drink, lads," said Gus. "I've put money behind the bar."

Gus went to join the others.

"Who's that with Luke?" asked Melody.

"Another DS from Gablecross," said Gus. "Good to see Luke is making new friends."

"Here they come," said Neil. "Come on, Blessing. What are the band like?"

"Covers," said Jamie. "No reggae or two-tone, but they're okay."

"I thought they were loud," said Blessing.

"When you're ready for another drink, Jamie," said Gus. "Just order what you like from the bar."

"Thanks, Gus. Tonight is a livelier affair than the get-together in the office the other Sunday. You should do it more often. We don't get many opportunities like this with my crowd."

"Too many retired coppers," said Gus. "Happier to sit at home with their feet up. Well, I never, look who's here."

Gus got up and walked to the bar to meet Vera and Divya Yadav.

"I wondered if you would make it," he said.

"I was ten minutes late," said Divya, "and the landlord let Vera's reserved space go."

"That could prove costly when the Butler clan hears the news," said Gus.

"Cheeky," said Vera. "He's already apologised."

"The drinks are on me," said Gus. "As soon as you get sorted, come and join us."

"You're very kind, Mr Freeman," said Divya.

Gus looked over his shoulder.

"Did my dad just put in an appearance? You can call me Gus. Not just when we're off duty, but also when I'm badgering you for data from the Hub."

"Thank you. You haven't been near us for days."

"I'm sure there will be an occasion early next week when we'll seek your help," said Gus. "We're swimming in treacle on our latest case."

"You told me we weren't talking shop tonight, Gus," said Vera.

"That's the plan," said Gus, "but I might slip into the old routine if we run out of topics."

It wasn't long before everyone was chatting more freely. Luke had plenty to say to his former colleagues about how things were in Swindon with his new accommodation. When Vera and Divya joined Melody and Suzie to discuss babies, Blessing left Jamie talking football with Neil and Alex to collar her boss.

"I had a thought when I was leaving work, Gus," she said. When she had explained what she meant, Gus agreed she had a point.

"It would explain a lot, Blessing," he said. "We'll follow that line of enquiry on Monday. I'll make a mental note."

"Don't worry," said Blessing. "I've set the alarm on my phone for a quarter past nine. I'll remind you if you haven't mentioned it by then."

Gus spotted Luke making for the bar with two empty glasses and joined him.

"Neil said you called the office the evening after I'd left."

"It's an odd feeling, Gus," said Luke. "I sympathise with the people we're supposed to be arresting. That hasn't happened before."

"What progress have you made in the short time you've worked at Gablecross?"

"I spent some of last week in Portishead, Gus. I'm playing catch-up compared to the others attached to this team. We're no closer to finding David Scott. As for the other senior officers of the charity, they appear to have surfaced at Larcombe Manor. Our latest surveillance exercise showed people working normally in the grounds and gardens."

"They can disappear into thin air one minute and reappear the next," said Gus. "Has anyone considered checking whether they ever applied for planning permission for an underground bunker?"

Luke laughed.

"I didn't have you pegged as a James Bond fan, Gus," said Luke.

"Well, unless David Copperfield has joined forces with David Scott and the others, I can't think of another way to pull off that trick."

"When I feel more confident of my standing in the squad, I might suggest it, Gus. Right now, they'd think I was bonkers."

Gus returned to rescue Suzie from the Mother's Union meeting. Luke took two fresh drinks back for him and Tom.

"Another drink, darling?" asked Gus.

"Yes, please," said Suzie. "We need to talk."

They got their drinks and walked through to listen to the four-piece group from a safe distance.

"Blessing was right," shouted Gus. "Why are we here?"

"Vera asked me how you were doing with the Katherine Alford case."

"She reminded me we shouldn't be discussing work when she arrived," said Gus.

"I summarised what we discussed last night," said Suzie. "Divya chipped in when I mentioned Dr Gray had found the body. Her husband, Arjun, met Dominic Gray at Great Western Hospital. Divya said Arjun thought he was arrogant but a highly competent doctor. He's worked at Savernake Hospital for over twenty years."

"I sense there's something more interesting, judging by the fact we needed to suffer this racket. Hendrix would turn in his grave if he heard that version of Hey Joe."

"Patience is a virtue, Gus Freeman. I've told you that before. Arjun said Dominic and Amy Gray have an unconventional lifestyle."

"Don't leave me hanging, Suzie," said Gus. "What does that mean?"

"It means you have another lead to follow on Monday. It might not be connected to your case, but we girls want to know what you find. We're always interested in salacious gossip. So now, forget work altogether and dance with me while you can still hold me close."

Chapter Eleven

Saturday, 29 September 2018

"WAKEY, WAKEY. RISE AND SHINE," said Suzie.

Gus risked one eye.

"It's Saturday. What's the rush?"

"We need to go shopping," said Suzie. "I heard what you said to Grace last night, that you intend to desert me this afternoon while you dig for victory."

"What time is it now? It's barely light."

"Dull and overcast, and it's almost ten," said Suzie. "We're too late for breakfast. Brunch will be at half-past ten. I'll be in the kitchen. You hit the bathroom."

Gus knew it was pointless to argue. So he rolled out of bed.

"I enjoyed last night," he said.

"Everyone did, Gus," said Suzie. "Blessing's singing will stay with me for a long time."

"I missed Luke and Tom leaving," said Gus.

"They were hoping to get back to Swindon to visit a club," said Suzie.

"The exuberance of youth," said Gus.

Thirty minutes later, they were tucking in to a cooked breakfast with all the trimmings. Suzie drove them into Devizes to visit the supermarket, and everything was tucked away in the fridge or freezer by one o'clock.

"How long will you be gone?" asked Suzie as Gus changed into his gardening gear.

"Are we visiting The Lamb tonight?" asked Gus. "If so, I'll head home by half-past four."

"Okay," said Suzie. "Try not to ruffle too many feathers."

"I'll be on my best behaviour," said Gus.

He walked along the lane, passed the pub, and walked through the gateway next to the village church. The clock was preparing to strike the half-hour.

"Hello, stranger,"

"Reverend Bentham, as I live and breathe," said Gus. "Are you about to leave, or will I have the pleasure of your company this afternoon?"

"I've been here for an hour, Gus," said Clemency. "Another minute or two, and I need to be on my way. Two parishioners asked for Holy Communion."

"I presume they're not confident of getting next door for tomorrow's scheduled service," said Gus.

"Afraid not," said Clemency. "Bert worked on his vegetable patch for most of the morning. He's back to his old self. You don't need to ask where he is now. The Lamb will miss his financial contributions when the time comes."

"I pray that's not for a few years yet," said Gus.

He opened his shed and brought out his canvas chair.

"Sitting down on the job, Gus?" asked the Reverend.

"I'm expecting company."

"Oh, lovely, Suzie's on her way. I didn't think I'd see her before tonight."

"Suzie and I will be in The Lamb by eight o'clock," said Gus. "No, one of my colleagues wanted a chat."

Clemency nodded towards the gateway.

"It looks like she's here. So I'll get going, do my duty, and see you later."

Gus glanced over his shoulder.

The Reverend mounted her bicycle and pedalled past the newcomer.

Grace Packenham was standing at the side of an orange Smart car. They hadn't heard it arrive, so he guessed it was the electric model. Grace was always smartly dressed at London Road. Either in her uniform or a tailored suit that wouldn't look out of place in the City.

Town and city dwellers always have a problem dressing for the countryside. Gus used to cringe when he saw the crowds at Cheltenham during Gold Cup week. Genuine country folk never had to try to look at home. It came naturally because whatever item of clothing they selected for the occasion had been weathered in advance. John and Jackie Ferris were a case in point. Gus doubted whether John had bought a new item of clothing in five years, but in a Barbour jacket, boots, and a trilby, he looked every inch at home as the country squire.

City folk bought the best clothes money could buy, turned up on the day with the sales ticket still attached, and looked like prats. Grace Packenham was something else. She'd made a valiant effort to dress casually in a beige blouse, cardigan, and a calf-length plum-coloured woollen skirt. But, when she fetched the fluorescent green wellington boots from the boot, Gus groaned.

"You haven't started work yet?" asked Grace as she carefully picked her way across the grass.

"We had a late night," said Gus. He nodded towards the canvas chair. "Careful how you sit. I didn't check whether I set it on a flat spot."

"Do you think it will rain?" asked Grace, perching on the chair before relaxing.

"Can you see the top of the hill in the distance?" asked Gus.

"Yes. Does that mean we're safe?"

"Not really. The rain comes from the same direction as the lane you drove along. Look to your left to see what's coming our way. If you can't see the hilltop, the rain has started."

"Can we discuss the case before that dark cloud reaches us?"

Gus ran through the salient points of the Katherine Alford case while cutting the pick of the crops he wanted to take home to the bungalow.

"I don't think much of how they handled things in 2008," said Grace. "DCI Davies and DI Barnett must have bullied ACC Cromwell. She's a far sharper cookie than your account suggests."

"We've got a list of items to check on Monday," said Gus. "It would help if at least one of them moved the case forward."

"It sounds like the original investigation stalled because of poor management," said Grace. "We won't get accused of that this time. So what will be my first task?"

"I hoped you would visit Anna in Dorchester on Tuesday. DS Hardy can go with you. That's no reflection on your abilities. Kenneth prefers us to hunt in pairs."

"Do you have a prepared list of questions?" asked Grace.

"Alex has a list of items where we're not happy with our answers thus far. So that will be your starting point. You've done this before, haven't you?"

"Not on a murder case," said Grace. "Or with an Assistant Chief Constable as one of the people whose answers we don't like. I can see why you travel in pairs."

"There's more than one reason for that, as you know," said Gus. "Someone needs to go with me because I don't have a warrant card. I ensure Lydia and Blessing work with a detective sergeant or me to help them learn. I team up with Alex and Neil for the same purpose. Now you've joined us, I hope you will do the same."

"Who do you think could have murdered Katherine?"

"I've got more names of people who couldn't have," said Gus. "Every lead we've followed has been a dead end. That means one of two things. Either someone lied to the detectives ten years ago and is still lying today, or we haven't dug deep enough to find the real motive for the killing."

"You think the killer's name is among the people from the original investigation," said Grace. "Why they did what they did remains a mystery."

"We might make a decent detective out of you yet, DI Packenham," said Gus. "Would you like a butternut squash?"

Monday, 1 October 2018

GUS AND SUZIE left the bungalow at half-past eight.

"Things should go more smoothly today after your good deed on Saturday afternoon," said Suzie.

"I'm glad Bert Penman wasn't there. He wouldn't have been able to resist poking fun at Amazing Grace's wellies."

"Usual time tonight?" asked Suzie.

"Five-thirty, give or take," said Gus.

Suzie gave Gus a wave as she drove through the gateway and into the lane. Gus followed in the Focus at a more sedate pace. As they neared London Road, he caught up with Suzie and watched her turn into the Wiltshire Police HQ.

Gus reflected on the weekend's events as he drove through the town centre. Grace accepted his gift of a vegetable, thanked him for spending time with her, and silently made her way up the lane in her Smart car and drove home. Gus realised he didn't know where that was, but Vera could probably tell him. No doubt it was one of her ex-husband, Monty's properties.

Gus worked on his allotment with his hands, and the case with his brain, until four. Then, he decided he wouldn't make any more sense from the clues he had at his disposal and returned home.

In the evening, he and Suzie ate at The Lamb with Brett and Clemency. Bert and Irene stopped by for the last hour and revealed that they'd been to the cinema in Devizes. Gus couldn't believe the change in his old friend. Bert would be booking tickets at the theatre next.

Sundays were designed to be a day of rest, and Gus and Suzie had taken full advantage. But, this morning, they both felt re-energized. Gus thought that maybe, just maybe, today they could make a breakthrough.

Gus turned into the Old Police Station car park and eased the Focus into the remaining space. The full complement of CRT vehicles was in a neat row. Many locals knew who occupied the offices above the charity shops, but strangers would be hard-pressed to match the assortment of cars to an elite team of detectives.

He called the lift to the ground floor and rode up to join the others.

"Morning, guv," said Neil. "A quiet thank you for Friday night. Melody had a great time."

"I saw the orange box downstairs," said Gus. "Where's the driver?"

"DI Packenham is in the restroom with Alex, guv," said Lydia. "He risked life and limb by giving her the tour and introducing her to the mysteries of the Gaggia."

"He deserves a medal, guv," said Neil.

"How are you this morning, Blessing?" asked Gus.

"Embarrassed, guv," said Blessing. "I had too much to drink on Friday night."

"Don't be too hard on yourself, Blessing," said Gus. "Axl Rose has a distinctive voice, which isn't easy to reproduce for a young woman. Try something less challenging next time."

"There won't be a next time, guv," said Blessing.

Alex and Grace emerged from the restroom.

"If everyone's on the same page, let's get started," said Gus.

He picked up his felt-tip pen and added the information received on Friday night to the list on the whiteboard.

"Where did that come from, guv?" asked Neil.

"I spoke with someone from the Hub at the weekend,

Neil. An observation from a reliable source that might be worth a look."

"Got it, guv," said Neil, remembering where that observation had originated.

Grace spotted the glances between the others. She realised she wasn't in the loop with this team yet.

"Can you work on the bus timetables, please, Blessing?" asked Gus. "Where might our mystery caller have come from, and was it possible they got to Marlborough between nine and nine-thirty?"

"OK, guv," said Blessing. "We mustn't forget they needed a way to make the return journey after midnight."

"True," said Neil, "and there would be no chance today. Things weren't any better ten years ago. The last bus would have been well before midnight."

"They could have taken a taxi," said Grace. "Many operators work until after two o'clock for customers leaving bars with late-night licences."

"Fat chance of anyone remembering someone calling for a cab ten years ago," said Lydia.

"Our killer wouldn't have stood by the Peugeot at West Woods waiting for his lift," said Alex. "They would walk to the A4 Bath Road, a more likely pick-up point."

"Which wouldn't be easier to remember after all this time," Lydia said.

"Dig out the facts, Blessing," said Gus. "If we have to discount our killer coming from outside the town, so be it."

"What's next, guv?" asked Neil.

"One for Lydia, I think," said Gus, "Ask the forensic accountants at the Hub to check whether Katherine Alford received significant sums between 2000 and when the balance of her mother's estate transferred into her account?"

"Right, guv," said Lydia. "I'll get them to include other sums paid into her account. Unless her possible employer paid her in cash, there should be a record of when she worked at home. Of course, it's possible someone else gave her a helping hand. Perhaps the person she described to Lily Faulkner as being like a brother."

"Good thinking," said Gus. "The cash-in-hand angle would be difficult to trace. That is why people who want to avoid paying taxes use it. Moreover, her husband had abandoned her, and one could imagine Katherine being tempted to hide an income from the authorities."

"Would that be a motive for murder, guv?" asked Blessing.

"People have killed for less, Blessing," said Gus, "but in this case, I don't believe it will. We're just following Lydia's suggestion that we ensure nobody can accuse us of not pursuing every possibility."

"It looks like I'm researching Katherine Alford's childhood," said Neil.

"Got it in one, Neil," said Gus. "Leave no stone unturned. What did she excel at in school? If her husband considered Katherine to have reached her academic peak at sixteen, she might have had other talents. Could she have utilised those to earn a steady income? Where did she work before her marriage? Did that firm employ outworkers?"

"What about the friend, guv?" asked Alex. "Is that my task for this morning?"

"We're off to George Lane later," said Gus. "I want to tackle Trefor Davies and Wayne Barnett on what we've uncovered. First, I want to see the list of people cautioned about nocturnal activities at West Woods. Then we'll ask Trefor where we can find Callum Brady. He may have left the police force, but he can't be too difficult to find. Something he remembers from his time with Anna Cromwell may hold the key to this case."

"I'll contact George Lane and make arrangements, guv," said Alex.

"Don't stand for any delaying tactics, Alex. It's later this morning, and no excuses."

Alex grabbed the phone.

"We're tight for time, Gus," said Grace. "Whatever this Brady character can tell us would be useful to have in our locker when we interview ACC Cromwell tomorrow."

"Dorchester's a long drive, Grace," said Gus. "We can squeeze Brady first thing in the morning and pass on anything relevant before you enter the ACC's office. No need to panic."

"I never panic. Are we working together on the final two items, Gus?" she asked.

"I'll check on Guy Faulkner first," said Gus. "Then, I'll confirm when Daniel Matravers tied the knot for the second time. Meanwhile, you could use your contacts around the county to learn more about Dominic and Amy Gray. Be discreet. We don't want to spook them. We're not interested if they're swingers. That's none of our business. The good doctor discovered a dead body at a spot he and his wife cycled past on several occasions. They live two miles away in a picturesque village and could be pillars of the local community."

"Then, you hear a whisper that they live an unconventional lifestyle," said Grace. "I suppose your legendary gut instinct tells you there's something fishy."

"I've no idea," said Gus, "but until you discover what form of unconventional we're talking about, Dr Gray and his wife stay on the list."

Gus sensed Grace thought she had been handed a task

that would prove a waste of time. That was true, it might, but he wanted her to realise teamwork meant that now and again, each of them would trawl through reams of paperwork and end up with nothing. TV crime shows had a lot to answer for, as people thought the job was glamorous. Instead, it could be a hard slog, often with little or no reward.

"DCI Davies will see us at eleven, guv," said Alex. "DI Barnett will be available whenever we finish that meeting."

"Excellent," said Gus. "We'll leave at twenty-five past ten. So heads down for the next sixty minutes, and if anyone's free at ten o'clock, they can get the hot drinks."

Blessing could see everyone was still working when the clock reached the appointed time, so she headed for the restroom. She stopped at Grace's desk for confirmation of her order.

"We'll get used to remembering you prefer green tea soon, ma'am," said Blessing.

When everyone had their drink, Gus asked for a brief progress report.

"A bus service from Swindon to Marlborough could have brought someone into the town centre when you mentioned, guv. Far less likely, the killer arrived from the Beckhampton direction. There was zero chance of leaving the town from anywhere close to West Woods after six in the evening."

"That suggests the mystery caller lived locally," said Alex, "and drove into town to meet Katherine."

"Have you discounted there being two cars?" asked Grace.

"The eyewitness saw just the Peugeot," said Neil.

"We didn't ask Bert Harris if he saw another car," said Blessing.

"Ovens and Park never noticed a car of any make at The Roebuck," said Alex. "Even though there had to be several."

"What about your task, Lydia?" asked Gus.

"Divya Yadav has accepted the challenge, guv. The Hub number crunchers will give us something by early afternoon."

"Good, and what have you found, Neil?"

"Katherine was a capable student, who never threatened the top grades in her exams, but was far from being as dim as Daniel made out. I hoped she would have been brilliant at Art or Handicraft, guv, but so far, nothing suggests a talent that brought in good sums of money."

"Any joy learning where she worked after leaving school?"

"At Savernake Hospital, guv, as a healthcare assistant. Back in the Eighties, she may have been termed an orderly. Katherine cared for patients, checked their vital signs, and assisted the nursing staff if required. As with every other group she came into contact with, they remembered Katherine as hard-working and friendly."

"We can rule out her brief working career having a connection to any work she carried out at home," said Alex.

"If Katherine did work at home, it was on something else entirely," said Neil.

"Could that be where the friend she mentioned came into her life?" asked Grace.

"Nobody picked up that task, guv," said Alex. "Maybe Blessing can ditch the bus routes and look closer at where Katherine grew up. We know she lived on the same side of town as Purlyn Acre when she was with her parents. What was Katherine's father's name? I don't recall seeing that. He died when Katherine was in her early twenties. Daniel

Matravers will have met him. We don't have many people to ask for information from those days, do we?"

"We've been fortunate the Chief Constable hasn't handed us a case from fifty years ago, Neil," said Gus. "But you're right. We need people who knew Katherine as a young girl. She would have been in her mid-fifties now, and Daniel Matravers didn't meet her until she was eighteen. Even so, he should have some insight. I haven't spoken to him yet. However, I learned something about Guy Faulkner, which was unexpected."

"Do tell, guv," said Lydia.

"I avoided asking Lily Faulkner for details and spoke with his former employers. Guy worked at the Honda factory for ten years before emigrating to New Zealand. The lady I spoke to in the HR department was doing the same job at the time. When asked why he was leaving, Guy blamed a relationship breakup. I asked whether the woman involved was married. She was surprised I didn't know Guy was gay. The affair had been with a married man."

"That confirms Guy wasn't Paul Alford's father, guv," said Neil.

"Plenty of gay men have fathered children, Neil," said Alex.

"Gay men who have children aren't doing so to make a statement about homosexuality or the role of families," said Grace. "They do so despite their homosexuality."

"How does any of that help us with our case?" asked Blessing.

"You haven't got the relevant pieces of the jigsaw, Blessing," said Gus. "I asked whether the lady in HR knew the name of the person involved. She said Guy hadn't given her any details, but it was someone who lived close to him in Marlborough."

"If the affair were with Daniel Matravers," said Lydia, "that would explain a lot."

"So would Daniel having a vasectomy and not telling Katherine," said Blessing.

"Did you get hold of Daniel Matravers yet, Gus?" asked Grace.

"He's not in the office today. We could visit him at home, but Alex and I are off to George Lane in a few minutes."

"I'll drive to Salisbury, guv," said Lydia.

"Neil should go with you, Lydia," said Gus. "He will be busy digging into Katherine's childhood for an hour or two. So perhaps you can fix a time this afternoon, Alex."

Alex nodded and checked if they had Daniel Matravers's mobile number.

Gus saw Alex making a call and crossed the office to Grace's desk.

"What can you tell me about Dominic and Amy Gray?"

"I discovered Dominic was born in Marlborough, Gus. Although he was six years her senior, he attended the same junior and secondary schools as Katherine Alford. His family lived on Blowhorn Street."

"Where's that? We didn't pass that on our travels."

"Half a mile from where Daniel and Katherine bought a house, based on the street map on our office wall."

"Interesting," said Gus. "Where did Mary Alford and her husband live, I wonder?"

"We need to leave, guv," called Alex. He was standing by the lift door already.

"I'll carry on digging, Gus," said Grace. "First, I'll confirm Katherine's father's name. Then I'll see whether Katherine and Dominic were near neighbours."

"Don't count your chickens," said Gus. "Six years is a

lifetime between two kids. We've heard from Emily, Paul, and Sophia that four years can be a chasm. Savernake Hospital is my best bet for their paths crossing."

"The dashing young Doctor Gray meets a teenage girl taking bloods and emptying bedpans on his ward rounds."

"Barbara Cartland made plenty of money out of stories of that ilk," said Gus.

"She was way before my time, Gus," said Grace. "Anyway, the timing's not quite right. They grew up in the same part of town, but he trained to be a doctor for six years after leaving school at eighteen."

"You've got your sums right," said Gus. "Katherine was twelve when Gray went to medical school and started the journey. She left school at sixteen. Hang on. Find out where he did his two years as a junior doctor. Could he have gone straight to Savernake? What was their speciality twenty years ago? His training could have been targeted for something important to him."

"That will keep me busy until you get back," said Grace.

Gus grabbed his folder and joined Alex.

"I'm driving, I see," said Gus. "Lydia brought you in from Chippenham this morning."

"It's far quicker, guv," said Alex, "but no less frightening."

Gus checked the clock on the dashboard. They shouldn't be too late arriving at George Lane station. However, he doubted whether Trefor Davies would notice.

Trefor was waiting for them when they reached Reception.

"Did you find something we missed?" he asked. "I've been trying to recall how we handled things all weekend without luck."

Trefor led them through to his office and closed the door.

"What was it you wanted?" he asked.

"Just relax, Trefor," said Gus. "We need information from ten, maybe fifteen years ago, relating to West Woods. You sent patrol cars there regularly for several years. Can you tell us whether there was anyone whose name cropped up on more than one occasion? Was anyone connected to the Katherine Alford investigation found there?"

"I'd need to get someone on that, Gus," said Trefor. "It would be in one of our filing cabinets, I suppose."

"Grab that PCSO on Reception and get them searching right away, Trefor. It could be important."

Trefor called the front desk and set things in motion.

"Was that it?" he asked.

"Far from it," said Gus. "Where did Callum Brady go after he left George Lane?"

"Callum, the one that got away," said Trefor. "He joined the British Transport Police and went to work in London. I had a contact number for him back then. He may have moved on, but it would be a start."

"If you could give it to DS Hardy, he can start hunting for him," said Gus.

Trefor opened a desk drawer and rooted around for thirty seconds.

"Here we are. Callum Brady was based in Islington."

Alex made a note of the number and left the room.

"How do you think Callum can help?" asked Trefor.

"We've got several additional scraps of information gleaned from people we've re-interviewed. Callum might remember something more or have an insight into the fresh evidence we've gathered. After we've spoken to Anna

Cromwell tomorrow, we can compare what they remember of the case."

"Anna was one of my successes," said Trefor.

"You've been here for years, Trefor," said Gus. "You moved to Marlborough from Pontypridd with your wife, Megan. Is that right?"

"That's right, poor Megan. We'd only been living here for eighteen months, and she was diagnosed with bone cancer. Megan had hidden it from me for months, and when she went to the doctor, there was nothing to be done. They treated her in Swindon at the Great Western for a while, and when she was closer to the end, they transferred her to Savernake Hospital. It was easier for me to visit her there. My superiors were very good. I could take time off to sit with her for hours on end. The pain she had to endure was terrible. The doctors did everything they could to make her comfortable, but I could see it in her eyes. I wanted to grab a pillow and end her suffering, Gus. So when Megan passed, it was a relief."

"It must have been a dreadful time, Trefor," said Gus. "When Tess died, it was so sudden, it knocked me for six, but I didn't have to watch her suffer. You married again, I heard?"

"Maureen, yes, lovely lady," said Trefor. "A local girl. Maureen sang with the community choir, and we both needed someone. She's been good for me."

"Does Maureen know about your concerns over your health?" asked Gus.

"She noticed I was forgetful. That was two years ago now. I fell asleep in a meeting at London Road last November. The room was warm, but that wasn't like me. Not in my prime."

"You ought to contact London Road, Trefor," said Gus.

"I'll have a word with Kenneth if you like; there could be problems if you try to soldier on until your official retirement date."

"I hoped to hang on until the end of the year when they close this place," said Trefor.

"Kenneth will make sure you leave with your reputation intact, Trefor," said Gus. "Help's available. Please take advantage of it. I'm sure you and Maureen will be better for it."

Trefor's phone rang.

"They've found a dusty file with the details you need, Gus," he said.

Two minutes later, Alex Hardy returned with a folder.

"Your lad in Reception handed me this, sir. I've spoken to Callum Brady. He's at Canary Wharf these days and asked me to pass on his regards."

"Can we take this file with us, Trefor?" asked Gus.

"No good to me," he replied. "Is that it then?"

"Leave everything to me, Trefor," said Gus. "Oh, one last thing. Which doctor looked after Megan at Savernake Hospital?"

Trefor stared at Gus for a second.

"Megan's GP visited her when she could, but her husband was with her for her final few weeks. I don't know whether you've spoken to them this week. Dominic and Amy Gray. They've been stalwarts in the town for three decades. I don't know where we'd be without them."

Gus and Alex were halfway out of the office when Gus asked his final question.

"Why did you put Wayne Barnett in charge of the Alford murder case, Trefor?"

"I thought it was the right thing to do, Gus," said Trefor.

Gus nodded. That made sense after what he'd heard this morning.

"DI Barnett has someone with him, guv," said Alex. "The lad on Reception told me it was Eve Northwood, and they shouldn't be long."

Gus had only met the redoubtable Ms Northwood once, but she left a lasting impression. Few GPs had the accreditation to stand in for a police surgeon and carry out a post-mortem. Gus wondered what had brought her to Marlborough. But he didn't have long to wait. The door opened, and Eve Northwood bustled into the corridor.

"Gus Freeman. What brings you here?" she asked. "Another unsolved murder case?"

"It's what we do, Eve. I was about to ask you the same question."

"A personal call. Wayne is my nephew."

Alex went inside to get Wayne Barnett prepared for what lay ahead.

"A small world," said Gus. "We're reviewing the Katherine Alford murder. I doubt you remember it from ten years ago. Were you involved in police work then?"

"No, before my time. I was working in Swindon and remembered the news reports. I felt sorry for the children, and I think there was a grandchild."

"Well, that's why we're here. Our progress is slow, but while there's hope."

"Forensics offered nothing if I remember right," said Eve.

"There wasn't much in the report apart from the basics," said Gus. "The time of death was midnight, give or take, and Katherine was strangled. If we knew a lot more about the victim, where she went after she left home, and who with, we'd be better placed to find her killer."

"If it's not there, we can't record it," said Eve.

"Who was the pathologist in those days? Can you remember?"

"That would have been when Stuart Fitzwalter was at Gablecross," said Eve. "Did you say ten years ago?"

"The end of June 2008," said Gus.

"You would need to check, but a locum might have been required. Stuart flew home to South Africa for his father's funeral that year. Peter Morgan could have come over from Devizes, or Dominic Gray, as he was on the doorstep."

"Dr Gray? He found the body," said Gus. "Surely, he couldn't do the post-mortem?"

"Why not?" asked Eve. "He saw the body in situ at the murder scene. If Dominic were on duty that week, it would have been sensible for him to maintain the continuity. He's an excellent physician."

"Does Gray still work for the police, if required?" asked Gus.

"Not since I offered my services," said Eve. "He's scaled back his involvement in the past five years and is due to retire at sixty. That must be coming up soon. Amy's a GP in the town, did you know?"

"Trefor Davies told me earlier," said Gus.

"It takes all sorts," said Eve. "Silly me, I mustn't gossip. I need to return to Gablecross. I wish you luck with the Alford case, Gus. Good morning."

With that, Eve Northwood scuttled along the corridor towards Reception.

Gus thought about what she'd said and joined Alex and Wayne Barnett.

"We're just looking through these cautions, guv," said Alex.

"Never thought anyone would bother digging back that far," said Wayne.

"What have you found?" asked Gus.

"Several names crop up more than once," said Alex. "Wayne identified the two women as prostitutes, long since retired, and one man who was caught with both women."

"Not at the same time, though," said Wayne.

"Are the names of any men frequenting West Woods related to our case?"

"We can't see any," said Wayne. "A long list of teenagers doing the horizontal tango, drinking underage, smoking weed. Sometimes all at the same time. But I don't reckon we'll find anything to conjure up a name for our killer."

"It was worth a shot," said Gus.

"Anything else you need?" asked Wayne.

"You attended the post-mortem with Anna Cromwell on Tuesday morning following the discovery of the body, didn't you?" asked Gus.

"That's right," said Wayne. "It was Anna's first. You know what it's like. We sit up top while they carry on below, telling you what they find. I told Anna to place her chair back from the window, far enough that she could see the guy's head but didn't see the gruesome stuff. That way, Anna held onto her breakfast. Most of the guys give a running commentary as they work. We were interested in the time of death, confirmation she was strangled, and whether he found anything to add to what forensics collected at the scene."

"Did you not recognise the person doing the post-mortem?" asked Gus.

"Why should we?" asked Wayne. "They all look alike in that room; head covering, mask, and scrubs."

"What if I told you it was Dr Gray? The man who called George Lane to say he'd found a body."

"You're kidding," said Wayne. "We let the uniforms get on with taking their statement. There wasn't any call for us to talk to them at the time. I probably wouldn't have recognised him, anyway. Lycra and a cycle helmet aren't a great look for a middle-aged bloke. I tried not to take much notice. The wife had a tidy body on her, though."

"Nobody followed up and spoke with Dr Gray and his wife at home, did they?" asked Gus.

"Trefor told us we probably wouldn't learn anything. They were busy people, he said."

"Dr Gray worked at Savernake Hospital at the same time as the victim," said Gus. "It's possible they knew one another when they were children. Their family homes were half a mile apart in Marlborough. Do you see where I'm going with this?"

"We missed more than I thought," said Wayne.

"I suppose you blame Trefor for not providing the needed support."

"I haven't done so far, but I would if push came to shove," said Wayne.

"We're speaking to Callum Brady later," said Alex. "He asked if you were still here."

"Nobody else would have me," laughed Wayne.

"Time for us to leave, Alex," said Gus.

Chapter Twelve

"THAT WAS AN ODD MORNING, GUV," said Alex. "I missed some of your conversation with Trefor and your chat with Eve Northwood. Do you want to bring me up to date?"

"Eve didn't know whether or not Gray did the post-mortem, but he's qualified and was on the reserve list in 2008. We need to check that out. She didn't think it odd for him to take charge. As for Amy Gray, everyone paints her as a wicked lady, but nobody gives details. Whether any of it is important, I can't decide."

"Callum Brady didn't have a high opinion of Wayne Barnett, guv. He was in awe of Anna Cromwell; however, I think he had a crush on her."

"A tad misplaced if Barnett's assessment of the ACC was correct," said Gus.

"Callum said that was because Barnett tried it on with Anna and received a knee in the crown jewels for his trouble. Barnett thought if a woman didn't fancy him, they must be gay."

"Let's get back to the office," said Gus. "I want to hear what the others have learned in our absence."

"Amazing Grace will have cracked the whip, guv," said Alex.

Gus slotted the Focus into the empty parking space. Lydia hadn't left for Salisbury yet. The church clock struck one o'clock.

"The boys are back in town," said Neil as Gus and Alex exited the lift.

"I'll give you our headlines," said Gus. "Then it's your turn."

Neil gave a low whistle when Gus told them Dominic Gray could have carried out the post-mortem on Katherine Alford. Blessing raised an eyebrow.

"We received the data I requested from the Hub," said Lydia. "Shall I tell you what it revealed?"

"Don't keep me in suspense," said Gus.

"Well, a month after the divorce, Katherine received a four-figure sum from her mother's savings account. Three thousand pounds."

"Right, that tided her over for a while," said Gus. "What about later?"

"Mary Alford transferred a similar sum eighteen months later. The balance of her estate was the last major sum to appear in Katherine's bank account before her murder. As you know, I also wanted to check the smaller amounts to see who made them, in case they were significant."

"Did she receive monthly payments from an employer?" asked Alex.

"Never," said Lydia. "If Katherine was doing temporary work, it may have been seasonal. Because, although week after week, she would withdraw the same amount in cash for her day-to-day expenses, sometimes, for weeks on end, she didn't need to visit the ATM. "

"Someone gave her cash," said Gus. "We can't tell who or what for. That's a shame."

"Apart from that anomaly, her bank account looked how one would expect," said Grace. "No extravagant expenditure and Katherine's weekly shop was at a budget supermarket."

"I've got more on Dominic Gray's childhood, guv," said Neil. "He lived half a mile from Katherine and had a younger sister, Alice. She was the same age as Katherine. They were best friends from primary school."

"Why haven't we heard her name before, Neil?" asked Gus.

"She died from leukaemia, aged twelve, guv," said Neil. "From a cancer of the blood that ninety percent of children survive today, but Alice wasn't so lucky forty years ago."

"I'm not surprised her brother chose to be a doctor," said Blessing.

"Hang on, I've just thought of something, guv," said Neil. "Let me check the file. Yes, I remember reading this out to you. Whoever carried out the post-mortem discussed the query about the coil with the victim's GP and learned they fitted her with her first IUD in the mid-Eighties."

"Dominic Gray's wife, Amy, works at a surgery in Marlborough," said Grace. "He spoke to his wife. Can that be possible?"

"When did Dominic Gray marry?" asked Gus. "Was Katherine Alford one of Amy Gray's patients? Was Amy another local girl? Marlborough's a small town, and perhaps there's a simple explanation, but coincidences concern me."

"Katherine can't be alone in coming into contact with Amy at the surgery and her husband at the hospital," said

Blessing. "Dozens of patients could be treated by both each year."

"Let's carry on with the checks I've indicated," said Gus. "I want to update my files while everything from this morning is still fresh in my mind."

"We're leaving for Salisbury now, guv," said Neil. "We should get back by five o'clock."

"Neil has insisted on driving," said Lydia, "so I'm not taking bets."

"Don't let Daniel Matravers wind you up, Neil," said Gus.

"The interview room at Bourne Hill is ready and waiting," said Alex. "Matravers will have his brief with him this time."

"I'll be good as gold, honest," said Neil. "I planned to set Lydia on Matravers while keeping an eye on his solicitor."

Gus watched the pair head to the lift. Were the mists clearing, or did they still have a way to go before they could identify Katherine's killer?

"We still haven't checked when Daniel married again, guv," said Blessing. "It might help Neil and Lydia if we can send that information through before they arrive at Bourne Hill,"

"We can text Neil and get him to ask as soon as Matravers enters the interview room Blessing," said Gus. "It might get him on the back foot from the start."

"I wondered whether knowing his choice of partner might put Neil on the front foot, guv."

Gus could see what Blessing was thinking.

"You're thinking of a civil partnership in 2006, perhaps?" said Gus. "Because Katherine and Daniel weren't in contact, except through their solicitors, the timing of any wedding would have been hearsay or conjecture on Katherine's part. How does knowing the answer help find our killer, though?"

"The more Daniel Matravers thinks we know, the better," said Grace. "Even if we're taking an educated guess in some areas. He might open up on matters he hid from you when you spoke to him before."

"Find out what you can, Blessing, and send the details to Lydia's phone. You have an hour."

"I'll give Blessing a hand, Gus," said Grace.

Gus and Alex concentrated on entering their reports into the Freeman Files. They didn't have long to wait before Grace interrupted them.

"Howard Sullivan, a forty-eight-year-old graphic designer, met Daniel in 2002, and the pair took advantage of the change in the law from December 2005. They've lived together since 2003 and registered their partnership in April 2006."

"Well done, you two," said Gus. "Pass the necessary to Lydia, and let's see whether that encourages Matravers to shed more light on matters."

Neil heard Lydia's ringtone as they drove across Salisbury Plain.

"Bob Marley?" he asked. "Are you a fan?"

"Only to annoy Alex," she grinned. "I change it once a month to something I know he hates. The SMS was Blessing, sending us news."

When Neil parked in the visitor's car park at Bourne Hill, he had one more string to his bow.

Lydia and Neil signed in, were escorted to the interview room, and sat waiting for their guests to arrive. There was a tap on the door, and Daniel Matravers was shown in, followed by a portly gentleman in a light grey suit. Neil could tell quality cloth when he saw it. Matravers must have deep pockets to afford this chap's hourly rate.

Neil went through the formalities in detail to ward off any complaints from Mr Ivan Twentyman.

"I hope this won't waste my client's time," had been his opening gambit.

"We know everything that happened while you lived in Marlborough now, Mr Matravers," said Neil. "There's no point hiding anything. You married Katherine, had a daughter and gave your neighbours the impression you were a happy, loving family. She quit her job at the hospital two months before giving birth to Emily, and you insisted she stayed at home and accepted there would be no more children."

"None of this is relevant," said Daniel.

"When did you first cheat on your wife?" asked Lydia.

"How old was Guy Faulkner when you two began your relationship?" asked Neil.

"Guy was eighteen," said Daniel.

"You had married Katherine two years earlier," said Lydia. "That happy, loving image was shattered after just eighteen months. The affair continued for twelve years until Guy emigrated to New Zealand. Which was the dominant factor that caused you to leave your marriage? Paul's birth in 2000 or the pain of losing the man you loved?"

"You appear to know much more than you did when you visited me last week," Daniel said. "Guy was hurt and upset. We had kept our relationship secret for so long. Guy couldn't believe it when his mother told him Katherine was pregnant."

"You swore to him sexual relations between the two of you had ceased, I presume?"

"I told him I did my duty as infrequently as possible,

and I'd had a vasectomy before I got together with Guy, so there was no way I could be the father."

"You were caught between a rock and a hard place," said Neil. "Guy didn't believe you, and you couldn't let Katherine know what you'd done. She hoped to have another child and had the coil removed when it was due for replacement. We know Katherine did that without your knowledge. She knew you would disagree. Did Katherine die believing you were Paul's father?"

"It's possible," said Daniel. "We had had sex for the first time in months. I didn't give it another thought, and then suddenly, she returned from seeing Dr Gray, telling me she was expecting. So I visited my GP at once to confirm nothing had gone wrong with my procedure."

"Would that be Dr Amy Gray who Katherine saw?" asked Lydia.

"That's right. When I arrived in Marlborough, I registered with a different practice and never switched."

"Did you and Guy plan a future together?" asked Lydia

"We didn't know that soon we might have enjoyed the type of relationship Howard and I have," said Daniel. "But Guy felt I'd betrayed him and moved to the other side of the world before Paul was born. I can't say whether I would have moved out to be with him. After returning home, I continued to function as a chartered accountant in Salisbury, but my social life was on hold. In time, I felt ready to move on, met Howard, and we will soon live in France as a married couple."

"Katherine's death must have come as a shock," said Neil.

"Of course it did," said Daniel. "I wouldn't have wished her harm."

"You remarked that we knew much more today than

when we spoke with you last week," said Lydia. "We still have gaps in our knowledge. For example, who did you suspect to be Paul's father?"

"I studied the boy's face, thought of men Katherine had known since I met her but could never see a resemblance to anyone. Paul was two when I left, and then I saw more of his mother in his features than anyone else. I can't help you, I'm afraid."

"Did you ever meet anyone Katherine used to work with at Savernake Hospital?" asked Neil.

"We bumped into Dr Gray and her husband in town when Emily was still in a pushchair. I hadn't realised Katherine knew him from her time there. But then, they were local children, and I was the odd one out. They may have known one another growing up. I sensed Amy Gray was desperate to have a child when we bumped into them. Apart from Dr Gray, I suppose the odd nurse or cleaner from Savernake lived on the estate and chatted to Katherine."

"If you think of a name before you retire to France, we would appreciate a call," said Neil. "For now, we've got what we need. Thank you for sparing the time to meet with us. Good afternoon."

"I hope you find Katherine's killer," said Daniel.

With that, he and Ivan Twentyman left the room. Neil gave them a minute to leave the building, and then he and Lydia followed.

"We didn't progress matters very far, did we?" said Lydia. "Apart from learning that Amy was born and raised in Marlborough."

"Every little helps," said Neil. "Let's get back and see if the others have had better luck."

As they travelled back across the Plain, Gus spoke to Callum Brady in Canary Wharf.

Callum went through the events of Sunday morning and recalled the interviews he'd been involved with over the following days. His version of the interview with Charlotte Ovens and Jasmine Park didn't throw up any anomalies. One point of interest came when Gus mentioned the eyewitness, Bert Harris.

"Bert Harris told you he saw Katherine Alford's red Peugeot as he walked his dog," said Gus. "We thought reports submitted by you and Anna Cromwell were confusing. It wasn't clear whether the car was heading towards you or away from you. When we spoke to Bert the other day, he said it was neither. He said the car sped past, left to right, at the top of the road he was walking towards."

"That could have been right," said Callum. "There were half a dozen boy racers on the estate roads that Saturday night. They were first reported near Savernake and continued causing a nuisance until after midnight. The old guy was adamant he'd seen the victim's car. I suggested to Anna it was the only one he recognised. She concentrated on the actual sighting of the Peugeot. Based on complaints received at George Lane, I expect there were others Bert Harris saw in the same part of the estate."

Gus thanked Callum for giving them his time and ended the call.

"Anything positive, Gus?" asked Grace.

"Far from it," said Gus. "Callum has muddied the waters. He's suggesting when Bert Harris saw the red Peugeot speed past the junction, someone could have followed it."

"I asked if we'd discounted that as a possibility," said Grace.

"I don't believe there was ever more than one car," said Gus.

"On what basis?" asked Grace. "A gut feeling?"

"Bert says there was one car. The ladies at the pub noticed nothing. So we proceed on the basis there was just the Peugeot involved for now."

"Neil and Lydia are on their way back, guv," said Alex.

"Good. Is everyone set for tomorrow?" asked Gus.

"I can't wait to drive to Dorchester with Alex to interview ACC Cromwell," said Grace.

"Alex, before you leave today, can you arrange an interview with Dominic and Amy Gray? Lydia and I will need the interview room at George Lane. I want to speak with them separately. The morning would be preferable. If you have any problems, use the big stick, and we can interview them under caution."

"Got it. guv," said Alex.

"I've got the missing details on Dominic and Amy Gray, guv," said Blessing. "Amy Winter was born in Marlborough in 1960. She went to Bristol University for a two-year foundation course in general training and a three-year specialist training course in general practice. Amy joined her current practice, aged twenty-four, a few weeks after Katherine and Daniel married. Katherine was registered there with an older doctor who looked after her parents. After he retired, they added Katherine to Amy's list. Emily and Paul followed in due course."

"When did Dominic Gray and Amy Winter marry?" asked Gus.

"In 1986, guv," said Blessing.

"Did Amy know Katherine before becoming a doctor?"

"Amy Winter was two years behind Dominic Gray and four years ahead of Katherine and Dominic's sister, Alice.

I'm sure they were aware of one another, guv, but I can't say whether the three girls were ever close."

"We can ask Amy Gray tomorrow," said Gus.

At five o'clock, with the following day's schedule in place, the team went their separate ways. They had no clue what shocks tomorrow would bring.

Tuesday, 2 October 2018

"ANOTHER DAY, ANOTHER COLLAR, GUS?" asked Suzie.

"I'm beginning to wish Neil had never dreamt up that phrase," said Gus. "We must keep following the invisible threads that have worked loose in this case. One of those threads could lead us to the killer."

"You aren't confident it will happen today," said Suzie. "I got that impression last night when we reviewed the case again."

"I'm sorry, sweetheart," said Gus. "Tonight, we'll discuss anything other than the Alford case."

Suzie looked out of the kitchen window.

"A cloudy start, with a glimpse of sunshine later. Let's hope that's what you've got in store too. How was it with Amazing Grace yesterday, by the way? Did you steer clear of any confrontation?"

"She might grasp the benefit of teamwork in time," said Gus. "Grace offered to help Blessing, unprompted, yesterday afternoon. I got the odd dig from her about relying on gut instinct rather than trawling through reams of statistics. So far, so good."

"We had better get going," said Suzie, finishing the last dregs of her coffee.

Gus grabbed his jacket from the kitchen chair and followed Suzie outside. Rain was in the air, not falling, but just hanging around, as it did in October. They drove into Devizes, and after Suzie had disappeared into the busy London Road car park, Gus continued to the Old Police Station office.

Alex and Grace were standing together in the car park. Lydia had gone upstairs already.

"We waited for you to get here, Gus," said Grace. "Do you have any last requests?"

"That sounds ominous," said Gus.

"I wondered whether you had any additional questions for ACC Cromwell. You've had the night to reconsider Callum Brady's observations."

"You would like to ask Anna whether they ever wondered if there was more than one car on the estate that night?"

"Perhaps we should follow your usual strategy, guv," said Alex. "Don't stick to a rigid set of questions if something the witness mentions open up a fresh path."

"We have to remember who we're dealing with, Alex," said Grace. "I don't want to make Anna Cromwell feel we're questioning her actions, even though they left something to be desired. She was young and let down by her superiors. They didn't keep her on the right track."

"You might as well not bother to go, Grace, if you can't get the answers we need."

"I didn't mean I wasn't prepared to ask the tough questions, Gus," said Grace, her cheeks reddening. "I meant we need a subtle approach to get what we want rather than stomping into her office with hobnailed boots."

"Whatever floats your boat," said Gus. "Just make sure

you can congratulate yourself on the return journey that it was good hunting."

"Don't worry, guv," said Alex. "We'll work it out—good hunting to you and Lydia, too, in Marlborough. Dominic Gray is first up. He's arriving at ten o'clock."

Gus watched Grace and Alex leave the Church Street car park. Then, two more cars arrived as he waited for the lift to descend to the ground floor. Neil and Blessing had squeezed into their parking bays by one minute to nine.

"Come on, you two," he said. "You can ride up with me. What will you do while Lydia and I drive to Marlborough, Neil?"

"We can ensure our files are up-to-date, guv," said Neil. "Also, I can check whether Amy Winter was friends with Katherine and Alice. Was there something else you had in mind?"

"Take a trip to see Bert Harris," said Gus. "Sometimes I've been wrong. Ask him whether he saw another car on the estate that night."

"It would be odd for there *not* to be another car some-where, guv," said Blessing. "I spotted dozens parked on driveways and the roadside when we visited Lily Faulkner and Bert Harris's houses. Of course, there wouldn't be trade vehicles late on a Saturday evening, but plenty of people would be on their way home from a night out or popping into town for a takeaway."

"Blessing's right, guv," said Neil. "Bert remembered the red car because he recognised it. Would he notice a black saloon or a white Mini behind the Peugeot?"

"It's best to ask, Neil," said Gus. "Rule 19 in Lydia's CRT bible; ask the daft questions and the sensible ones. Our superiors can't accuse us of not exhausting every possi-bility then."

Lydia was sitting on the edge of Gus's desk when they exited the lift.

"We need to go straight back down again, guv," she said. "It's a devil to get an appointment with a doctor. We can't keep him waiting."

Gus nodded at his desk. Lydia was sitting on his folder. She grabbed it, and Gus turned on his heel.

"We'll see you two at lunchtime," said Gus.

"Another day, guv," said Neil.

"Don't go there, Neil."

Gus didn't argue with Lydia when she told him she was driving them to George Lane.

It was their best chance of reaching there before ten o'clock.

Lydia stopped as close to the front door of the police station as possible and studied the car park.

"That's his car," she said. "It has to be."

"A two-year-old Mercedes E-class Estate," said Gus. "I wonder what he'll be driving when he retires?"

"A golf trolley?" asked Lydia.

"We know very little about Dominic Gray," said Gus. "He was a keen cyclist a decade ago."

The duty sergeant signed them in when they entered the building and informed them that Dr Gray was waiting in DCI Davies's office.

"All very cosy," said Gus as they walked along the corridor.

"Their paths must have crossed a lot over the years, guv," said Lydia.

"I imagine so," said Gus. He tapped on Trefor's door but didn't go inside.

Trefor saw Gus and Lydia through the half-glass door

and waved. Dominic Gray stood, shook Trefor by the hand, and came into the corridor.

"Good morning, Mr Freeman. You are Lydia, I presume. Trefor told me what to expect."

"The interview room is further along the corridor, sir," said Gus. "I don't know whether you're familiar with the station layout."

"I've visited the old place often but never sat on the opposite side of the table from a top detective before."

They entered the interview room, and Lydia followed procedure, explaining who was present and why, and reminded Dominic Grey that the conversation was being recorded

"I thought this was a friendly chat," he said.

Gus took stock of the man on the other side of the table - medium height, medium build, clean-shaven. He didn't wear glasses, but Gus couldn't rule out contact lenses. Despite the grey hair and a few wrinkles, Dominic Gray looked fitter than most men his age. His suit and general demeanour convinced Gus they were dealing with a sophisticated, articulate professional.

"Let's start from the events of Saturday ten years ago," said Gus. "The night Katherine Alford died. You told police you had been working."

"It's a day I'll never forget," said Dominic. "I'd spent the day at the hospital with a patient. Of course, one always has post-operative concerns to consider, but when I drove home in the afternoon, I was happy we'd weathered the storm and, given time, they would recover fully. Amy had spent the day making various trips but was home when I arrived. She cooked us a meal, and because we had planned an early night, we indulged in two glasses of wine. Little did we know."

Gus saw Lydia make a note.

"The hospital phoned you before nine, is that right?" asked Gus.

"Yes, we'd not long sat down in the lounge. I wanted to check our bicycles over first. We spent thirty minutes in the garage making sure everything was shipshape for the morning. Then I received a call every doctor dreads. My patient's condition had rapidly deteriorated two hours after I'd left. I needed to get there as soon as possible, but I wasn't fit to drive. I asked for a car to be sent to collect me. The ten minutes I had to stand around waiting wouldn't have made any difference. My patient died well before I reached Savernake."

"You stayed there long after that, though, didn't you?" asked Lydia. "Why was that?"

"It was my duty to complete the relevant documentation," said Dominic, "Once I'd done that, I checked every step I'd taken from the first moment I set eyes on the poor chap. Had I missed something? What could I have done differently?"

"How did you get home, sir?" asked Lydia.

"I called Amy and told her what had happened. My wife had drunk as much wine as I had, so I needed to cadge a lift home. Someone was travelling my way and kindly dropped me outside our gateway, and I went indoors. Amy had gone to bed. I went upstairs to tell her I was home and needed a stiff drink. So I had a large whisky, went over the details of the case again, and didn't go to bed until the early hours."

"The alarm woke you both at six," said Gus.

"Too early, after the night I'd had," said Dominic. "We stuck to our schedule. We cycled past the caravan site and were near the car park at West Woods when I spotted the car."

"Did you recognise it?" asked Gus.

"Why on earth should I recognise it?"

"It belonged to Katherine, your late sister's best friend. Before she married Daniel Matravers, Katherine worked at Savernake Hospital. She didn't have a car then, but surely your wife would have seen the red Peugeot in the car park at the surgery where she works? I thought perhaps she might have mentioned it in passing. After all, Katherine and Amy saw one another frequently, such as when Daniel insisted Katherine use an IUD to prevent falling pregnant. Certainly, Katherine, Emily, and eventually Paul would have needed to visit the doctor for various illnesses. Yet neither of you recognised the car as you passed the car park."

"Context," said Dominic. "Perhaps Amy *had* seen the car at the surgery but didn't make the connection when we spotted it in the countryside."

"When you looked inside the car, you must have been shocked to find it was Katherine."

"I was intent on not leaving fingerprints," said Dominic. "Her hair had fallen across her face. Then, however, I realised I knew who it was, and I told Amy to stay by the roadside."

"But you didn't tell the uniformed officers you knew the victim. Why not?"

"To avoid the type of questions that you're asking now. The police look for those closest to the victim for suspects. They would have tied us up at West Woods for hours. We went home because Amy couldn't face a long cycling trip after the shock."

"You could tell Katherine had been strangled?"

"Telltale signs," said Dominic. "Don't forget I gained

the extra accreditation to perform autopsies. So I'd seen that type of injury before."

"Could you give us the name of the person who brought you home from Savernake that night?" asked Gus.

"I can't recall the name," said Dominic. "They worked at the hospital in a minor capacity, but where they are today, heaven knows."

"Convenient," said Lydia.

"How well did you know Katherine?" asked Gus.

"Our paths crossed during our childhood. Alice was six years younger than me. We didn't share the same friends or interests. I suppose Katherine visited our home between the age of five and eleven. After Alice's untimely death, I didn't see Katherine again until I worked at Savernake. Then, one day, I saw a face I thought I recognised on a ward round. But, of course, Katherine looked a lot different at seventeen. She was now a beautiful young woman holding a bedpan. We exchanged words from time to time, and then she married and left. I don't recall the next time we had occasion to speak."

"You were with your new wife, Amy," said Lydia. "Katherine and Daniel were with baby Emily in town, and you stopped to talk."

"Gosh, what a memory someone has. That would be Daniel, I presume. You have been busy."

"You have no idea," said Lydia.

"Although you had known the victim since she was five, you didn't recuse yourself from the post-mortem," said Gus.

"I had little option," said Dominic. "Stuart Fitzwalter was abroad, and the deceased needed to be examined as soon as possible to determine both time and cause of death. I wanted to give Trefor and his team the best opportunity for a quick resolution."

"We noticed you and Trefor are friends," said Lydia.

"We met when Trefor's wife, Megan, reached us at Savernake. They had done all they could for her in Swindon. He knew Megan had gone there to die. Doctors watch too many brave people suffer terribly for far too long. We watch those closest to them falling apart and wish we could do more."

"Why did nobody visit you for a second interview?" asked Lydia. "You gave a statement to the uniformed officers at West Woods, but none of Trefor's detectives got in touch."

"I imagine Trefor thought we could add nothing further," said Dominic.

"When do you retire?" asked Lydia.

"At the end of the year. We have no plans to do a moonlight flit if that's what you're asking. Instead, we'll be in Clench Common, tending to our garden, cycling around the country lanes, and spending time with friends."

"I think we can stop for now," said Gus. "Thank you for taking time out of your busy day, Dr Gray. We will need to speak to you again. So. we'll be in touch."

"You will need to see me again? Heavens, I can't imagine why. We found a dead body, that's all. I trust you will consult Trefor."

"I report to DS Mercer and the Chief Constable," said Gus. "There will be no need for consultation. One last question: did you resolve the problem over the sudden death of your patient that night? Was there an internal investigation?"

"I can't see how it could assist in your enquiries into Katherine Alford's death," said Dominic, "but, yes, everything pertaining to the treatment prescribed, the operation, and the patient's aftercare was looked at with a fine-toothed comb. Unfortunately, the patient died of complications following major surgery, but nothing I'd done contributed to the outcome. May I go now?"

Gus nodded.

Dominic Gray rose from his chair and swept from the room. As Gus and Lydia waited for Amy Gray to arrive, they heard Trefor Davies's door close along the corridor.

"What did you make of that, guv," asked Lydia.

"He never mentioned the light cotton gloves," said Gus. "I believe we can reduce the field of runners to two."

Epilogue

GUS AND LYDIA discussed what they'd learned and waited for their next guest to arrive

Dr Amy Gray was a tall, solid-framed individual. Gus couldn't quite fathom why she seemed familiar. Where had he seen her before?

"We meet again," said Lydia.

"West Woods and The Oddfellows," said Gus.

Amy Gray was one of the two ladies they saw on their trip around the Manton estate.

"I expect to find a new Honda Jazz in the car park," said Gus.

"I parked in the spot vacated by my husband," said Amy. "Dominic was not happy when he drove back to the hospital."

"Hiding the truth from the police is not recommended," said Lydia. "We keep asking uncomfortable questions until we hear it."

"We can make this brief with your cooperation, Dr Gray," said Gus.

"What do you wish to know?"

"The question is, rather, what do we know already?" said Gus.

"Oh dear," said Amy. "I was afraid of this from the moment I saw you at West Woods."

"When did you meet Dominic?" asked Gus.

"We grew up on the same street. I always loved Dominic. He didn't notice me until I was sixteen. Dominic was home from school that summer after his A-levels. Alice died from leukaemia in the spring, and he always looked sad. After that, we started seeing one another. I hoped it was serious, but I wasn't sure if Dominic felt the same. Finally, he told me he wanted to be a doctor because he wanted no one to suffer as his sister did."

"Were you and Alice friends?" asked Lydia.

"We barely spoke," said Amy. "Alice and Katherine were close friends. I had friends of my age, as they did. But my focus was on Dominic. He left home to start his medical career, and I was heartbroken. I followed his lead two years later. I'm not ashamed to admit I chose the profession because I wanted to be near Dominic. I would have followed him to the ends of the earth."

"Did you see one another over the next five years?" asked Gus.

"University life can be all-consuming," said Amy. "I filled what little spare time I had and stopped dreaming of Dominic. The boys involved didn't complain."

"What happened after you left Bristol?" asked Lydia.

"When I came home at the end of my first year as a junior doctor at the Great Western, Dominic was still working at Savernake. He was living with his parents, but I could tell he was a troubled soul. He and Katherine were thick as thieves, although she was dating someone, and it was serious. After Katherine and Daniel married, Dominic and I rekindled our relationship. The feelings we had for one another grew, and we married in 1986. Only one thing prevented it from being the perfect marriage. Ever since I was a young girl, I had been desperate to have children. After two years of trying, we got ourselves checked. There was nothing wrong with either of us. We had options, of course, but I wanted a natural birth. My physical needs were greater than Dominic's. It wasn't just other men I wanted. I needed women, too. The men were a means to an end. There had to be a man whose sperm was compatible. As I sought a mate, my life became a constant rollercoaster of emotions. I experienced a great high followed by a devastating low when my period arrived. I needed a woman's arms around me in those terrible days. It took me back to the days when I had my first periods, and my mother held me close and told me she loved me."

"We heard rumours of an unconventional lifestyle," said Gus. "I didn't imagine it would take that form. We don't judge. You were Katherine's GP, I believe?"

Amy Gray nodded.

"I was the family doctor for over twenty years. Katherine and her mother, Mary, were on my list. Katherine saw me when she needed a replacement IUD. I could never understand why she let Daniel tell her what to do with her body. Then, one day, Katherine arrived at my surgery and announced she wanted to have her coil removed, not replace it with a new one. I couldn't fathom what had changed. Was she having an affair? Had Daniel relented, and were they trying for a second child?"

"So, you looked after Katherine through her pregnancy with Paul," said Lydia. "That must have been difficult for you. Not just with Katherine, but other women who seemed to pop out little ones to order."

"I thought I was reconciled to my fate," said Amy. "I hadn't changed my ways, and the variety kept the demons at bay."

"Then, Emily was your next patient from the Alford family," said Gus. "An unmarried mother at eighteen."

"Those were the pregnancies that made me the angriest," said Amy.

"Were you shocked when Daniel walked out on Katherine and the children?" asked Gus.

"Dominic and I didn't know him well," said Amy. "He always struck me as an odd choice for Katherine."

"Did you see Katherine much between that time and the night she died?" asked Gus.

"She brought Paul with her when she made an appointment. Emily came in with Sophia, but her mother didn't come with her. I can't recall every visit, but they had no more ailments or concerns than one would expect. It was a difficult time for Katherine when Mary was ill. The cancer treatment left her very weak, and Dominic told me Mary faced a slow, painful decline."

"Dominic treated Mary Alford as well?" asked Gus.

"Savernake is a mere satellite to the Great Western Hospital now, but it had decent facilities for a small town such as Marlborough years ago."

"When was the last time you saw Katherine?"

"Out at West Woods, in the springtime. Paul was five, perhaps. It must have been over the Easter holiday weekend. Katherine spotted me with a friend, waved out, and I acknowledged her. We didn't speak."

"Ironic that the next time you saw her was at West

Woods again," said Gus. "Do you want to tell us about that?"

"We had planned a cycle ride to Bath that morning. Dominic and I had ridden for just five minutes when he called me to stop. I was twenty yards ahead of him, and he'd spotted a car in the car park. I wanted him to leave it. What business was it of ours? But Dominic insisted he reported it to the authorities. So I looked after our bikes while he messed around with the camera on his phone. Then, he realised there was someone in the car."

"You both spent a long time perfecting this story, didn't you?" said Gus. "The pertinent details never change. I warned you from the outset that we know what happened. I understand why after listening to you this morning. Only one thing bothers me. What special talent did Katherine Alford have that made her vital to Dominic?"

"Oh dear," said Amy, "I told my friend in The Oddfellows that day that you looked like a bloodhound, who, once he's caught the scent, never stops hunting. I think I need my solicitor now."

Lydia suspended the interview, noted the time, and stopped the recording.

"I'll speak to Trefor Davies, Lydia," said Gus. "Can you sit with Dr Gray until her solicitor arrives?"

Lydia nodded. She hoped Gus would let her know what the heck was going on.

Gus knocked on Wayne Barnett's door.

"Can you spare us a minute, Wayne? I'd like you to sit in on my conversation with Trefor."

"Sure," said Wayne. "What's going on?"

"I think it's time you knew the truth," said Gus.

Thirty minutes later, Wayne returned to his office and searched for the number of a business on the South

Marston Industrial Estate. Once the arrangements had been made, he drove to Swindon to meet with Paul Alford.

As Wayne walked through Reception, he passed Dr Gray's solicitor, Edward Vickers.

The PCSO on duty escorted Mr Vickers to the interview room.

"Can I have fifteen minutes with my client, please?" Vickers asked as soon as he entered the room.

"You may," said Gus. "We have cautioned your client. Dr Gray knows the charges we intend to bring against her and her husband."

"You mean Dominic is involved? I represent them both. Do you intend to arrest him, too?"

"We informed Dr Gray we would need to see him again. He didn't ask for legal representation when he was here earlier this morning. He was unaware of how much we had learned."

Lydia wondered how Gus could keep a straight face when he said that. She made a mental note never to play poker with him.

Gus and Lydia went outside to wait in the corridor.

"I asked Wayne Barnett to sit in with me when I spoke with Trefor," said Gus. "I wanted Trefor to tell us the truth about Megan's death. But I realized when we were listening to both Dominic and Amy, there could only be one explanation for Wayne being put in charge of the investigation and not getting the support he needed."

"Trefor didn't want the case solved? That makes little sense, guv," said Lydia.

"Consider what I told you earlier," said Gus. "Trefor wanted Katherine's killer found. He didn't want Dominic Gray's activities under the microscope. If he'd let things take their proper course, the entire business could have been wrapped up a decade ago."

"I'm still in the dark, guv," said Lydia.

"Wayne has gone to collect a DNA sample from Paul Alford," said Gus. "Does that help?"

"You said we had reduced the field of runners to two. I couldn't work out why that should be Dominic and Amy Gray. Since we've spoken to Amy Gray, she obviously has something to hide. You believe Dominic was Paul's father?"

"Without a doubt," said Gus. "I'm sure Amy realised it too."

"Gosh," said Lydia. "What did that do to Amy's head when he'd never been able to get her pregnant? She'd slept with heaven knows how many men. Did Dominic know Katherine had had the coil removed? Was he desperate to be a father, too?"

"We have plenty of questions to ask them, with their solicitor present. However, we need to be careful how we tread. Amy's the weaker link. I think she'll crack if we lay out the facts and fill the gaps with the likely sequence of events based on the new knowledge we've gathered."

"I can't wait to hear it," said Lydia. "You seem to have the answer to everything. Can you explain the light cotton gloves now?"

"There were no gloves, Lydia. Come on, let's get back inside. They've had time to decide what they're going to do."

Lydia restarted the recording and added Edward Vickers' name to the persons present.

"A simple yes or no for my first question, Dr Gray," said Gus. "Did you mention to your husband that Katherine had asked for her IUD to be removed?"

"Yes," she replied.

"You asked for your solicitor when I mentioned Katherine's special talent. Are you prepared to tell us what that was now?"

"When Katherine and Alice played together at Dominic's home, he noticed her ability to copy Alice's handwriting. For example, Alice wrote a sentence from a book or the lyrics of a song. Katherine wrote the same words underneath. Dominic said it was uncanny."

"That's solved the mystery, thank you," said Gus. "I'll take you through the true events now of Saturday evening. Jump in if I miss something."

Lydia held her breath.

"The phone call from the hospital came as a shock to Dominic," said Gus. "He truly believed his patient was on the road to recovery. You both had a drink with your meal, so he asked for a lift to Savernake. When he arrived, your husband completed the necessary documentation, checked his notes, and realised his error. At nine-thirty, he called Katherine, desperate for her services once more. Another forged document to put him in the clear when the inevitable investigation occurred."

"Dominic had no alternative. One tragic mistake on drug dosage would destroy everything he'd achieved in the past thirty years."

"Katherine rushed to Savernake, thinking she was assisting him as she had for years. Was the first occasion while she still worked at Savernake Hospital?"

Amy nodded.

"For the tape, Dr Gray."

"Yes, it started as long ago as 1983. There were others over the next twenty-five years."

"We haven't identified everyone yet, but we know Megan Davies and Mary Alford were among the patients Dominic helped."

"Dominic had watched his sister dying," said Amy. "He vowed never to let anyone in his care suffer longer than necessary. Dominic described himself as their one true friend."

"We'll talk to your husband about that," said Gus. "Let's return to what happened around a quarter to ten on Saturday night. Katherine altered a document or created a new one, and Dominic agreed to pay her whatever she asked. Then she realized Dominic wasn't releasing a patient from their pain; he was covering up his blunder. That wasn't their agreement. We know they left Savernake and drove to The Roebuck pub. I imagine Dominic persuaded her not to go to the police. That took time, but you knew that, didn't you?"

"Dominic needed a lift home from the hospital," said Amy. "I thought I'd be safe to drive, and I drove from Clench Common into town on my way to Savernake. I passed the Roebuck and saw them talking outside. Katherine's car was parked at the roadside a short distance from the pub. I sat and waited for them to leave."

"You had guessed Dominic was Paul's father. However, your husband never gave you cause to believe he was having an affair."

"I challenged him when Paul was perhaps eighteen months. Dominic swore they had only had sex the one time. A moment of weakness, he said, after she'd forged another signature that would mask yet another death."

"That must have hurt you deeply," said Lydia.

Amy hung her head.

"Where did you go after they left the pub?" asked Gus.

"I couldn't make out what was happening. I thought Dominic would have persuaded Katherine to take him home, but they were driving around, arguing."

"Then they headed for Clench Common, and you followed?"

"Dominic didn't know I wasn't home," said Amy. "He got Katherine to stop yards from our gateway. I saw him creep inside the house, and then I followed Katherine. I caught her, flashed my headlights, edged past her in the lane and forced her to turn into the West Woods car park."

"You got into the passenger seat and told her you knew she had just helped him cover up a fatal mistake."

"It was obvious," said Amy. "Why else would he have called her?"

"Did you tell her you suspected he was Paul's father?"

"She laughed. Dominic had pleaded with her to have sex a hundred times, but she had never fancied him. He needed her to forge another signature, and she realised that if she got pregnant, it might finally rid her of Daniel. She knew he had struggled to hide that he was gay for years. She slept with Dominic that one time. He meant nothing to her. Dominic was just a means to an end."

"A motive with which you were familiar," said Gus. "You strangled her."

"She laughed at me," sobbed Amy.

Gus stood up and left the room. Wayne Barnett was walking along the corridor.

"Everything done?" asked Gus.

"We'll get the results in due course. I asked the lab to get a wiggle on."

"I think you should do the honours, Wayne," said Gus.

He explained why Amy Gray had murdered Katherine Alford.

"You had better hope the DNA results back you up," said Wayne.

"They will," said Gus.

"What about Dominic Gray?" asked Wayne.

"We'll recall him as soon as we're through with his wife. That interview will take much longer. Mercy killing has become a hot issue. We have other charges we can hold him on while we dig deeper. His wife says he's been convincing himself his cause is just, and he's the patient's one true friend."

"Can I sit in with you for that interview, Gus?" asked Wayne.

"I don't see why not. What will you do about Trefor Davies in the meantime?"

"I've asked DS Mercer for advice on how to charge him. He was never directly involved with what Gray did, but he knew his wife had died sooner than expected. He felt he owed the doctor a favour and did his best to drag our attention away from him."

DOMINIC GRAY ARRIVED at George Lane at three o'clock. Edward Vickers spent fifteen minutes with him before joining Gus, Lydia, and Wayne in the interview room.

"We'll start with the murder of Katherine Alford," said Gus. "Your wife has confessed to strangling Katherine at West Woods. She followed you home from The Roebuck, watched you walk indoors, and then chased the Peugeot to the car park. Amy knew about your campaign of mercy killings at Savernake Hospital. She had guessed Katherine's forgery skills had proved invaluable to you, but she didn't want to accept you had been unfaithful. Ironic, considering your unconventional marriage. Her undying love for you meant she could reconcile the deaths of patients like Megan Davies and Mary Ward, but she couldn't bear hearing Katherine say you were just a means to an end."

"All very interesting, but can you prove any of this?"

"Amy hasn't told us the details of the conversation you had when she returned home from West Woods yet, but she was keen to get everything off her chest. Perhaps you would like to do the same?"

"No comment."

"If that's how you want to play it, I'll tell you what I think Amy will say. You asked her where she'd been. Amy told you she'd seen you together and realised you were always closer than you had said. Katherine had confirmed what Amy had dreaded, that you were Paul's father. Amy also knew you were covering up a fatal mistake you'd made that day. A mistake she threatened to take to the authorities. Each of you had something over the other. So, you sat down and devised a plan. You used that route often enough to know it wasn't a huge risk to wait until seven o'clock the next morning before appearing to discover a dead body. Amy stayed away from the Peugeot while you checked for evidence. Because the regular pathologist was away on compassionate leave, you did the post-mortem. The time of death you recorded was incorrect. Katherine died close to eleven o'clock, not midnight. Amy's initial statement said she was in bed when *you* reached home at around a quarter past eleven. That was when Amy arrived home. You were sat at home at eleven, wondering where she was and waiting."

"I think I need a minute with my client," said Edward Vickers.

"As you wish," said Gus. "By the way, Dr Gray, you might have got away with it if you hadn't tried to be clever by mentioning the light cotton gloves in the report. Something felt off from the moment I read that."

"Mea culpa," said Dominic.

When they resumed the interview, Dominic Gray confessed to helping his wife cover up her involvement in Katherine's murder.

"Trefor Davies will testify against you," said Gus. "We'll get your superiors to check the death of every terminally ill patient you've ever treated. Other charges will follow, Dr Gray, of that you can be certain."

"Give me some credit, Mr Freeman. Trefor Davies has dementia, and he'll never be a convincing witness. Katherine was an excellent forger. What a pity you can't charge her. I'll take my chances with a jury if you ever get enough evidence for the CPS to take it to trial. Times have changed. I was doing the patient and their loved ones a favour."

Gus nodded to Wayne Barnett. He lamented the lack of a warrant card at times like this. While Wayne charged Dominic Gray, Gus and Lydia slipped away for a final word with Trefor Davies.

"How's it going, Gus?" asked Trefor.

"We may have to accept we can't win them all," said Gus. "English law recognises a doctrine where doctors can administer pain-killing drugs to relieve suffering, even if the result is the patient's death. But they murder if they give drugs intending to kill the patient. So I believe Dominic Gray injected his patients with diamorphine, attributing the cause of death to cancer when he signed the death certificates."

"Dominic didn't mean to kill anybody, Gus," said

Trefor. "I hope the media don't portray him as another Harold Shipman."

"Gray believes he will find a sympathic jury. He may be right, but the other charges will stick. DI Barnett tells me he's spoken to Geoff Mercer about your actions in the case."

"I'll have more time to spend with Maureen now. That's something."

"We're sorry to see you go like this, Trefor. No hard feelings," said Gus.

"Get on with you. The only unsolved murder on my patch since I moved from Pontypridd is done and dusted."

Gus shook Trefor's hand, and he and Lydia walked outside into the warm sunshine.

"Do you think Dominic Gray's right, guv? A jury might think he did the right thing?"

"We haven't uncovered every death involved yet, Lydia. You started that process when you got the forensic accountant's report. I counted the number of gaps where Katherine didn't visit the ATM after 2000. There were five occasions where Dominic could have paid for her forgery skills. Amy told us she believed the first occasion was twenty years earlier. When Wayne Barnett picks up the case and makes up for lost time, he might find deaths that don't fit the pattern. On the other hand, Wayne might uncover enough to convince a jury to think twice about letting Dr Gray off scot-free for playing God."

Lydia drove them back to the office.

"Alex and Grace are back from Dorchester, guv," said Lydia.

As the lift doors closed and they rose to the first floor, Lydia turned to Gus.

"How do you think Grace will take it when we tell her, guv?"

"I hope she'll remember teamwork means that now and again, each of us will trawl through hours of work and end up with nothing."

"And if she doesn't?" asked Lydia.

"Will you be my one true friend?"

vinci-books.com/whisperedtruths

Murder in paradise: a love shattered, a village haunted.

In a quiet village, Mark Fennell and Helen Roker's new beginning turns tragic when Fennell is found dead. Months later, seemingly consumed by grief, Roker's body is discovered in her bath. As suspicions rise, Gus Freeman and his Crime Review Team uncover secrets at a distant caravan site.

Turn the page for a free preview…

Whispered Truths: Chapter One

Tuesday, 2 October 2018

Gus took a deep breath as the lift doors opened. He and Lydia stepped into the office.

"Welcome back, you two," said Neil.

"You look worried, guv," said Blessing. "We hoped you might be the bearer of good news."

"Have you heard from Grace and Alex yet?" asked Lydia. "We thought they would be here by now."

"Alex texted me thirty minutes ago," said Neil. "He reckoned it was a wasted journey. He said you would be happy that Amazing Grace asked the right questions, but Anna Cromwell's answers didn't advance our cause. Alex didn't believe they were closer to finding Katherine Alford's killer."

"It was unlikely they would find the answer in Dorchester," said Gus. "Unless DI Packenham ignored my assertion there was only one car on the housing estate when Bert Harris walked Biggles."

"You've learned there was another car?" asked Blessing. "Who saw it?"

"Grace and Alex are on their way home," said Gus. "They should be here in the next half-hour. Lydia and I will update the Freeman Files with the information we gathered during our two interviews this morning. I suggest you and Neil get your records straight, too. What were the headlines?"

"We visited Bert Harris, guv," said Neil. "He was having one of his vague days. Because our last visit wasn't in the newspapers, Bert needed reminding who we were and what we'd asked him last time. Blessing got Bert on track after a few minutes, and we went over what happened as he returned home from Coldharbour Lane. We were careful not to put words in his mouth."

"I asked Mr Harris to close his eyes and see Katherine's red car," said Blessing.

"Bert repeated what he told us the other day, guv," said Neil. "The Peugeot drove across the junction at the top of the road, travelling from left to right."

"I asked him whether he'd heard any other cars nearby," said Blessing. "Either before or after he saw the red car."

"Bert said it was the sound that made him look up," said Neil. "He'd been enjoying a quiet stroll with Biggles. They'd stopped by a lamppost, and when he glanced up, he spotted a car he recognised and then carried on walking home."

"I asked Mr Harris to keep his eyes closed, guv," said Blessing, "and describe what he saw next. He told us he had to wait for another car to pass him before crossing the road. I asked if he could remember what colour it was and whether he had seen the driver. He told us the car was dark, perhaps grey, and the driver was female."

"We believe it was a Honda Civic," said Gus.

"Not a Jazz then, guv?" asked Lydia. She looked puzzled.

"What aren't you telling us, guv?" asked Neil.

"They didn't start making the Jazz in Swindon until 2009, Lydia," said Gus. "My guess is Amy Gray switched to the Jazz later, but back in 2008, the Civic was a readily available model for the good doctor. We can ask Wayne Barnett to check."

"Are you going to tell Neil and Blessing what we know, guv?" asked Lydia.

"I haven't heard everything they have to tell me yet. What did Bert say happened next?"

"He made his way home and went to bed," said Blessing. "Mr Harris confirmed he had never seen the second car on the estate before."

"We have to remember how Bert came to respond to the TV appeal, guv," said Neil. "The police wanted to hear from anyone who saw Katherine's Peugeot on Saturday night. Bert remembered he had, and that was the only car he told them about."

"How does Amy Gray connect to the sighting of the cars, guv?" asked Blessing.

"All in good time, Blessing," said Gus. "What was the other task you two handled?"

"We dug into Amy's background, guv," said Neil. "She lived closer to Dominic Gray in Marlborough than Katherine Alford, but Amy fell somewhere between the two age-wise. All four children went to the same local schools. So, they would have been aware of one another but moved in different circles because of their age."

"Katherine and Alice were great friends," added Blessing, "but we found nothing to suggest Amy was ever close to the two younger girls. I spoke with several former sixth-form pupils from St John's who were in Amy's year. They remembered her as the quiet, studious type, but they all agreed Amy had a crush on the dashing Dominic. A couple of those former students are still registered as patients of Amy Gray at the town surgery."

"Did any of those women have anything to add?" asked Gus.

"Amy's reputation as a man-eater was well-founded, guv," said Neil. "Nobody suggested she has ever carried on with one of her patients."

"Is that it?" asked Gus.

"Pretty much, guv," said Neil. "We started updating our files before you got back. Give us fifteen minutes, and we'll be finished."

Neil looked towards Blessing, and she nodded.

"I'll get the coffee," she said. "I wish Grace and Alex would hurry. I want to know what's going on."

"I'll come with you, Blessing," said Lydia. "Believe me. I was in the same situation ninety minutes ago."

The files were soon done and dusted, and the coffee mugs were back on the shelf beside the Gaggia. Ten minutes later, Gus heard the lift descend to the ground floor and prepared for the ice storm that was sure to follow.

Neil dispensed with his customary cheery quip when Grace and Alex arrived in the office.

"Welcome back," he said.

"I hope the rest of you had more joy than we did," groaned Alex.

"It sounds like a quick debrief is in order before updating your files," said Gus. "I'm sure you asked the right questions, Grace, so why didn't ACC Cromwell provide you with telling answers?"

"Anna treated us very well, Gus," said Grace, flopping

into her chair like a petulant teenager. "She was polite and eager to assist in our cold case review but didn't tell us much we didn't already know."

"I doubt Wayne Barnett ever received a Christmas card from her, guv," said Alex. "The ACC took great pleasure in listing the number of black marks against Wayne during their investigation. However, we sensed the story Callum Brady told us was true. Wayne made a pass at Anna Cromwell, and she rejected his advances."

"Wayne's an idiot," said Gus. "However, all was not what it seemed at George Street."

Grace turned her head towards Gus at that remark.

"If you picked up gossip, or fresh facts this morning, it could have helped," she said. "Why didn't you update us?"

"Meetings with witnesses and potential suspects have a habit of moving at a snail's pace for ages, then suddenly racing at one hundred miles an hour, ma'am," said Lydia, "as you well know."

"I can't think of much we learned this morning that might have helped you, Grace," said Gus. "Neil and Blessing arrived here just after you left the car park en route to Dorchester. As it turned out, hearing Neil's background on Amy Winters and how she fitted into the scheme of things would have been vital. But, unfortunately, we weren't to know that until we'd started interviewing her husband."

"Lydia looks like the cat that got the cream, guv," said Alex. "It strikes me we're several steps behind you in this investigation."

"Lydia was right about a missing piece of the jigsaw producing a sudden acceleration in progress," said Gus. "What I thought would be a brief social conversation with Eve Northwood turned the case on its head."

"Are you telling us you've found Katherine Alford's killer?" asked Grace.

"That's only half of what we learned this morning," said Lydia.

"I must admit to an error," said Gus. "It didn't seem likely another vehicle was involved when Katherine died. My head told me Katherine met her killer soon after leaving home, and they stayed in the car throughout, except for a brief stop at The Roebuck. We knew Katherine worked at Savernake, and however brief the time their careers over-lapped, she and Dominic Gray could have known one another. But, unfortunately, I didn't give that snippet of information sufficient thought."

"It was Dominic Gray who found the body," said Grace.

"Yet when the uniformed officers took his statement, he didn't tell them he recognised the deceased," said Gus.

"Dominic Gray was at Savernake Hospital the evening of the murder, guv," said Alex. "His wife said he arrived home not long after eleven. How could he have been with Katherine that evening at all, let alone at West Woods after midnight? Why would Katherine rush out to meet Dominic, anyway?"

"You'll have to fill in the gaps, guv," said Lydia. "They don't have the missing pieces of the jigsaw."

"They're still looking at the wrong picture on the box, like the rest of us, guv," said Blessing.

"I'm more in the dark now than I was on Monday morning," sighed Grace.

"Wayne Barnett has plenty to do yet to determine when it all started," said Gus. "It's easy to understand how Dominic Gray's views on end-of-life suffering evolved after losing his only sister to leukaemia. We had learned Katherine and Alice were the best of friends. I didn't realise how those facts connected until we spoke to Dominic Gray. Once the first domino fell, the cascade continued until the full picture was revealed. There was no time to consider whether to call the office or text Alex to keep you two in the loop. I'm sorry, but we kept watching the dominos falling."

"If there was any hesitation," said Lydia. "Gus gave a slight nudge that encouraged Dominic and Amy Gray to tell us the full story," said Lydia.

"You think Dominic killed Katherine and Amy helped him cover it up?" asked Grace. "What possible motive did he have? Why would his wife stand by him, anyway?"

"We need to go back further than the night of the murder, I'm afraid," said Gus. "Trefor Davies's wife may not have been the first when she died of bone cancer at Savernake Hospital. But Dominic Gray handled her pallia-tive care while she was there. We learned that Amy Gray was Megan's doctor. The Alford family had been registered with the same practice for many years. When we read the statements from West Woods in the murder file, there was nothing to indicate the two cyclists were so closely connected to our victim."

"Remind me again how Katherine's mother died, guv," said Alex.

"Cancer, Alex," said Gus. "Amy Gray referred her to the Great Western Hospital in Swindon. The aggressive treat-ment she received there only delayed the inevitable, and Mary transferred to Savernake."

"Where Dominic Gray tended to her in her final weeks," said Lydia.

"The mists are clearing," said Grace. "When did Katherine realise Dominic Gray was responsible for her mother's death?"

"Don't jump to conclusions, ma'am," said Blessing. "We don't have enough information yet."

"When we left Trefor's office to speak to Wayne Barnett, I asked Trefor why he put Wayne Barnett in charge of the Alford murder case," said Gus. "Trefor told us he thought it was the right thing to do. After listening to the other conversations that morning, it made perfect sense. When we went to speak to Wayne, Eve Northwood was in his office, so we waited in the corridor. I was surprised to see Eve so far from Gablecross, but it appears she's Wayne's aunt. I have no idea why she was visiting him, but Eve told me Dominic Gray had performed a similar role to her in the past. Dominic Gray had been on standby to perform post mortems if the regular pathologist was absent."

"How did that impact the Alford case?" asked Grace.

"The regular coroner had flown home to South Africa for his father's funeral at the time of the murder," said Gus.

"If Dominic Gray did the post-mortem, that opens up several possibilities," said Alex.

"Go on," said Gus.

"The coroner's role is to establish the time and cause of death, guv. If Dominic Gray and Katherine were in a relationship, and she died after an argument, he could manipulate the facts to give him an alibi."

"Surely, Anna Cromwell and Wayne Barnett would have recognised him when they attended the post-mortem?" said Grace.

"I asked Wayne why they didn't notice, and he shrugged and said they all looked alike in a mask and scrubs. Wayne reminded me it was Anna's first post-mortem, so she had her eyes closed for most of it. When they were at West Woods two days earlier, her focus was on the Peugeot. Wayne Barnett was hungover and paid scant attention to the uniformed officers taking statements from the two cyclists."

"Why didn't Trefor Davies get Barnett and Cromwell to do a follow-up interview, guv?" asked Alex.

"Trefor Davies guided them in another direction," said Grace. "He realised Dr Gray had brought his wife's suffering to a premature end and didn't want anyone to probe too deeply."

"Right," said Alex. "So that's what was going on. Even if Katherine realised something similar had occurred with her mother, it doesn't explain why Dominic Gray called her that night or why she dropped everything to meet him. What was the nature of their relationship?"

"When I studied Katherine's bank account, there was just one anomaly," said Grace. "Katherine didn't always need to withdraw cash. So we reckoned someone was paying her for services rendered. Was Katherine black-mailing Dominic Gray?"

"A moot point, Grace," said Gus. "This case should be a lesson learned. How was Katherine portrayed in the murder file? What was it you said, Blessing?"

"Katherine was a devoted mother-of-two, guv," said Blessing. "Nobody had a bad word to say about her, whether members of her family, friends, or neighbours. So I queried how a woman who appeared to be a saint could anger someone so much they strangled her."

"Why *was* Dominic Gray paying Katherine cash then, guv?" asked Alex.

"As with other aspects of this case, you need to analyse the distant past, Alex," said Gus. "Alice and Katherine were best friends as kids. They spent a lot of time playing together, often at Alice's home. Dominic remembered Katherine had an unusual skill. She could reproduce a copy of anyone's handwriting, apparently at will. So when they met at Savernake Hospital, Dominic realised he could contact Katherine whenever he needed a signature forged. Katherine needed the extra cash after Daniel Matravers walked away from their marriage. We may never know how often Dominic Gray shortened the suffering of a dying patient in his care, but I suspect the cost of a signature rose steeply from 2000 onwards."

"Katherine wasn't as saintly as I believed, guv," said Blessing.

"I've just remembered something," said Grace. "A footnote attached to the post-mortem referred to the IUD, and the coroner said he'd discussed the matter with the victim's GP. We did not know that signified Dominic Gray had spoken to his wife."

"We followed the threads from the initial investigation and concentrated on the relationships between Daniel and Katherine, Katherine and Emily, and even Emily and Paul," said Gus. "Both investigations sought a lover, a casual employer, anything to explain who Katherine had dashed out to meet and why."

"It was a person Katherine thought of as being like a brother," said Lydia. "As thick as thieves one minute and at arm's length the next, but never on intimate terms."

"Or so we thought," said Gus. "We'll get to that in a minute. But first, I want to explain how my insistence there was never a second car kept us from asking the right questions earlier in the piece. Bert Harris said Katherine's car sped past him, travelling left to right, as he walked towards the junction. Callum Brady conceded that Anna had concentrated on the actual sighting of the Peugeot, even though they both knew half a dozen boy racers were reported to be causing a nuisance until midnight around the town. Callum Brady said Bert Harris might have noticed another car, but Anna discounted it as irrelevant as he didn't recognise it."

"So, who was driving the other car?" asked Grace.

"Amy Gray," said Gus.

"She must have known what her husband was up to and followed him," said Grace.

"We interviewed Dominic Gray first," said Gus. "Everything followed the familiar path of events we had read in the murder file. The hospital rang that evening to tell him his patient was dying. Dominic Gray went to Savernake in a vain attempt to save him. He completed the necessary documentation and then returned home, where he spoke to his wife just after eleven o'clock."

"Dominic and Amy drank wine with their evening meal," said Lydia. "He took a taxi to Savernake. When we asked how he got home, he claimed he'd called Amy and told her what had happened. Someone happened to be travelling his way and gave him a lift."

"That sounds convenient," said Neil. "With slight variations to the statement in the murder file."

"Dominic stuck to the story he and his wife rehearsed for what happened on Sunday morning," said Lydia.

"When I asked why Amy didn't recognise the car, Dominic was screwed," said Gus. "He tried to bluff his way out of trouble, but it didn't make sense that Amy wouldn't have seen the red Peugeot at the doctor's surgery. He was further on the back foot when I suggested he must have been shocked to find the victim was Katherine, someone he'd known since childhood."

"Dominic said he'd realised it was Katherine after working inside the car for several minutes," said Lydia, "but he still didn't tell the uniformed officers he knew the victim."

"He tried to fob us off by saying he hardly met Katherine when they worked at the same hospital and couldn't recall the last time they'd spoken," said Gus. "I couldn't get my head around Katherine's random cash deposits. Nor could I accept it was acceptable for him to do the post-mortem despite Eve Northwood saying it made sense to maintain continuity from the crime scene."

"Dominic Gray had ample opportunity to mislead the original investigation," said Grace. "When did the murder take place?"

"An hour earlier than reported," said Gus. "We didn't get confirmation of that until we interviewed Amy Gray. By that time, I'd unpicked Dominic Gray's version of events on Saturday night and Sunday morning, and she suspected I had the upper hand."

"I imagine you presented Amy Gray with a modified version that suggested you knew far more than you did," said Grace. "She fell for it."

"Amy was a far weaker opponent," said Gus.

"Gus sat back and let Amy tell us the full story," said Lydia. "My overall impression was Amy was relieved it was over."

"Amy would have done anything for Dominic," said Gus. "They both wanted children, but it didn't happen for whatever reason. Dominic didn't object when his wife slept with other men in the hope of conceiving. As far as Amy was concerned, Dominic never looked at another woman until Katherine took Paul into the surgery one day."

"Katherine and Dominic *were* having an affair," said Grace. "How did they keep it under wraps for so long? Lily never suspected a thing, nor did Katherine's daughter, Emily."

"Did Amy mention to Dominic that Katherine had asked for her coil to be removed, guv?" asked Alex.

"Amy Gray confirmed she had, Alex," said Gus. "That was wrong, but she couldn't have known what would follow. Katherine and Daniel's marriage was falling apart for obvious reasons, and she had never had feelings for Dominic. But, unfortunately, the same couldn't be said for him. Dominic had pursued her ever since they met again at Savernake. We can only guess at Katherine's motives, but the one occasion she relented and they had sex resulted in her getting pregnant."

"No wonder Daniel left," said Grace. "What did happen on Saturday night? I can't quite put the pieces together."

"The medical emergency was genuine," said Gus. "Dominic had made a fatal mistake on drug dosage. He needed Katherine to forge another document to stop his illustrious career from disappearing down the drain."

"Katherine thought she was helping him with another cancer patient," said Lydia. "Dominic had watched his sister dying and refused to let anyone suffer longer than necessary."

"Amy drove into town on her way to the hospital to collect Dominic," said Gus. "She saw Katherine and Dominic talking outside the pub, waited, and followed Katherine's car when they left. That was the grey car Bert Harris had to wait for until he could cross the road."

"So, Katherine and Dominic argued on the way to West Woods, and then he killed her," said Grace.

"No, Dominic was guilty of many things, but not Katherine's murder," said Gus. "He told us he'd called Amy to explain what had happened to his patient. That was a lie.

She didn't know a thing; therefore, he didn't know she wasn't home. Katherine dropped him at their house in Clench Common and headed for Bath Road to make her way home. Amy chased the Peugeot through the lanes and forced Katherine to stop at the car park at West Woods. When she joined Katherine in the car, Amy told her she'd known Paul was Dominic's child for years. She accused them of having an affair. Katherine put her straight. She had slept with Dominic once, and he meant nothing to her. He was just a means to an end."

"Gosh," said Grace.

"Amy couldn't listen to Katherine laughing at her," said Lydia.

"Amy strangled her, not Dominic," said Grace. "I didn't see that coming."

"Trefor Davies didn't come out of things too well, guv," said Alex.

"He's asked DS Mercer if he can retire earlier than planned," said Gus.

"You look puzzled, ma'am," said Lydia.

"I don't see how you explain the white cotton gloves," said Grace.

"Did Amy Gray wear them, Lydia?" asked Alex. "Were they lightweight driving gloves?"

"Perhaps the time of death wasn't the only misdirection Dominic Gray included in the post-mortem report," said Gus. "Time to update these files and then get off home."

Grab your copy...
vinci-books.com/whisperedtruths

About the Author

Ted Tayler is the international bestselling indie author of The Freeman Files and The Phoenix series. Ted lives in the English west country, where his stories are based. He was born in 1945 and has been married to Lynne since 1971. They have three children and four grandchildren.

His thought-provoking mysteries appeal to readers of Sally Rigby, Joy Ellis, Pauline Rowson, and Faith Martin. His action-packed thrillers are a must for fans of Mark Dawson and J.C. Ryan.

Gus Freeman's cold case investigations are carried out with reasoned deduction rather than bursts of frantic action. In each of the twenty-four books, unsolved murder is accompanied by romance, humor, and country life. The core message in the twelve Phoenix novels is that criminals should pay for their crimes. Unfortunately, the current system fails to deliver the correct punishment, so Phoenix helps redress the balance.

Acknowledgments

The love and support of my family; without them, this would have been impossible.